THE *Dragon's* DISCOVERY

(Lochguard Highland Dragons #6)

Jessie Donovan

This book is a work of fiction. Names, characters, places, and incidents are either the product of the writer's imagination or are used fictitiously, and any resemblance to actual persons, living or dead, business establishments, events, or locales is entirely coincidental.

Books by Jessie Donovan

Asylums for Magical Threats
Blaze of Secrets (AMT #1)
Frozen Desires (AMT #2)
Shadow of Temptation (AMT #3)
Flare of Promise (AMT #4)

Cascade Shifters
Convincing the Cougar (CS #0.5)
Reclaiming the Wolf (CS #1)
Cougar's First Christmas (CS #2)
Resisting the Cougar (CS #3)

Kelderan Runic Warriors
The Conquest (KRW #1)
The Barren (KRW #2)
The Heir (KRW #3)
The Forbidden (KRW #4)
The Hidden (KRW #5 / Summer 2019)

Lochguard Highland Dragons
The Dragon's Dilemma (LHD #1)
The Dragon Guardian (LHD #2)
The Dragon's Heart (LHD #3)
The Dragon Warrior (LHD #4)
The Dragon Family (LHD #5)
The Dragon's Discovery (LHD #6)

CHAPTER ONE

*A*listair Boyd stood next to his mother, Meg, inside the great hall on Lochguard and almost wished the roof hadn't been replaced yet.

Scotland wasn't the warmest of places, but he didn't mind the rain, wind, or a combination of both. However, he wanted an excuse—any excuse—to leave and not have to meet the group of ten females who would partially become his responsibility. Not because he regularly shirked responsibilities, but rather he suspected his mother wanted to matchmake.

She'd tried to pair him up for years, and Alistair had made it his mission to leave any and all gatherings early. He had no intention of taking a mate.

His dragon spoke up. *You used to dream about meeting human females, and now a whole group of them are here.*

That was before, and you know it.

Before referred to almost three years ago, when Alistair had made a vow to stay away from and avoid sleeping with any female. He'd failed the one female he'd cared about most, and he couldn't risk that happening again.

His beast huffed. *We did everything we could to help Rachel. Enough with the moping. Even if you pretend not to want it, I need a female. Our hand doesn't compare.*

Alistair resisted glancing over at his mother. *Let's not talk about masturbation standing next to Mum, aye?*

Then at least look at the human females and think about giving them a chance. The whole point of them coming to Lochguard is so that some of the single Lochguard members can find mates.

It was true—the Department of Dragon Affairs, or DDA, was trying something new. Instead of sending one human female at a time and requiring her to take a male until she was pregnant, they were sending a group of ten to mingle freely, with no requirements of sex. The hope was that human-dragon pairings would happen more naturally and cause fewer problems in the long run.

Alistair replied to his dragon, *We're to educate them about dragon-shifter ways and nothing else.* Finlay Stewart, Lochguard's blond-haired clan leader, walked out onto the raised dais at the front of the room. *Now, hush. We need to listen to Finn in case he decides to accidentally add any "extra" duties for us.*

His dragon snorted. *Nothing Finn does is by accident.*

Alistair mentally grunted and watched as Finn raised his arms, calling for silence. As soon as the hall was mostly quiet—Lochguard wasn't known as the quietest of clans—Finn projected his voice into the hall. "I can think of no better day to celebrate having the new roof finished, and not just because of the wee storm outside."

As if on cue, wind rattled the windows. Alistair wouldn't put it past Finn to have someone doing it for him, to make a grand show.

Lochguard's leader was intelligent, skilled in handling the clan, and would die to protect them all. But he was also a charmer and performer who tended to act over the top on purpose.

Finn continued, "After the lively year we've had, I imagine all of you are getting a wee bit bored with the calm, aye? But no longer! The group of potential female mates has arrived, along with their chaperone, Dr. Kiyana Barnes."

Murmurs arose, even though everyone knew this day had been coming for weeks. Finn ignored the rumblings and continued, "While the females will stay for a few months, mingling with the single dragons wanting a mate, Dr. Barnes will be with us a wee while longer. Six months, in fact. She'll be here to observe our clan and collect information to better inform both the DDA and the general human population in the UK about our kind."

Some louder grumbles rose up, mentioning a book about dragon-shifters by a human named Melanie Hall, as well as a videocast series by another human mated to a dragon-shifter, Jane Hartley. Both of which had already helped the humans better understand their kind.

Finn shook his head. "Those were good starts, but not enough. Dr. Barnes isn't mated to a dragon-shifter, and it will offer a unique perspective. Especially as she's an anthropologist and will be trying to take an objective look at how our clan works."

Alistair had spent most of his life dealing with objective facts. He may be a school teacher now, but he'd once been the head scientist and research lead on Lochguard. To say he was skeptical of the social sciences, like anthropology, was an understatement.

His dragon sighed heavily, but Alistair was good at ignoring his beast when he wanted to do so.

Finn motioned toward the back of the stage. A group of females came out to form a line behind him. While one was as nice as the other, it was the female at the end, with curly, black hair and light brown skin, that caught his attention.

She stood taller than the rest, but that wasn't what garnered his attention. The others were mostly focusing on one point in the distance or the ground, but the female with curly hair was scanning the crowd. Every once in a while, she'd pause, study something, and then her gaze would move again.

Alistair would bet everything he owned that she was the female sent here to study them.

His beast grunted. *We've suffered preconceptions from humans for decades, if not centuries. Don't judge her before you meet her.*

It's not because she's human.

Still, at least she's not afraid. I rather like that about her.

Warning bells went off in Alistair's head. *Och, no, don't even think about it.*

Why not? She's bonnie. Not to mention brave to come live with us for six months. After all, stories say we eat humans for dinner.

If you make a crack about eating her, in a name-screaming way, I will toss you into a mental prison, aye?

His beast chuckled. *I'd like to see you try. It's been years since you've built one, and you're out of practice.*

Before Alistair could reply, Finn spoke again as he motioned to the females. "Behind me are the brave lassies who've agreed to come to Lochguard for a few months and are open to mating—marrying—a dragon-shifter. Let's show our support and welcome them to our clan!"

To Lochguard's credit, they cheered and clapped. Since there had been a reception before the meeting, where there had been quite a bit of alcohol, Alistair bet most everyone was happier than usual.

Including the two older dragonmen standing near his mother.

Not wanting to think of his mum and her two males—or, at least everyone suspected they were her two males—he clapped politely.

His mother nudged his side and whispered, "Maybe you'll fancy one of them."

"I thought you were done trying to matchmake," he drawled.

"Aye, I was. But with all those single females coming at once? There may be hope for you yet, Alistair."

It was on the tip of his tongue to say there was more to him than finding a mate, but decades of experience had taught him that arguing with his mother was pointless. She always found a way to win, no matter if she was in the wrong.

The female he'd noticed with the dark, curly hair moved to stand next to Finn, a microphone in her hand. Once Finn quieted the clan again, she spoke, her accent marking her from somewhere in the south of England. "Hello, Lochguard. As Finn said, my name is Kiyana, but feel free to call me Kiki."

Kiki didn't suit her; his mum had once had a dog named Kiki.

His beast spoke up. *Why do you care?*

Not wanting to think of why he did, he focused on the female's next words. "While I'll be observing your clan, I hope to get to know many of you on a more personal level as well. I've worked for the DDA for many years, and I know most of the rumors about you aren't true."

A few people laughed, and one male—he thought it came from the direction of one of the MacAllister siblings—blurted, "Then which are true? The ones about how big our—"

Someone smacked the male to quiet him. Definitely one of the MacAllisters then, since the mother of the five siblings often acted as their censor. Well, for the youngest four. The eldest child was one of the most level-headed dragonwomen he'd ever met.

His beast snorted. *I wish the mother wouldn't censor them. It's much funnier when they say what's on their minds.*

To her credit, the human female Kiyana grinned and replied, "If you want to know exactly what I'm talking about, then we'll have to sit down for a chat at some point, right?"

His dragon muttered, *I told you she's brave. If we're not careful, one of the MacAllisters will snatch her up.*

And why should that matter? I'm not looking.

But you agreed to stay at one of the parties for at least an hour.

Only to stop Mum from asking ten thousand more times.

Kiyana continued, "But sincerely, thank you for welcoming us into your clan. I know there have been some rocky ties between Lochguard and humans in the past, but all of us"—she motioned to herself and the other females—"are here of our own free will. Again, thank you, and I look forward to talking with you in a bit."

Finn clapped, and so did most everyone else. Kiyana went back to her spot on the stage, at the end of the line of humans.

Their clan leader took center stage again. "Aye, well, now that the formal remarks are finished, it's time for a party! The humans will be mingling with everyone else, so be on your best manners. After all, each has a Guardian here tonight to ensure their safety. And I'd rather not have to deal with any fights, especially since I always have my hands full with my cousins as it is."

Protests came from where the MacKenzies—his cousins—were standing on the other side of the hall.

Finn ignored them. "I officially declare the start to the gathering." He motioned toward the side, and music filled the air.

Alistair turned and took a step toward the door—he wasn't required to meet the human females until the following day—but his mother's hand clamped on his wrist. While his mother was in her sixties, her grip was firmer than some of the males his own age.

She asked too sweetly, "Where do you think you're going?"

He took a deep breath and tried to keep his voice level. "I have to prepare for tomorrow. You know I have to teach the human females about dragon-shifter ways."

His mother tsked. "You're always prepared two days ahead of time. Humor your old mum, won't you? At least meet with them. You did promise me an hour, no?"

His mum's words might seem like a request on the surface, but they were an order. One that he had to follow or risk her meddling even more into his life.

To the point she'd invite all of the females to dinner and he'd be the only other guest.

He envied others with parents who didn't need to know everything about their children's lives.

His beast spoke up. *Saying hello to the humans won't hurt anyone.*

You're supposed to be on my side.

I am. It's not even six o'clock. And Mum's right—you have everything prepared for tomorrow. For once, can't we just have some fun? It's been years since we stayed long enough at a clan gathering to even dance.

Since he was clearly outnumbered and the last thing he wanted was for his mother and dragon to work as a team against him, Alistair sighed. "Okay, Mum. I'll stay for a wee bit, but not the whole night, aye?"

"Maybe you'll have so much fun that you'll forget about wanting to leave. Now, come on. We need to greet the human females before the others do. Lorna MacKenzie may have mated all her children now, but I can't risk Sylvia MacAllister's three sons all snatching the best females in the bunch."

Alistair wanted to say that the females weren't for snatching, but decided against it. The argument wasn't worth it.

Following his mother, he did his best to not glare or look overly bored. Just because he wasn't interested in a mate didn't mean he should be rude to the humans.

⁓⁓⁓

Dr. Kiyana Barnes did her best to keep her jaw from dropping as she looked from one dragon-shifter to the next. It wasn't the first time she'd been on a dragon clan's lands. However, it had been more than five years since the Department of Dragon Affairs had given her anything but desk assignments.

Not that she hadn't deserved them. After all, she'd screwed up big time five years ago by becoming involved with one of the dragon clan members she was supposed to be observing.

It hadn't been love, which had made the mistake all the worse.

But tonight, well, tonight was her second chance. While it was partially luck on her part that no one had really wanted to live with a dragon clan for six months,

Kiyana had also spent years learning as much dragon-shifter history as she could. That, plus her past five years of stellar work reviews, had resulted in her obtaining the post.

Of course, she was more than merely an observer this time. She also had to help take care of the other human women. One of whom, Julie, currently hid behind Kiyana.

Being gentle wasn't her way, but she tried her best and whispered, "What's the matter? You were excited about coming to Lochguard, more than any of the others. So what happened?"

Julie replied, "I know, but now that I'm here, it's so much more real. They're all so tall, and fit, and, well, are you sure they won't turn into dragons and snap me in two?"

Kiyana's first thought was to tell the other woman to snap out of it. No one was going to shift inside the great hall and possibly knock down the walls or roof.

Remember, they haven't been around dragon-shifters as much as you, Kiyana. Play nice. With the reminder, she smiled and spoke as gently but firmly as she could. "Listen, Julie. Not only do you have your elder, ex-military brother coming here to watch over you, do you really think Lochguard will risk starting a war with the humans? Let alone do something as silly as shift inside a building?" She wanted to add they'd wait until a new moon, so no one could see, but resisted the joke. Julie probably wouldn't see it that way. So, Kiyana continued, "This is a party. Maybe a glass of wine will help you calm down and allow you to merely enjoy yourself."

Julie opened her mouth but promptly closed it. Kiyana looked ahead of them and noticed the gray-haired dragonwoman standing next to a tall man, the tattoo on his arm marking him a dragon-shifter. It was hard to miss the toned muscles of his chest and arms, which was another thing dragon-shifters tended to have, their muscles developed from a combination of flying and training.

While he wasn't movie-star handsome, there was something about his face that made her want to study it. Maybe his square jaw, or even his eyes—one was blue and the other brown. However, it was the patently fake smile on his face that made her lips twitch. He didn't want to be here, but the older dragonwoman had a firm grip on the man's wrist.

The older woman spoke first. "Och, sorry to startle you lasses, but I wanted to be one of the first to welcome you to Lochguard. My name is Meg." She gestured to the man at her side. "And this is my son Alistair. My unmated son, aye?"

Kiyana swore she heard a sigh from Alistair, but when she looked at his face again, it was the same fake happy smile as before.

Meg spoke again. "So what is the ginger-haired lass's name, then? I know the doctor because she spoke, but not the bonnie lass behind her."

Kiyana shouldn't care how the dragonwoman described Julie as bonnie but not her. When it came to traditional ideals of Scottish beauty, Julie had it all—red hair, blue eyes, and even a smattering of freckles.

She, on the other hand, was none of that. Kiyana was confident in her looks and with her body, but the older woman's words still stung.

Pushing down the unintended offense since attracting a dragon-shifter male wasn't part of her assignment, she forced herself to keep smiling. After all, she wasn't going to risk her standing in the DDA again by sleeping with a dragonman.

Julie spoke up, now standing right at Kiyana's side instead of behind her. "I'm Julie. Nice to meet you, Meg."

Meg released her son, gave him a look that probably conveyed something Alistair would understand but Kiyana wouldn't, and then Meg put an arm around Julie's shoulders. "Och, no, it's me who's pleased to meet you. Come, tell me a wee bit about yourself." She glanced at Alistair. "Come join us in a few minutes, aye?"

Alistair muttered, "Yes, Mum," before Meg and Julie moved toward the drinks table.

Kiyana probably could've made polite conversation if Alistair hadn't raised his eyebrow at that moment and said, "Go ahead, say what's on your mind, lass. Otherwise, you'll burst."

Grinning, she answered, "I think your mother wants to have you mated by the end of the night."

"Well done on saying mated and not married. I hope the others are as well informed."

She frowned. "Does that matter? It's not as if we've been welcomed onto dragon lands whenever we please."

The man shrugged his broad shoulders. "It probably doesn't matter to most, but my full name is Alistair Boyd. I'm to be your cultural liaison and educator."

She'd known the other women would have to attend classes primarily with Alistair Boyd. However, the man in front of her wasn't a stodgy type with glasses and tweed suit jackets. "I hope you don't teach whilst bare-chested, too. Otherwise, the women aren't going to be able to focus for at least a few days."

He smiled slightly. "Only a few days, aye? A little flexing would probably make it last at least a week." She rolled her eyes and he continued, "Well, I suppose I'll have to wear a shirt, then. I can't be distracting the humans longer than necessary." He motioned toward his dark blue outfit, which was a long length of material wrapped around his waist and thrown over his shoulder. It was similar to the Scottish plaids of old. "However, I would think if you're here to study us, you should already know what this is."

Needing to prove she wasn't an idiot, Kiyana put on her best professor voice. "Every dragon clan has a traditional outfit. In the UK and Ireland, the outfits are similar to plaids of old. They were originally a means of being cost-effective. After all, a long length of cloth could be cut into needed lengths. However, the practice never changed, even with modern-day technology that could allow any design or color one wished. In some regions, such as Scotland, some dragon clans and human villages would order the same color and share one long length." She paused and raised her brows. "Is that enough or should I go into how there were a few skirmishes over who gets what color?"

The corners of his mouth twitched. "No, that should be enough. It's a good thing you're here on another job or mine might be at risk. I usually teach history to the children here."

It was hard for Kiyana to imagine the large, muscled man teaching youngsters, but he had no reason to lie. After all, in her experience men liked to pretend they were something quite a bit more macho when they did lie.

Lochguard's clan leader, Finn, walked up to them and lightly slapped Alistair on the shoulder. "I didn't pin you as part of the welcome committee." He winked at Kiyana. "I hope he's not giving us a bad name."

Alistair grunted, and Kiyana smiled. "No. We were discussing the history of your traditional outfits, as a matter of fact."

Finn blinked. "Oh, aye?" He glanced sideways at Alistair. "I hope you're not boring the lass."

Kiyana spoke for herself. "No. It's rather interesting to talk with someone who knows as much as me."

Alistair muttered, "I know more."

Finn barked out a laugh. "I'm not sure that's a contest you want to get into, Dr. Barnes. Alistair here is something of a bookworm, and knows more about dragon-shifter history than anyone else I've met."

Kiyana jumped in. "Call me Kiyana or Kiki. Dr. Barnes is too formal."

Alistair stated, "Kiyana suits you better."

She blinked. "Um, okay?"

Finn studied Alistair a second before nodding. "Kiyana it is. Now that I've confirmed you're not bored to death, I have a few others to check up on. The female with Meg Boyd looks like she wants to flee. I'd better go take care of it."

Once they were alone again, Kiyana asked, "Why does Kiyana suit me better?"

She probably shouldn't have questioned him as she wasn't on Lochguard to form close social relationships with the dragon-shifters. However, something told her Alistair liked honesty. And for some reason, she wanted to be honest and open with him right then.

Before warning bells could go off in her head, Alistair replied, "It's a beautiful sounding name, full of depth. And even though I've just met you, I think you're a female of depth, aye?"

Depth of personality wasn't usually the first thing people noticed about her. Alistair Boyd was interesting indeed. "I am. But my mother always called me Kiki. I think it was the compromise. My father wanted the name Kiyana, to name me after his dead sister, and mother

19

wanted something easier to say. Hence, two names for one woman."

"I'm sorry about your aunt."

She shook her head. "I never met her. She died in Jamaica before my dad came to Britain. I always wanted to be called Kiki as a girl, to fit in better. But ever since university, I've preferred Kiyana. Not only because I want to honor my aunt's memory, but also because I'm not afraid of being different any longer. If I were, I wouldn't be living on Lochguard for six months, now, would I?"

"Then why introduce yourself as Kiki?"

She shrugged. "I guess I wanted to try to fit in a little more, and it makes me less stuffy-sounding."

Alistair didn't reply right away, and it gave her a moment to realize how much she'd revealed about herself. Usually it took five dates to share that much information. And yet, Alistair Boyd's mismatched eyes weren't uncomfortable, bored, or even patronizing. No, she swore they were asking her for more information.

Then his pupils turned to slits and back. She'd seen a dragon-shifter talk with his inner beast before, but not for years.

Not for the first time, she wanted to know what it was like to have another personality inside your head. It was something she'd never experience, and no amount of questioning or observing would give her a true understanding of the special relationship between the human and dragon halves of a dragon-shifter.

Alistair's pupils turned round again. "It's a brave thing to come here for six months, aye, I'll give you that. However, I don't know where else you've studied my kind before, but Lochguard isn't reserved or wary. They'll be in your business at every opportunity, wanting to befriend you or try to match you up with their children. And before long, you won't be able to maintain the distance necessary to objectively observe us. In other words, I'm giving you fair warning that your term here will probably be cut short. Maybe even because you end up fancying a dragon-shifter here."

His words were like a slap in the face. There was no way he could know about her past and her mistake in dating a dragonman before. As far as she knew, no one outside the DDA had access to that information.

Before she could probe him to see how he knew it, his mother returned with Julie at her side. "Alistair, you've kept the lovely Julie waiting. Come. She's agreed to the first dance."

"I don't dance anymore, Mum. You know that."

Meg raised her brows. "Have you turned into a male who goes back on his promises?"

Kiyana looked between the two. She was beginning to see what Alistair meant, about Lochguard being nosey.

Of course, her mother was far away, in Bedford. Meaning Kiyana didn't have to worry about her mother asking if she would marry any time soon, for the umpteenth time.

At that moment, Alistair looked directly into her eyes. His mother glanced between them, and her expression turned curious.

Not wanting his mother to attempt matchmaking—Alistair was an attractive, intelligent man, but she wasn't going to ruin her career, no matter how much someone tried to pair her off—Kiyana took a step back and scanned the crowd. Finding one of the other humans, she said, "Excuse me, but I need to check on the others. I trust you'll keep an eye on Julie for me?"

"Aye, we will," Meg stated.

21

And with that, Kiyana turned and walked a little faster than normal to one of the other human women. She needed to put as much distance between her and Meg Boyd as she could.

Starting tomorrow, Kiyana would be more careful and focus on her job inside the clan. While learning more about the dragon-shifters was tied for her top priority, she needed to avoid being alone with single dragonmen if she could manage it.

Alistair Boyd would be at the top of her list of who to steer clear of. She couldn't avoid him completely since he was the liaison, but she would keep those meetings short and to the point. No more sharing bits and pieces of herself, for one.

And she most definitely wouldn't stare into his eyes and wonder what he was thinking.

Chapter Two

The next morning, Alistair paced at the front of the empty classroom and tried not to look at the clock again.

His dragon spoke up. *Why are you nervous? You teach every weekday, and then some. This isn't any different.*

But it is different, aye? Knowing Mum, she'll pop in and invite the humans to dinner.

She didn't even get that far last night with the ginger-haired female. She might be playing it safer with us, afraid she'll never get another daughter-in-law and by extension, another chance of finally getting a granddaughter.

His brothers had all had boys, which wasn't unusual since the dragon-shifter population skewed male. *She's set on matchmaking again. I can tell from how happy she was last night.*

Again, we don't have to mate any of them. Even if it's just sex, it's better than nothing.

So accommodating you are.

I try.

The door at the back of the room opened. Seeing Faye MacKenzie's curly brown hair, he relaxed. She was one of Lochguard's co-head Protectors. Not only that, she was happily mated and pregnant. In other words, he was safe. His mother wouldn't rock that boat, and not just because Faye was the daughter of her frenemy, either.

"Can I help you, Faye?"

She entered and walked to the front of the room. "Er, there's been an incident."

Both man and dragon became alert. "What happened?"

"Oh, it's nothing too serious. No one died, or anything. But it seems one of the human females hooked up with a male dragon-shifter last night and left this morning."

"Aye, well, you said they didn't have to mate anyone."

Fay shook her head. "No, but judging from those who talked with her last night at the gathering, I don't think she came to Lochguard for a mere one-night stand. However, this morning she went to Finn, asked to go home, and he could do nothing but let her go."

While he didn't think any of the males on Lochguard would hurt the humans, he asked, "She wasn't abused, was she?"

"Och, no, not that we can tell—she denied it, as did the dragonman she slept with. However, the human female was anxious to leave. I don't know if it's because the male's inner dragon came out to play and scared her—Finn's still trying to get the details—or if it was something else. Still, in case of the former, Finn has a favor to ask of you."

Crossing his arms over his chest, Alistair raised an eyebrow. "A favor, aye? And yet, he couldn't bother to ask me himself."

Faye stood tall and placed her hands on her hips. "Finn can't do everything, and you know that. Besides, Grant and I have just as much say in running the clan under certain circumstances as Finn does."

Grant was Faye's mate and the other co-head Protector. "I know that, aye? But Finn is supposed to be in charge of the humans, which is why I mentioned it."

She harrumphed. "If that's your way of apologizing, then I accept. It'll make things easier."

He resisted a sigh. Faye was an intelligent, strong female who could hold her own. But every once in a while, her temper flared, and Alistair didn't want to deal with it. That was her mate's problem, not his. "So what is it you want, lass? Try as I might, I can't read minds."

Her lips twitched. "Believe me, you don't want to hear my pregnant dragon's thoughts."

Clearing his throat, he made a motion with his hands for her to continue. "So what is it you need?"

The amusement faded from her eyes. "Instead of lessons inside the classroom, Finn wants you to hold some outside with the children and teenage dragon-shifters. He thinks that maybe having the humans interact with younger dragons will make us less intimidating, and give them time to acclimate to flashing dragon eyes."

He nodded. "Aye, that could work. Although usually David teaches anything to do with inner dragons, shifting, or flying."

"And he'll keep doing it. However, there needs to be another teacher there explaining things to the humans. Since you're the cultural liaison, Finn wants you to do it."

At the mention of one of his many titles, he asked slowly, "So will their liaison be there, too?"

"Kiyana? Yes, of course. Why?"

"No reason," he bit out quickly. "I just like to be prepared and know how many will be there. That way I can make enough copies and handouts."

Faye snorted. "Ever the teacher, aren't you? Although I'm not sure those will work in the wind and rain outside at the moment." She grinned. "Finn thought it a good idea for the humans to experience a usual day in the Highlands, too. That way, they can't say he didn't give them all the information if they find mates and decide to stay."

He waved a hand in dismissal. Alistair could teach without handouts if need be. "Fine, fine. When and where do I need to go?"

"The training area, in an hour. I'll check in with you after."

Faye left before he could ask anything else, and Alistair sighed again. He hoped he didn't have to deal with the females when it came to complaints, fears, or the like.

His beast spoke up. *Kiyana will do it.*

The female from the night before, who hadn't even tried to hide her knowledge from him, flashed into his mind. Alistair thought she wouldn't be afraid of flashing dragon eyes, especially since she'd seemed so interested in his the night before.

His dragon spoke again. *I say we should give her a private session, and I can make our pupils flash as much as she wants.*

Not going to happen, dragon. Because you'd then suggest showing her what you could do, if you took control.

I think she's interested, but you won't even give her a chance.

No. Now, drop it.

His beast huffed. *For now. But if she gives any sign of encouragement, I may have to take control or risk never having a female again.*

Since ignoring his beast was the best way to shut him up, Alistair did exactly that.

He may have to talk with Kiyana, but he wasn't going

to be as friendly or open as the night before. If his beast was right, Alistair wouldn't encourage her. He had more important things to do with his time, such as continue researching his secret project.

Just remembering his project strengthened his resolve. If he'd been able to solve the mystery a few years ago, he might've saved Rachel. Even though she was no longer with them, he would fight on in her memory. That was far more important than sating his dragon's lust with a bonnie female.

⌒⌒⌒⌒⌒

Kiyana pulled the hood of her raincoat tighter around her face and tried not to let the drizzle ruin her day.

Not just because her hair went from curly to a frizzy poofball whenever it rained heavily, but more because she'd already failed one of the women in her group.

Maybe it was true Cheryl had wanted to merely hookup with a dragonman one time and leave. But from what little she could get out of the woman before she'd been escorted and driven off Lochguard's land, it had seemed, at least to her, that the woman's fleeing was a result of flashing dragon eyes and a growly change in voice more than anything else.

Since she'd had sex for a little while with a dragonman years ago, Kiyana had experienced the fascinating phenomenon once before. The man from her past had tried his best to hide his beast from her, no matter how much she encouraged him to let the dragon take control of his mind.

While part of her had been curious to learn more, part of her had wanted the growly beast to take control and give her the kind of sex she had only dreamed about in the past.

However, as she and the remaining women reached the area which was partially shielded from the wind by walls of rock, Kiyana put her sex memories to the side. Scanning the surroundings, she noticed a tall dragonman probably in his forties standing at the back, as well as five or six children trying their best not to look over their shoulders.

At the sight, excitement bubbled up inside her. Kiyana had never witnessed a child shift into a dragon before, and she hoped she'd get the chance soon. True, it was as the liaison for the women and not as someone who could watch uninterrupted from the sidelines, but it was still better than nothing.

They had just stepped inside the walled area when a familiar male voice filled her ears. "We're to stay along the back wall."

Turning around, she came face-to-face with Alistair Boyd. If she expected him to be dressed more than the night before, she was wrong. His chest was bare, the rain causing rivulets to run down his chiseled muscles.

Damn, he was fit.

Her gaze trailed lower, to his tight-fitting jeans. Before she could help herself, she blurted, "Those are going to be bloody difficult to get off later."

Alistair grunted, and she met his gaze again. Like the night before, his pupils changed to slits and back to round. She wondered if his dragon was talking about her or not.

Grunting again, he looked over her head and motioned toward the other eight women. "Come closer to me, so I can explain things as they progress."

The women hesitated. However, Julie moved first, and a second later, the others followed suit.

Julie stood right next to Alistair and leaned in, displaying her wet cleavage to his full view. "Is this okay?"

Somehow, Kiyana contained an eye roll. It seemed Julie was no longer afraid of at least one particular dragon-shifter.

However, Alistair's gaze didn't drift downward, but rather above the women's heads to the children. "Aye, but you may want to turn around so you can watch. Otherwise, I could do this lecture inside, where it's warm and dry."

As if on cue, the rain fell harder. Kiyana muttered, "You lot are cheery considering the weather here."

Alistair must've heard her because his eyes found hers. "When the sun's out, the light glimmering on the loch, combined with the sky reflecting on its gleaming surface, fills you with enough good humor to last months, or more."

She hadn't expected Alistair to be poetic. Maybe there was a hidden depth to him he kept tightly packed away from almost everyone else.

They stared at one another a few beats until the teacher up front clapped his hands and said, "All right, lads and lassie, it's time to review what goes into a shift."

The only girl in the class turned to look at them and then back at the teacher. "Do we have to do it with them there? It's weird having people watch. My dragon is shy and doesn't want to be watched."

The teacher smiled. "A shy dragon? Come, now, we know she's not. The humans are here to learn."

The little girl looked at Kiyana and the others again, before turning back around. "Then why are they at the back?"

The teacher shrugged. "So they don't get in the way."

One of the little boys spoke up. "But you always say we learn better if we sit up front. The humans should come up front."

The others murmured the same, and Kiyana smiled. Dragon-shifter children weren't all that different from human ones. Sure, they could shift into magnificent creatures while humans couldn't, but their curiosity and forthrightness were the same.

The teacher looked at Alistair, and Alistair surveyed the group of women. "Would you prefer being up front?"

Julie nodded. "I would. They're cute, and no matter what people say, I don't think they'll hurt us."

The little girl cried out, "It's humans who hurt us!"

Julie shook her head. "No, I don't think so."

"It's too, true! My mummy said so."

Kiyana sensed the back-and-forth could go on for a while. Even though it wasn't her place, she blurted, "How about we agree that everyone here won't hurt each other? That should be good enough."

All of the dragon-shifter children turned and stared at her with wide eyes.

Thankfully it was Alistair who stepped in. "That's a brilliant idea. Lasses, let's head toward the front. Maybe David, the teacher, can introduce you to the wee ones."

The women all walked briskly to the front, but Kiyana took her time. True, she was just as excited to watch the young dragons as any of the others, but she wanted to observe, if even for a short while, how the women interacted with the dragon children. Especially as the little girl didn't wait for her teacher's permission to walk up to Julie and start blurting out questions.

Alistair's voice came from right behind her. Due to her hood, she had to strain her ears to catch his words. "I thought you were supposed to observe and not interfere?"

She stopped, and Alistair gently bumped against her back and arse. For a second, she sucked in a breath at his hard, warm body against hers. However, as he stood there, not moving, her skin grew too tight and her heart raced.

She was no longer cold from the wind and rain.

But nearly as soon as the heat burned, it vanished. Alistair suddenly stood two feet in front of her. Their eyes locked, and she couldn't pull her gaze away. Maybe she imagined the heat and desire in his eyes, but she didn't think so.

And maybe if they'd met under different circumstances, she would've closed the distance between them, placed a hand on his bare chest, and tilted her lips upward.

Too bad that could never happen. Kiyana had worked too bloody hard to climb back up the DDA's ladder. No matter how sexy Alistair Boyd was, or how one molten look could make her insides flip, she couldn't act on it.

Ever.

Clearing her throat, she shrugged. "The DDA didn't think it through when they made me their liaison in addition to the observer-slash-documentarian. So I'll have to do the best I can, and once the other women all decide to stay or go home, I can finally get to work."

Alistair searched her gaze, his pupils flashing, and she willed her heart to slow the hell down. His dragon most definitely didn't think about her in *that* way.

He couldn't.

With a grunt, Alistair turned and walked toward the group of women. As he went about helping with introductions, Kiyana tried to look away. But even when she could force her gaze to one of the adorable schoolchildren, they almost instantly darted back to Alistair's broad shoulders and square jaw.

And his chest. Damn, the warm, solid chest she'd felt against her back for the briefest of moments.

Someone said her name, loudly, and she blinked before finding Julie. The other woman shot her a puzzled look then asked, "Aren't you coming, Kiki?"

"Kiyana," Alistair stated.

All eyes turned toward the towering dragonman. Julie managed to say, "Pardon?"

"She prefers Kiyana. The children should learn her real name and not the ridiculous nickname."

The human women all exchanged glances before zeroing in on Kiyana.

Thank goodness for the distance and the hood pulled close around her face. They probably couldn't see how uncomfortable she was. No shuffling of feet or biting of lips for Kiyana. No, she started tugging strands of her hair straight, releasing them, and doing it again.

Wanting the focus off her, Kiyana clapped her hands. "Enough about me. We're here to talk with the children. Now, shall we finish the introductions? I'm Kiyana."

As the kids each jumped in to share their names, she did her best to focus on the little balls of energy. Throughout the entire exchange, she felt Alistair's gaze on her back, but she refused to turn around. She most definitely wouldn't turn around.

And if she kept running into him or being near him, she might slip in her resolve and do something stupid. So, the first chance she had, she would encourage Julie to be the leader of the group of women. If Julie was up for the task, then she only had to report back to Kiyana, meaning less time Kiyana had to interact with the clan members.

Yes, that would be the best option. And with Kiyana out of the way, maybe Alistair would go after one of the other women.

Although why that thought left a sour taste in her mouth, she refused to acknowledge. Her work was too important to her. And as she'd learned the last time she'd dallied with a dragonman, a heated look didn't mean forever. She needed to remember that.

CHAPTER THREE

*A*fter the outdoor session with the children, Alistair had thankfully been able to teach his other lessons to the humans in a classroom. The women were mostly eager to learn, and the familiarity of teaching, quizzing, and fostering discussion made time pass easily.

Well, for the most part. He had a hard time not looking at the door to see if Kiyana would show up or not.

Even now, when he was sitting inside the clan's archive building, he was tempted to look at the door despite the fact she probably didn't even know about the place's existence.

His dragon spoke up. *Go find her. I know I saw heat in her gaze the other day.*

You keep saying that, but it still doesn't matter to me. Besides, this afternoon is the first time we've been able to work on our secret project for weeks.

His beast grunted. *The information you're searching for may not even exist.*

I'm not giving up.

Alistair looked back at the dusty, barely legible book in front of him. Since few people visited the clan's archives, it was one of the quietest places on Lochguard, and therefore one of his favorites.

He'd just managed to decipher a passage about centuries-old treaties when a female voice—a Southern English female voice—filled the space. "What are you doing here? I thought you had lessons since it's a weekday."

His dragon sat up tall and spread his wings at Kiyana's voice. However, Alistair didn't give the beast time to suggest they woo the female into his lap. Not looking up from his book, he shrugged. "Every third Wednesday of the month, the students go volunteer with the elder dragon-shifters and help them with whatever they need."

Amusement tinged Kiyana's voice. "From the few pensioner-aged dragons I've seen, they're more than capable of doing things themselves."

"Maybe. Still, they have much to teach us. Not everything is found in a book."

A fact Alistair was all too aware of himself.

"Are you going to keep your back to me for the entire conversation?" the human asked.

Alistair decided to be as blunt as she was. "I thought this would be a universal sign shared between humans and dragons, one that says leave me alone."

She laughed, the deep sound washing over him, making his dragon hum and his cock go semihard.

His beast spoke up. *Why resist her? You haven't been this attuned to a female since Rachel.*

At the mention of his late girlfriend's name, his body cooled instantly, as if ice water had been dumped over him.

Turning, he gave his best stern look, one he'd perfected over the years with his students. "I wasn't making a joke. I'm working on an important project."

Curiosity flared in Kiyana's brown eyes, ones he was fast becoming able to read. She asked, "What are you researching?"

He shouldn't tell her. Hell, he hadn't told anyone.

His dragon murmured, *And it's a lonely endeavor. Tell her. What could it hurt?*

She would keep asking questions and might even want to help. So I most definitely don't want to tell her.

And then Kiyana was next to him, squinting at the page of his book. "*The History of Dragon Clan Treaties: 1700 to 1860.*"

He closed the book. "You have good eyesight for a human."

Kiyana peered closer at the cover. "Why are you reading that? Do Lochguard and the other clans in the UK want to form treaties with dragon-shifters in other countries?"

"If we did, I wouldn't tell you."

She didn't pay his clipped tone any heed. "Is the book proprietary knowledge, forbidden to humans?"

Try as he might, Alistair couldn't lie. "No."

She nodded. "Then when you're done with it, I'd like to read it."

He frowned. "Why?"

She raised an eyebrow. "Are you going to tell me why *you're* reading it?"

"No."

"Then until you share, I have no reason to tell you my reasons, do I?"

His dragon hummed. *I like her. She's not afraid of us and treats us as if we were merely another human.*

You just want me to sweet talk her so that maybe she'll kiss us.

What's wrong with that? Imagine pulling her close, kissing her lips, jaw, neck, and down to her hard nipple...

The image flashed into his mind. Alistair closed his eyes and growled to his beast, *Don't do that.*

Why? She's not going to crawl under the table and check the current status of our cock.

Kiyana's voice interrupted his inner conversation. "Most dragon-shifters can easily talk with their dragons and jump right back into a conversation with someone else. Is it different for you?"

His dragon hissed, *Of course not. Tell her.*

Opening his eyes, Alistair drew in a breath at how close Kiyana stood. If she leaned a few inches closer, her breast would brush his shoulder.

And if he turned his head and lowered it a little, it'd be at the perfect height to suckle her nipple through her top.

Stop it, Alistair. Nothing can come of it, he mentally told himself. Of course, his dragon snorted.

Careful to keep his voice even and not husky, he shook his head and answered, "No, I can talk as easily with my dragon as anyone else. Maybe I was trying to send another subtle signal for you to leave, but somehow you're still here."

"Well, you haven't actually asked me to leave."

His dragon chuckled. *She's right.*

"Will you leave, then?"

She tilted her head. "That depends. Will you let me know when you're done with that book?"

Fuck, if he said yes, she'd leave but then he'd be forced to talk with her again. Somehow, he didn't think she'd take too kindly to him sending a student on his errand. If Finn got word of him avoiding Kiyana, then his clan leader would probe. And no one wanted to be prodded and questioned by Finn. Charmer he may be, but he was tenacious, too.

His dragon sighed. *Stop being a coward. Just let her know we'll bring it to her. It's not that difficult.*

Alistair grunted. "Fine, I'll let you know when I'm finished with it. Although you'll have to bribe Jhanvi—she's in charge of the archives—heavily to even think of taking it out of this building."

Kiyana stepped toward the nearest bookcase, and Alistair tamped down his disappoint at how her scent diminished. He watched as she ran a finger over the nearest shelf of books, carefully touching each spine. "I like it in here and don't need to take the book out of the building. Besides, I wouldn't do anything to revoke archive privileges. There's so much knowledge here, stuff that most humans haven't had access to in decades. I almost wish I could stay here my entire time on Lochguard. Not to avoid everyone, but the knowledge will be brilliant, I know it."

His beast said, *She appreciates books as much as we do.*

Maybe, he conceded.

That kind of female is a rarity. Are you really going to ignore her and risk never finding another one who shares such a major passion of ours?

He watched as Kiyana continued to read the spines on the shelf above her. Her profile was just as beautiful as her whole face. The urge to kiss every curve and line of it exploded through his body, his lips throbbing in anticipation.

Kiyana met his gaze and froze. After a beat, she faced him and shook her head. "Sorry, but not going to happen, Alistair."

He blinked. There was no way she could've read his mind. "What the bloody hell are you talking about?"

She gestured between them. "Us. The desire is plain in your gaze, but I can't. Just know that I can't, no matter how much I may want to."

His dragon roared. *Then she does want us. Why can't we have her? Ask her. Ask her now.*

Since he was curious as well—even Alistair had some pride—he asked, "Why not?"

As they stared at one another, sadness flickered in her gaze. "Because if I do, I'll lose everything. My job, my career, my whole life's purpose. Things may be changing between most humans and dragons, but employees of the DDA still aren't allowed to dally with dragons if they wish to remain in the organization."

His dragon growled, *It wouldn't be a dalliance because that implies once or twice. That's not enough. I want to know her better.*

The words gave Alistair an idea, one he should instantly toss away. And yet, if he was to truly understand humans better and pass on the knowledge to his students, he shouldn't shun all of them.

And so far, Kiyana fascinated him the most.

Not to mention with her not wanting to sleep with him, it created the perfect barrier. Alistair would never push something that would cause harm, which meant he'd never have sex with Kiyana and ruin her dreams.

He spoke up. "Then no sex. None. I promise you that."

She searched his gaze. "Just like that?"

"Aye. But is there anything in the rules about being friends?"

Pausing a second, she tapped her chin. It took everything he had not to stare at her long, graceful finger as she did so. "Not that I recall."

"Good. Then we can share information. Once a week we can meet here and ask each other questions. No touching, no heated gaze, just two people engaging in a professional relationship."

His dragon hissed. *I don't like that, not at all.*

To me, it's the perfect solution. After all, sex is off the table. And neither of us are dishonorable enough to take everything away from her, aye?

Of course not. Maybe some rogue dragon-shifters don't have honor, but we most assuredly do. It doesn't mean I won't try to think of a way around it.

You do that. Although I somehow doubt you have a vast knowledge of the DDA's policies.

Then maybe I'll work on changing that.

Kiyana's voice interrupted his conversation with his dragon. "I hope I don't come to regret this, but okay. We'll try it." She narrowed her eyes. "But at the first heated look, I'm out of here and I do my best to steer clear of you."

"I'll try to hold back, but I can't always control my dragon's emotions. Unlike my human half, he doesn't understand why we should hide emotions."

At the spark of interest in her eyes, Alistair knew she wanted to know more.

And while his dragon may cringe at a platonic relationship, it worked well for him.

His beast spoke up. *And what about Mum? She'll ask questions if she finds out.*

Good point. Alistair focused back on Kiyana. "And maybe one more caveat, aye? I have no interest in finding a mate, but my mother will continue to foist females in my direction with the hope of me changing my mind. So if she asks, I'll tell her I have someone. I won't mention names, but maybe we can humor her?"

"I can't risk that, Alistair. Forgive me, but even I've already learned how much of a gossip your mother is."

"Aye, she is that. But I will merely tell her we're friends, nothing more. However, she may wink at you occasionally, thinking she's cracked our secret. Still, if there is no proof of a romantic entanglement, the DDA can't reprimand you."

"Add any more conditions, and we'll need to draw up a written contract so I can remember them all," she drawled.

His lips twitched. "No more stipulations, I promise. And look at it this way—the less time I have to argue with my mother about finding a female, the more time I can answer your questions."

"You're good at dangling the carrot, aren't you?"

He chuckled, surprising himself.

Alistair hadn't laughed much over the last few years.

However, before he could sort through that thought, Kiyana spoke again. "Okay, then meetings here once a week it is. But we should both try to arrive as inconspicuously as possible. That way fewer will notice the coincidence of us both being here at the same time. Maybe your mother won't ever find out."

He grimaced. "Unfortunately, the female who runs the archives is friends with my mum. Even if she weren't, Meg Boyd has a way of finding out anything and everything that happens on Lochguard."

Well, except for Alistair's secret project and his late girlfriend. Both of which he managed to keep from her, but only because he knew his mother so well.

Kiyana tugged a section of her hair straight, released it, and repeated the gesture. He was sure it meant something—probably discomfort or an internal struggle—but all he could focus on was how long her hair was when stretched out. It would be past her waist if it were straight.

Although he preferred it curly.

Not wanting to dwell on how he had a preference, he focused instead on her words as she stated, "Well, at any rate, I suppose asking most of my questions to one dragon-shifter will help me from forming social relationships with many more dragonmen and women. So doing all of this should be worth it, I think. I get the knowledge I want and can mostly keep a distance from the rest of the clan."

His dragon jumped in. *I don't want her to keep her distance. But still, she needs to say yes. If I find a loophole where she can keep her job, then maybe she'll change her mind.*

Even if there is one, I have no interest. A mate will detract from our work.

His beast huffed. *You always say that. But there is more to life than books.*

"Alistair, are you listening?"

He blinked. "Sorry. My dragon is quite chatty at times."

She slid into the chair opposite him. Even with her scent invading his nose, he managed to keep his body from responding.

Their arrangement might just work after all.

His beast shook his head but remained silent. When Kiyana leaned forward, he did his best to ignore her breasts pressing together. "Talking with your inner dragon is one of the things that fascinates me the most. Is there anything in the archives about inner dragons? Such as studies done in the past? That way I could have a foundation of knowledge before asking you for more details."

Alistair admired her zeal of learning. "I can't say I've looked for that sort of information before. Layla—Dr. MacFie—might know more about that since it's related to her field."

She craned her head around, surveying the rows of bookcases. "I may look here first. Nothing against your doctor, but I like to start with historical knowledge and work my way forward. It's not the most popular approach in my field, but I like getting the bigger picture, complete with a historical perspective, instead of focusing on just the present."

He scanned his memory for what little he knew about the social sciences, and social anthropology in particular. "Aren't you supposed to interview people? Watch how they interact, and interview some more?"

"That's the simplistic approach used decades ago. It's a lot more complicated than that now."

Alistair resisted a grimace. He really didn't want to go into ethics and philosophies surrounding anthropology.

Kiyana laughed. "Judging from your face, you would rather be shut in a room with a million gnats than have me tell you more."

"A million is a touch much, aye? A thousand, on the other hand, and then you'd be right."

She grinned, revealing a beautiful smile and a dimple on one side of her face.

For a split second, Alistair's heart stopped beating. Kiyana was one of the most beautiful women he'd ever seen.

Not only bonnie but also intelligent with a sense of humor.

If not for their agreement and his honor, he might be in trouble.

When his dragon remained firmly quiet, further unease settled in his stomach.

Kiyana stood. "Well, I'm going to look around and see what I can find. We'll start next week then, around the same time?"

He bobbed his head and watched as Kiyana walked away from him. His gaze zeroed in on her hips and arse.

She'd be nice to take from behind.

Not that he ever would. Alistair opened his book and tried to keep reading. However, he couldn't manage to comprehend a single paragraph until Kiyana left the building.

That alone should make him wary, but add in his dragon's restrained glee, and Alistair hoped he hadn't underestimated the depths of his honor. Because if he had, he might do something stupid, like eventually try to kiss Dr. Kiyana Barnes.

Which, of course, could never happen.

CHAPTER FOUR

As Kiyana walked home from the archives, she couldn't help but smile. Not only had she discovered a book on old Lochguard mating dances—who knew such a thing existed—she also now had a source to ask all her questions.

Being honest had seemed to work with Alistair. However, she never expected him to take her refusal so easily, not to mention suggest they meet once a week to share information.

Although why he needed information on humans, she didn't know. For his students, yes, but maybe it had something to do with his secret project. The one related to the barely legible book on 18th- and 19th-century treaties.

So wrapped up in her thoughts, Kiyana didn't see Meg Boyd until she bumped into the older woman. Thankfully Meg didn't fall over, and once they were both solidly on two feet again, Meg took her hand. "Come with me, lass."

"I don't think—"

"Now."

The cheerful, nosey woman from the night of the party had vanished, revealing steel beneath Meg's surface.

Not wanting to fight the old woman in public, she allowed Meg to drag her inside a cottage. Since Meg walked in without knocking, Kiyana assumed it was hers. The pictures of her three sons on the wall proved her theory correct.

However, the hall wasn't enough, and Meg pulled her into a small side room, one filled with a sofa, a small desk, and a chair. Only once she tugged Kiyana inside and locked the door did she drop her hand and speak again. "My Alistair wants you."

She blinked. "Pardon?"

"Don't deny it, lass. I know my son, and he hasn't ever shown as much interest in a female as he has with you. So tell me, how can I help?"

Meg's suggestion was more than merely winking and nudging her side. Surely Alistair would understand Kiyana's need to be honest. "You can't. My role here is to watch over the females and observe enough so I can write papers and maybe even a book to help humans better understand dragon-shifters."

"It's because of your contract, aye?"

The old woman was full of surprises. "Er, yes. How did you know that?"

Meg waved a hand. "There's a way out of that."

She frowned. "How in the world do you know that?"

Raising her brows, Meg's gaze turned dead serious. "Everyone thinks I'm merely a busybody, meddling in everyone's business. And maybe that's true to an extent, but I have a secret, too, lass. Ever since Rosalind Abbott became the DDA Director, I've been secretly working for the DDA, too, on the sly."

Kiyana's jaw dropped. Since when did the DDA start hiring dragon-shifters? Not only that, but without letting anyone else know?

Meg tilted her head. "I can see you're confused, and I don't blame you. Only Finn knows the truth, although I suspect his mate does, too. That may be a wee violation, but Arabella is a clever lass who wouldn't do anything to hurt the clan, so I forgave Finn for it."

Kiyana's brain spun, and she tried to make it stop long enough to let her ask a question. However, Meg just pushed on, revealing what it must've been like for Alistair growing up. The older dragonwoman said, "Circling back, I work for the DDA, and I reviewed your contract. On the surface, aye, you aren't allowed to date or sleep with any dragon-shifter, male or female. However, they left something out, something important. A point any lawyer would say works in your favor."

She should walk away from the whole crazy mess, but her curiosity burned. So, she asked, "What is it?"

Meg leaned in and whispered, "You're allowed to keep working if, using the human term, you're engaged. So, if you promise in front of the clan that you will be mated— say, as soon as your work contract is over—then you can do what you like with my son *and* keep your position within the DDA."

Kiyana merely stared at the dragonwoman. It took a second, but she finally made her mouth form words, "You want me to pretend to be Alistair's fiancée?"

Meg nodded. "Aye, that I do. You're my last hope, lassie. After all, he's turning thirty soon and while some dragonmen age well—like my own beaus—Alistair draws deeper into himself by the day. Soon, he'll be unreachable. You may be his—and my—last chance."

Kiyana didn't like how Meg dismissed her son so easily. Alistair was a bit mysterious, sure, and also liked to spend time reading dusty books in the clan archives. But he was sociable enough with the human women she'd accompanied, and he didn't seem like a complete recluse to her.

Meg prodded, "So, will you do it, lass? Pretend to be my Alistair's female?"

She'd have to handle the situation carefully. "I barely know him."

"Aye, I know. But don't deny you feel a pull toward him. I'm not sure if you're his true mate or not—not even I can judge that—but it's possible. Besides, even if it doesn't work between the two of you, then you can spend the time asking him all sorts of questions. I did my research on you, and I know you've been crawling your way out of the mistake you made five years ago. This will avoid that, and give you what you really want—the chance to maybe mate a dragon-shifter."

Meg Boyd was most definitely not who Kiyana had thought she was.

The entire scheme was crazy. She'd known Alistair less than a week and had spent maybe a few hours with him.

And yet, remembering how his heated gaze found hers, full of desire she'd never seen on another man, made her wonder if he was her happy ending. Ever since she'd been a child, Kiyana had wanted to live with the dragon-shifters. Her work had been the closest she'd come to achieving that, so she'd thrown her whole weight behind it.

However, times had changed from over twenty years ago. Human females didn't have to jump hoops or join the sacrifice program to be with a dragon-shifter in the UK, or so the last few years had shown even if it wasn't established law yet.

This could be her chance to belong where she had always wanted to be *and* keep her career.

Kiyana was on the verge of agreeing to the ridiculous plan, but then she remembered something important. "Shouldn't Alistair have a say in this?"

Meg smiled smugly. "If you agree, then he'll say yes."

"Because you'll force him to."

"Och, no, I'd never do that to my son. He'll say yes because on some level, his dragon recognizes how you are what he needs. My son changed drastically a few years ago for reasons not even I have discovered yet. But you, lass, you have helped bring a little of the old Alistair back. So if you say yes, he won't be able to resist."

Kiyana was skeptical of him not being able to resist. Sure, they were attracted to one another, but he'd made it plain that he wasn't looking for a mate.

And yet, having both a constant information source and maybe even a fuck buddy would be a plus, too. Not quite her happy ending, but it would definitely make her six months on Lochguard that much better.

Not to mention after her assignment ended, she could always leave, her and Alistair never having to see each other again if their relationship soured.

You really are crazy, Kiyana. And yet... She cleared her throat and stood up tall. "*If* Alistair agrees of his own free will, I'll talk with him and go from there. That's the best I can do."

Meg patted her cheek. "Clever lass. You'll do." The dragonwoman moved to the door and paused in opening it. "Come over for dinner tonight, around seven. All three of my lads will be home, and I'll find time to talk with Alistair. That way, we can start sooner rather than later."

It was on the tip of her tongue to say it would be okay to wait a day or two, but Meg opened the door and moved down the hallways. "Come, lass. I'll point out the exact passages in your contract that pertain to this scheme.

That way you'll be prepared."

As she followed Meg to another room upstairs, Kiyana's heart rate kicked up. Not only was her time on Lochguard vastly different from what she'd expected, but it may also change her life in ways she never imagined.

Ever since her screw up five years ago, she'd been careful about every decision. Rash ones tended to get her into trouble.

However, as Meg showed her the verbiage that could change her life, Kiyana remembered her father's words about needing to enjoy life more.

So, armed with legalese and a determined dragonwoman's enthusiasm, she embraced her late father's advice. Maybe, just maybe, the leap would land her to the destiny where she belonged.

⌒∽⌒∽⌒∽

Alistair took a deep breath and entered his mum's cottage. He and his brothers may be grown males, but once a week they all attended dinner at their mother's house.

Aye, not going would cause a month-long headache which none of them wanted. But it was also a way to keep grounded to his family. Even Alistair recognized he'd pulled away from them after Rachel's death.

His dragon said, *That's because you never talk about it.*

And I won't, until I find out how to stop it from happening to others. If other clan members find out about her condition, they could panic at the return of the inner dragon disease, and I don't want that.

His mum's voice drifted from the kitchen. "In here. I need to have a wee chat with you, Alistair."

His mother's chats were either about his lack of a mate, lack of children, or a lecture on how locking himself up with books all the time wasn't good for him.

He wasn't sure which of the three would be the day's topic.

Usually his dragon would make a witty or sly remark. However, his beast remained silent.

That meant Alistair was on his own against his mother for the lecture, and possibly the evening.

Entering the kitchen, he found his mother checking on something in the oven. Once she finished, she turned, placed a hand on one of her hips, and didn't bother with small talk. "I know who you fancy, and I've found a way for you to be with her."

He blinked. "What the bloody hell are you talking about?"

She clicked her tongue. "I'll ignore your language because what I have to say is more important." She took a step toward him, unafraid of how he towered nearly a foot above her tiny—for a dragon-shifter—form. "You like the Kiyana lass, don't deny it."

He opened his mouth, but she didn't let him say a word. "And aye, of course you'll deny it. Partly because you're dead set on never finding a mate. And partly because you know the rules surrounding her position."

Alistair usually allowed his mother to natter for a bit as he let it roll off him. But not this time. "How do you know any of this? And how do you know what I want?"

"I'm your mother, so of course I know what you want. I suppose there are mothers out there who don't pay attention to their children or some such thing, but I am most assuredly not one of them."

His dragon broke his silence to snort.

Alistair's mum didn't even draw a breath before adding, "You won't tell me why your personality and entire demeanor changed a few years back. I always ask, and you avoid it. Maybe it's because you need time to overcome what happened—I suspect something extreme and unpleasant took place—but I've come to terms with that. Well, mostly. But denying your dragon for years is selfish, Alistair, and you know it. Maybe humans can take a vow of celibacy, or what have you, but not dragon-shifters. He'll go mad before much longer."

Damn, his mother had brought up one of the we-never-talk-about-it topics. "I'm not talking about my sex life with you, Mum."

She shrugged. "You don't have to. I know everyone in the clan, even the newer humans, and have a fairly good idea of who is shagging who, when, and how many times."

Holy fuck, was his mother really telling him she had a clan-wide sex timetable?

No, no, no. He didn't want to know that.

His mum came even closer, poking his chest with her forefinger. "It's been more than three years. Any longer, and you could turn rogue, if the right set of circumstances cropped up. I've decided a mate may not be in your future if you continue on your own path. So I've fixed a new course for you."

Since his mother crossed her arms and arched an eyebrow, it was the cue that he could talk for a minute or so.

Sometimes he envied other dragon-shifters with mothers who didn't pry into every detail of their lives. Truth be told, only the MacKenzies had a mother similar to his, so most of the clan was fortunate.

Pouncing on his chance, he replied, "Arranged matings haven't happened in over a century, Mum. And Finn won't force it. Besides, Hamish and Graham are mated with children. Isn't that enough? What I do with my life should be my problem."

His dragon finally chimed in. *And what about me? Are you going to brush me off, too?*

Of course not. But you know I made a vow, and I won't break it. No sex until I find answers and/or a solution.

His mother huffed. "Stop being so stubborn. Your father was like that, too."

He sighed. "Using father to guilt-trip me won't work, Mum. He always encouraged us to find our own path, and having a mate and children isn't mine."

"Why? That's the one question I can never get an answer for. Why, Alistair? You used to talk about how much you wanted a family someday, and then suddenly, you never do. It's related to what happened three years ago, isn't it?"

"Aye, maybe. But I'm not ready to talk about that."

"And how long will it take? If it were only you, then aye, you could take all the time in the world. But don't neglect your dragon."

Alistair usually could hold his temper in check with his mother, but this evening she kept pushing. His patience snapped. "There are more important things than finding some female to woo into bed and shag. I have something important I have to do, Mum. Something that I need to solve, to keep the promise I made to someone on their deathbed. Can't you just leave it alone?"

At that moment, Kiyana stepped from the adjacent dining room into the kitchen. "Just drop it, Meg. He's hurting, and shouldn't be pushed."

He frowned. "What the bloody hell is going on? Why is Kiyana here?" He pierced his mother with a glare. "Start talking, Mum, or I swear I won't come over for dinner again until I'm forced."

Once his anger cleared, Alistair would realize he couldn't follow through with his threat. But for now, it made the most sense. It might also help his case.

And so, as he looked between Kiyana and Meg, he waited for some fucking answers.

Kiyana hadn't meant to eavesdrop. Meg had asked her to wait in the small office they'd been inside earlier, one that was apparently soundproofed.

But as she stared at the walls with exactly three pictures and tried her best not to look at the time every three seconds, she'd grown anxious.

After all, she was someone who, once they made a decision, tried their hardest to make it a reality as soon as possible.

Waiting wasn't her style.

So she'd started with cracking the door open. She heard two voices, and wondered if it was Alistair or one of his brothers conversing with Meg.

Then the male voice had grown louder, clearly upset. Slowly, she'd inched out of the room until she'd been standing in the dining room, rooted to the spot as she listened to Meg and Alistair's heated conversation.

It became apparent rather quickly that Meg had either misjudged Alistair or had used the wrong tactics to bring up the agreement.

Regardless, it was enough for Kiyana to step into the kitchen and end the madness. She'd meant it earlier, about not forcing Alistair. Whatever heat he'd displayed before had been split-second lust, and nothing more.

She'd let her girlhood fantasies cloud her better judgment earlier. She'd be careful not to let it happen again.

So when Alistair asked what was going on, Kiyana somehow managed to speak before Meg could. "I'm here because your mother asked me to be here. She made a proposition earlier, one that tugged on a dream of mine, which then made me hasty. But don't worry, I see now you have no interest in me or any other woman, and so I'll back away."

Alistair frowned. "Interest in you?" He looked at Meg and back to her. "Will someone tell me what the fuck is going on?"

Meg beat her to the punch. "Kiyana and I had a lovely chat earlier, one concerning you. She was all set to be your pretend mate-to-be, but you've ruined that now. If I didn't love you so much, I'd wash my hands of you, Alistair."

Alistair's mismatched eyes bored into hers, and she did her best not to step back. Alistair may be a teacher, but he was still a dragon-shifter, which meant he was part animal. His steely voice bit out, "What. Is. She. Talking. About?"

Used to the fierceness of his gaze, she raised her chin a fraction and never looked away. "It seems your mother has an eye for legal contracts and noticed a loophole inside the DDA's terms when it came to mine. I won't tell you how she knows about my contract as that's something you'll have to ask her. But just know that she's correct in that if I am engaged to a dragon-shifter, I can keep my job and be with them, at least until I marry—mate—the dragon-shifter. Even if you didn't want me physically, the situation would give us a chance to share information. I also thought it'd help keep your mum off your back."

"Och, now wait—"

Kiyana ignored Meg. "But I said I wouldn't force you, or trick you, and so I rescind my offer. Unless there's anything else you need to know, I should be going."

Alistair stepped closer, until he was near enough she could feel the heat from his body. Even with his flashing pupils, Kiyana didn't look away. Correction, she couldn't look away. Alistair's eyes were full of anger, yes, but heat, confusion, and something she couldn't define.

Maybe her initial gut feeling had been right.

He murmured, "You're not going anywhere until we talk more about this."

"About what? Your mother made an offer, one that I should've dismissed immediately but didn't. I heard your protests and decided to call it off. There's really nothing more to discuss."

Leaning another inch closer, Alistair said, "There is much to talk about. Just not in front of my mother." He moved away and looked at his mum. "You and I will revisit this later. But right now, Kiyana and I need to talk."

"About what?" Kiyana asked.

He put out his hand, palm up, and waited. "Not here."

She raised an eyebrow. "While I appreciate you trying to be nice and not just grab my hand, I can easily walk out that door and ignore you."

"You don't want to do that."

His voice wasn't threatening, but rather...husky.

Kiyana resisted a shiver and made her brain work. Maybe Alistair had changed his mind, but did she still want the ridiculous situation proposed by his mother?

The responsible thing to do was to walk away and pretend the day had never happened.

And yet, as she watched Alistair's pupils flash between slits and round, she burned to know what he was thinking.

The instant she placed her hand in his, Alistair tightened his grip and guided her down the hall. He threw over his shoulder, "See you later, Mum."

They hit the cool evening air, but she barely noticed. Every inch of skin that touched Alistair's sizzled, the electricity moving through the rest of her body.

And all she did was hold hands. If he kissed her, she might explode.

No, Kiyana. Focus.

The short trip from Meg's house to another cottage she assumed was Alistair's took less than five minutes. She used the time as best she could to think with only her brain and not also her lady parts. Whatever Alistair needed to discuss, it had to be done rationally. No more allowing her childhood dreams to make everything appear rosier than it really was.

And definitely she couldn't allow her hormones to get the best of her, either.

Kiyana thought she'd gotten herself under control. At least until Alistair pulled her inside the house, shut the door, and caged her body with his arms. While they weren't touching, she could feel his heat surrounding her. Her heart rate kicked up as her body temperatures rose.

Crazy as it sounded, time slowed as they stared at one another, too.

When Alistair finally spoke, his breath danced across her lips, stoking the fire inside her even hotter. "Now, lass, I think it's time for you to be honest and straightforward with me."

"About what?"

His eyes dropped to her lips. "Were you really going to be my fake mate-to-be?"

She swallowed. Her lips tingled as she replied, "Yes. But as I mentioned, I've called it off. I won't force it."

Alistair met her gaze again, and his pupils flashed more rapidly than before. "What if I want it?"

"Pardon?"

He moved his face another inch closer. "I've tried my best to ignore you, Kiyana. Even though you're the most bloody beautiful woman I've ever seen, not to mention smart and with enough backbone to even stand up to the likes of my mother, I didn't want to ruin your career. That gave me the perfect excuse to throw up a wall between us. But now? Now that I know there's a way for you to be mine *and* keep your job? I'm not sure I can forget that, lass." His gaze dropped back to her lips. "And I very much want to kiss you."

If she had any ounce of reason left in her brain, she'd tell him to let her go.

However, with his body so close and his scent overwhelming her, not to mention the want in his eyes, there was no way Kiyana could say no. She may be a strong woman, but not that strong.

Especially when it was something she wanted more than she'd wanted anything in a long while.

So she tipped her lips up toward his and whispered, "Then do it."

Without missing a beat, Alistair closed the distance between them and kissed her.

⚬⚬⚬⚬⚬

Alistair's dragon may have been badgering him about kissing Kiyana, but he was honest enough to admit he wanted her. More than he'd originally thought, especially when the human had threatened to leave his mother's house without another word.

But now she stood in front of him, her body a few inches from his, inside his cottage.

The air was electric, and one touch would probably start a fire. One that would have long-term consequences.

Rational Alistair should realize that, step back, and create a plan.

However, his beast growled, *No, don't you fucking walk away. She's here and she wants us. Kiss her. Now.*

He should demand more answers. Hell, Alistair always asked for more information.

There was also something in the back of his mind, a reason he shouldn't kiss her. Something to do with no sex.

However, Kiyana's scent was a drug, one he wasn't sure he could fight against.

So when she tipped her luscious lips up and told him to kiss her, Alistair didn't fight it.

The instant his lips touched hers, an overwhelming want coursed through his body. One he'd never felt before, one he wasn't sure he could fight.

Kiyana opened her mouth and he explored every inch of her delicious heat with his tongue, needing to learn every bit of it, wanting her to remember his taste forever.

Pulling her up against him, he groaned at her breasts pressing against his chest. He snaked a hand to her lovely arse and rocked her lower body against his.

He hissed at the friction against his cock at the same time his dragon roared, *More, more, I need more. Kiss her, fuck her, claim her over and over again.*

Kiyana moaned, and his need intensified. Fuck, if he wasn't inside her soon, he'd die.

And in that moment, Alistair's brain put it all together. *She's our true mate.*

Yes. So kiss her, fuck her, claim her. She is meant to be ours, forever.

His inner beast pushed for him to strip her and thrust between her thighs, but somehow Alistair drew on every iota of strength he possessed to break the kiss and release Kiyana.

His dragon roared, and Alistair tried his best to construct a mental prison. It wouldn't hold long, but maybe long enough for Kiyana to run.

Not just to save herself, but to help Alistair from betraying everything he believed. A kiss might have been okay, but sex wasn't. And once his dragon got out, there'd be a mate-claim frenzy, which would be nonstop sex until Kiyana carried his child.

He was an idiot for even kissing her in the first place.

Gritting his teeth, he ordered, "Get out."

Kiyana, his lovely human, didn't budge but frowned. "What? Why? You were clearly into me two seconds ago."

His beast pounded harder. In a few minutes, he might not be able to control his dragon until Kiyana was pregnant.

He retreated further, until his back hit the wall. "You know dragon-shifters. If you don't leave, my dragon will take control and I can't stop him. Not until you're pregnant."

Her eyes widened. "Wait, I'm your true mate?"

Roaring louder, his dragon launched against the sides of the mental prison. It wouldn't be long now.

Alistair nodded. "Now, go. Find Finn, explain it, and stay away from me."

She paused for a few seconds, each one giving his dragon more chances to break free. He ordered, "Leave. Now."

She responded quietly, "What if I said yes to it all?"

His dragon tried harder to escape, clawing at the prison, his lust and need seeping through. "No, I can't... please don't make me."

He swore pain flashed in her eyes, but it was gone before he could blink.

He'd hurt her. Bloody hell, he'd hurt her. "It's not what you think..."

"No, don't explain. That just makes it worse." She finally went to the front door. "I'll find Finn and leave you be."

Within seconds, he was alone. Alistair raced to his bedroom, typed out a quick text message to the clan's doctor, and curled into a ball on the floor. He didn't know how long he could hold off his dragon, but he hoped it was long enough.

Otherwise, he'd probably break the vow he'd made to himself concerning Rachel, and that was one thing he could never do.

CHAPTER FIVE

*K*iyana didn't cry often. But as she half ran, half stumbled to Finn's house, tears prickled her eyes.

Being rejected was never easy, but it was infinitely worse when Kiyana turned out to be someone's true mate—one determined by fate to be a good fit—and he still didn't want her.

Stop it, Kiyana. You know he didn't want a mate. That's nothing new.

If only the words would stick. Yet as she remembered Alistair's tongue stroking hers as he rocked her against his hard cock, it just didn't make sense. There had to be a reason for his rejection. There had to be.

And if she could figure it out, it might help the sting and ease her pain a little.

She finally reached Finn's cottage, the light in the front windows a good sign. Normally she'd take more care about noise since Finn and his mate had young children. But Kiyana was in no state to remember niceties, and pounded on the door with everything she had.

Finn opened the door with a frown. It instantly vanished when he saw her face. "Kiyana, lass, what's wrong?"

Since she'd ran the entire way and wasn't a runner in any way, shape, or form, she took a second to catch her breath before answering, "It's Alistair." A few more breaths. "He kissed me...true mate...doesn't want me."

Arabella appeared behind Finn, pushed him to the side, and took her hand. "Come in, Kiyana. Sit down and tell us what happened."

Kiyana didn't budge. She'd caught her breath enough to not have to gasp out words any more. "No, I can't. He told me to tell Finn. I think he needs help."

Finn and Arabella shared a looked before Finn met Kiyana's gaze again. "You come in and sit with Ara. I'll see to Alistair myself."

Arabella had managed to get her inside the cottage before Finn turned around and asked her point blank, "Did you want him?"

Tears threatened to fall again, but she held them back. She couldn't form the words, but merely nodded.

Finn grunted, looked at Arabella, and left.

Then Arabella looked at her with sympathetic eyes, and Kiyana couldn't keep it together. Tears tumbled down her cheeks and she lost all semblance of reason.

She had zero claim to Alistair Boyd, but it hurt. Damn it, it still hurt.

⌘⌘⌘

Alistair had resorted to curling on the ground with his eyes closed, trying to keep control of his body. No matter how often he tried to patch up his mental prison, it wasn't long before his dragon burst free.

Where is she? She is ours. I need to claim her. Over and over. Until she carries our young.

No. She is gone.

63

His dragon roared. *Then I will take control. I will find her. She wants us, and I will claim her.*

No. I can't.

His beast hissed. *Your stupid vow. You've wasted three years of our life on that vow. You brought this on yourself, denying me. Now, I will take charge of our life. Kiyana should be ours, wants to be ours, and I will claim her.*

His dragon tried to wrestle control of their mind, using every mental trick of force he could manage. The beast tried to expand his presence until Alistair would be trapped in a corner, but Alistair fought back.

Then his dragon roared on and on, trying to exhaust the human half who couldn't take such noise for long periods.

Alistair hummed to help block it out.

And so the battle continued until something pricked his arm. He opened his eyes to find Dr. Layla MacFie standing over him, a needle in her hand.

His dragon's voice grew weaker. *No, no, no. Don't silence me. Kiyana is what we need. She should be our future. Don't lose someone else.* The dragon's voice was barely a whisper. *Don't let the past haunt you forever.*

His mind fell blissfully quiet, and Alistair moved to slump against the wall. Layla's voice filled the room. "Your dragon will be silent for a few days, at most. Care to tell me what the bloody hell is going on?"

Finn's voice came from the doorway. "I'd like to know that, too. Especially since Kiyana showed upon my doorstep nearly in tears. What the fuck did you do, Alistair? Leading on a female isn't your style, so you'd better start talking."

Too exhausted to do anything but lean against the wall, Alistair remained on the floor.

Even without his dragon roaring and battling him every turn, it was difficult to make his brain work. It was probably more a result of exhaustion than the drugs Layla had used.

Finn squatted next to him, his voice full of steel. "If you kissed her, you were interested. And she admitted she was, too. So why the fuck did you send her away in tears? And none of the secretive bullshit you've been spouting for years now, either. It wasn't a top clan priority, so I let it lie. However, it's a priority now. Why did you turn away Kiyana Barnes?"

He'd kept his secret for years. Kept it from everyone he knew, hoping he could be the male Rachel had needed to fulfill a vow.

And here he was, years later, still no closer to the truth. His clan leader was furious, he'd hurt the one female he'd actually wanted for the first time in years, and he'd pissed off his dragon.

All for the sake of his vow.

Maybe, just maybe, it was time to ask for help.

Finn had been one of his best friends, years ago. Things had happened, their paths had diverged, but maybe he was the friend he needed again. And so he replied, "I made a vow three years ago that I wouldn't have sex until I found the answers I needed. Sex with Kiyana would've smashed that promise, destroying the male I've become. I couldn't do it, Finn. I just couldn't do it."

Finn's gaze never wavered from his. "What vow, Alistair? Maybe I can help."

No matter if Finn was clan leader now, he was the same male from before. One who would help Alistair without hesitation.

Normally his dragon would urge him to share the truth. But this time, Alistair made the decision on his own. "Just over three years ago, my girlfriend—a dragon-shifter named Rachel—died of some sort of inner dragon disease." Layla opened her mouth, but Alistair shook his head. "I won't go into the specifics right now. However, there was talk of a possible cure in the Amazon Rainforest. But no matter what I did, I could never reach the clans living in and around there. The lack of communication lines became obvious, and Rachel slowly wasted away until she died."

He paused, doing his best to push the memories away. He was too exhausted to sort through them in front of others.

However, as Finn stared at him with curiosity and no anger, he found the strength to add, "I couldn't save her, but on her deathbed, I vowed I'd do anything to open communication lines between the different clans around the world. Until I could assure something like this wouldn't happen to someone else because of not being able to talk with other dragon clans, I would dedicate my free time to research a solution. To do that, I added a bit to the vow for myself—no sex until I found answers."

"And so that's why you rejected Kiyana."

He nodded. "I couldn't do it, Finn. Aye, I want the lass, but I can't turn my back on something so important. Until I discover how clans can be open with each other and are willing to help one another, I can't think of myself. Too many people could die if I put off or give up on my project. The thought of another Rachel slowly wasting away is too much for me."

Finn's voice was softer. "Why didn't you come to me for help? Even before I took over the leadership, I would've helped you, Alistair."

Since shaking his head required too much effort, he merely replied, "There were so many other problems, not to mention there's still a lot of prejudices surrounding other clans outside the UK. Once everyone found out Rachel was from America, it would've made things even more complicated."

"America?" Finn echoed.

"Aye, we met during university. I don't know if you remember when I took that research trip three years ago, but that's when I took a ship to America, to be with her during her last days."

Finn ran a hand through his hair. "Alistair, fuck, you should've told me about this." He opened his mouth to protest, but Finn continued before he could say a word. "But the past is the past, and we have to deal with the future. Times have changed from three years ago, and you bloody well know it. Your plan actually aligns with something Sid and Gregor are doing down on Stonefire."

Gregor Innes had been Lochguard's head doctor until he mated a female dragon on Stonefire. Alistair hadn't heard much about the dragonman since he'd left Scotland. He frowned. "What are you talking about?"

Layla finally spoke up again. "Aye, it's true. Sid and Gregor are trying to form a worldwide medical association for dragon-shifters. They've been working on it for a wee while now."

"I had no idea," he murmured.

"Exactly." Finn lightly smacked the side of Alistair's head. "Which makes you an idiot. You didn't have to do this alone, and you won't have to, either, going forward." Finn stood and placed his hands on his hips. "But for the moment, we need to discuss Kiyana Barnes."

"I still can't claim her, Finn."

"Your bloody vow, aye? I doubt you could've fulfilled it yourself, even if you reached the ripe old age of one hundred. Are you willing to sacrifice your entire life to this vow? It's obvious you cared about this Rachel a great deal, and I respect that. But if she cared even half as much about you, then she would've wanted you to be happy, Alistair. Kiyana seems a good sort, your dragon wants her, and more importantly, she wants you, too. Granted, not all true mates end happily ever after, but I can tell you that it did for me. Arabella means the world to me. Don't you want a chance of that for yourself?"

His first thought was that he did. His mother had been correct earlier in that he'd always pictured himself with a mate and children. A family to love and hold close, and hopefully steer to a less chaotic existence than what he'd experienced during his own childhood.

Then Rachel had died, along with his hopes.

But now, he might be able to have the future he'd once dreamed of. Of course, it meant he'd have to break his vow.

Could he really do it? After all these years, could he live for more than information and always searching for a solution?

Finn's voice filled the room again. "I see you debating it. Although I should warn you, it might take a wee bit of groveling if you truly want the lass. You hurt her, Alistair. And you need to fix that."

The thought of Kiyana crying and in pain because of him made his stomach churn. He may not know her well, but she deserved better than that. Much better.

And yet, he remembered how she'd been willing to be his pretend mate for six months. Maybe, just maybe, she would still agree to be with him.

All it would take was for him to break his vow.

Rachel's final words to him came rushing back. *"Be happy, Alistair. I love you, but I'm leaving you soon. Please, find another person to make you smile and laugh. Life's too short to brood and be angry. Just...find happiness."*

Bloody hell, he'd loved her so much and she'd been taken far too soon from him. However, Rachel was gone. There was no way to bring her back.

And if Finn and the others helped him, he could still work on fulfilling his vow while not throwing away his possible second chance at happiness.

His heart squeezed. Fuck, it was harder to take the leap than he wanted. And yet, he wanted to. Oh, how he wanted to.

Squatting back down, Finn gently squeezed his shoulder. "I vow we'll help you with your mission, Alistair. With two, or more, clans working together, we'll get it solved a hell of a lot quicker. Right now, I'm more concerned about the fate of one of my clan members. I won't ask again, so here's my last time: Do you want Kiyana as your mate?"

Maybe he should've anguished longer, hesitated, and wrung his hands. But with the weight lifted from his shoulder a little—Finn always followed through on his promises—Alistair nodded. "Aye, I think I do."

"Right, then we need to take care of this soon. Layla will help you as much as she can in containing the mate-claim frenzy until you're ready." Layla nodded and Finn added, "Ara and I will keep Kiyana at our cottage for the night. Tomorrow morning, I expect you to show up early and be ready to explain yourself to the only person it matters—Kiyana."

"Aye, I'll be there," he stated.

"Good. Then I'm going home. I won't contact the other clans for help until we talk a bit more in depth about all of this. But I will help you any way I can, I promise."

"I know you will, Finn."

Finn gave him one last long look and then left him alone with the clan doctor.

As Layla asked him questions and explained how they'd keep his dragon silent, he barely paid attention. His mind whirred with his decision and what it meant for the future.

Even though he wanted to jump right into the sudden change in his life, it wouldn't be easy. While he'd apologize first, Kiyana would want the full truth.

And even if it tore open his heart to bring up the past and answer her questions, he would do it. Otherwise he may end up alone and never have a chance with the human female.

A few weeks ago, that wouldn't have bothered him. But now, knowing there was a chance to have the life he'd once dreamed of, he didn't want to end up alone. His dragon deserved better, and maybe one day, he'd forgive himself for not fulfilling the vow himself and accept he did, too.

CHAPTER SIX

*A*t some point, Kiyana had fallen asleep out of exhaustion. So when she woke up in a strange room, it took her a second to remember everything that had happened.

But as her eyes fell on a portrait of Finn and Arabella's three children, it all came crashing back.

The kiss with Alistair, his refusal, and her staying with Lochguard's leaders.

She wanted to focus on the rational side of it all. After all, few humans experienced even the beginnings of a mate-claim frenzy with a dragon-shifter. That was something she could maybe write about one day, interview others who'd gone through it, and put together a full picture.

And yet, her usual zeal for research didn't rush forth.

Maybe if it'd ended differently—who could turn down hot, dirty sex with a dragonman?—she would be smiling and thinking of who to talk to or what information she needed to form a proper thesis. Something along the lines of how mate-claim frenzies worked, if they produced happy marriages, and so much more.

However, it hadn't ended with sex and bliss the evening before. Alistair had pushed her away even when she agreed to it, and she'd suggested it not out of academic curiosity, either. No, Alistair Boyd had a pull over her she'd never felt before. Almost as if she learned more about him and discovered his secrets, she might fall in love with him.

Not that it mattered.

While she didn't think she could ask for a reassignment, Kiyana would just have to find a way to stay as far away from Alistair as possible.

Which meant she needed to get up and talk with Finn and Arabella. If she was to continue her job, she would need their help.

However, forcing herself out of bed wasn't easy. She'd much prefer to stare out the window for a while, thinking of nothing and everything.

Of course a baby growled and something scuttled past her door. Arabella's voice was gentle yet firm. "Freya Jocelyn Anne Stewart, get back here right now."

Another growl, louder this time, came through the door. Unable to ignore her curiosity, Kiyana tiptoed quietly to the door and cracked it open.

Her jaw promptly fell open. A tiny golden dragon stood at the end of the corridor, in front of a window with her wings outstretched.

I thought dragons didn't shift until they were older. Glued to the spot, Kiyana watched as Arabella inched forward. "You know jumping out of the window isn't safe and you can only do it when Daddy is waiting for you below. Since Daddy is busy right now, you can't jump out of the window."

The baby dragon swiveled her head to the window and Kiyana gasped.

Both Arabella and the little dragon must've heard, because they both looked straight at her.

The little dragon squeaked and plodded up to her door. Kiyana opened it the rest of the way and the dragon immediately jumped to put her front paws on Kiyana's legs. Unsure of what else to do, Kiyana scratched the little one behind the ears. The golden dragon leaned into her touch.

Arabella sighed. "It seems my daughter likes you, which is a first. Usually she only allows my mate or brother to do that whilst she's in her dragon form."

Kiyana couldn't move her gaze from the adorable little face below. "I didn't think they shifted so young."

"They don't. I'm just the lucky one, I guess."

While on the surface the words might seem sarcastic, she could hear the love in Arabella's voice. "Did you call her Freya?"

"Yes. The triplets were asleep last night, but this is one of them—our only daughter, Freya. Her brothers will probably sleep a few more hours, as they're a bit lazier. Or, rather, act more like babies than Freya does."

She smiled for the first time since everything that had happened with Alistair the night before. "She's beautiful."

Arabella squatted and picked up the squirming dragon baby, bumping her nose against the tiny dragon snout before kissing it. "Thank you. Did you want to come downstairs and help me feed her?"

She hesitated. If Kiyana went downstairs, she'd have to face reality once more.

However, Freya squeaked again—Kiyana assumed it'd become a roar at some point when Freya was older—and she couldn't resist the little one's charm. "Okay."

Freya jumped out of her mother's arms and into Kiyana's. She stumbled, but managed to keep from tumbling back.

Arabella shook her head. "If Freya wants you to carry her, then it shall be. Otherwise, it'll be nothing but a headache and someone jumping out the W-I-N-D-O-W the first chance she has."

Adjusting her hold on Freya, Kiyana said, "I can manage. Although hopefully she grows out of being carried because she must already weight at least two stone."

"If my mate has his way, she'll be carried a while yet. Finn likes to spoil her." Arabella motioned. "Come on. The sooner we feed her, the sooner she should fall asleep and shift back into her human form."

As they walked, Kiyana asked, "Why does she shift so early?"

"That is a long story, and one I can tell you later after she's asleep. Otherwise, she'll listen and get ideas again. I love my daughter, but she's too clever for her own good."

Freya squeaked again and Kiyana laughed. "Maybe she'll be a charmer, like Finn."

"Then I feel for whoever ends up as her mate." Arabella smiled to herself. "Although given how surly many of the dragon-shifters are, maybe she'll do one of the surliest some good."

They reached the kitchen and Freya jumped down, sprinted around the table, and stopped in front of what looked like a rather large dog food bowl.

Arabella fetched something from the refrigerator and said, "Freya also likes to eat in her dragon form more often than not, hence the bowl. I worry she doesn't get enough nutrients, but the doctor says she's doing brilliantly. As long as she eats in her human form twice a day, too, there shouldn't be an issue."

After the dragonwoman placed some cooked meat and vegetables into the bowl, she turned to Kiyana. Somehow she tore her gaze away from the tiny dragon chowing down her food as Arabella asked, "What about you? Would you like some breakfast? I promise I won't serve it in a dog food bowl."

Kiyana's lips twitched. "Tea would be fantastic."

"I'll add some biscuits."

"Do you have any chocolate ones? It's definitely a chocolate kind of morning."

Arabella grinned. "A female after my own heart. Sit, I'll get everything ready and give you plenty of chocolate to choose from."

As the dragonwoman went about her task, Kiyana realized how mundane it was. Even being part dragon didn't completely erase the human half of things. She'd known that, of course, and yet it was fascinating to see in real life.

She'd been about to ask a few questions when Finn walked in. "There's my bonnie daughter, in her wee dragon form."

Freya looked up, food stuck to her chin, and squeaked.

Finn chuckled. "We'll have to work on that roar of yours some more, lassie. Now, finish your breakfast."

Without missing a beat, Freya went back to eating.

It seemed Freya really was a daddy's girl.

Too bad Finn's next words destroyed the almost peaceful morning Kiyana had managed. He stated, "Alistair will be here shortly."

"Why?" she asked quickly.

Finn's gaze never left hers. "He and I had a wee chat last night, and it seems the reasons he was so against a mate-claim frenzy aren't as big as he thought they were. He wants to come and talk with you, Kiyana. What happens after that is up to you."

Her heart rate kicked up. Did they just let mate-claim frenzy-mad dragons run amuck? "I-I don't know. He was barely coherent last night. How are we supposed to talk at all?"

Arabella sighed. "Sometimes, Finn, I think you make things overly dramatic on purpose." The dragonwoman's gaze moved to hers. "A mate-claim frenzy can be contained by silencing the dragon with drugs. Not forever, mind you, if administered carefully. But long enough to allow the human half to function for a bit."

Kiyana looked between the couple. "I still don't understand. He said he didn't want me, and I'm not about to beg him for it."

Finn grunted. "And rightly so. If he has at least two brain cells inside his head, he'll plead a bit." She opened her mouth to ask another question, but Finn continued, "I can't tell you his reasons, but just listen to him, aye? If after that you still want to send him away, I'll do everything in my power to keep him away from you for your stay here. I vow that on my mate and children's lives."

To an everyday human, the vow might seem worthless. But mates and children were valued highly in dragon-shifter society, making it a solemn one indeed.

Kiyana couldn't believe she was even considering it. She'd packed away everything the night before, and then some more this morning. She'd almost returned to normalcy with Arabella and little Freya.

Talking with Alistair would bring everything back and possibly weaken her rational resolve to stay clear.

Arabella sat next to her and touched her shoulder. "If nothing else, think of it as an interesting bit of research. You'll see what a dragon-shifter is like without their dragon."

Given what she knew, it wouldn't be a happy time for Alistair. "I'm usually not thinking clearly when Alistair is around. So I'm not sure that's a good argument."

Finn shrugged. "Not being able to think when someone is around can be a good thing, lass. Trust me, it sometimes helps when reason goes to the wayside and you have to rely on feelings and instinct. To be honest, that's how our dragons work all the time."

Kiyana decided to be blunt. "Why are you so determined for me to give Alistair a chance?"

Finn raised his brows. "Honestly? Alistair and I were once close friends. I know the kind of male he is, and even with the changes that happened three years ago, he's a good one most of the time—we all have our off days. Besides, you are his fated mate, meaning you're supposed to be his best chance at happiness. I want my friend and clan member to have the chance to be happy, and if we're all fortunate, you could be, too."

Looking at Finn, Arabella, and then little Freya, Kiyana briefly imagined her living a similar sort of life. One with her and Alistair downstairs at breakfast, their son or daughter playing on the floor. Maybe even Alistair's nosey mother paying an early visit to spoil her grandchild.

To some it may seem mundane. But to her, it would be perfect.

Could she risk her heart again, though? If only she understood inner dragons better, such as how much effort it took to fight one off during a frenzy. For all she knew, Alistair could've been fighting with everything he had the night before just so he wouldn't touch her.

Which made him a little nobler than she'd originally thought.

If nothing else, she could sate her curiosity. It wasn't as if talking with the man meant she'd sign over her life forever.

Taking a deep breath, she replied, "One meeting, that's it. If he pushes me away again, hurts me, or anything else negative, I won't give him another chance. I know some women can keep overlooking a man who pains them, but I'm not one of them."

Finn bobbed his head. "As it should be. I'll let you have your tea and biscuits first whilst I wrestle this wee one back upstairs. After that, I'll send Alistair a text message to come over."

As Finn scooped up his daughter and disappeared from sight, she could hear the strong clan leader singing a silly song to his daughter. Such a contrast to the strong, well-controlled leader she'd seen in TV interviews.

Every day dragon-shifters kept surprising her.

Maybe Alistair would, too. Although she wouldn't know for sure until he came. So Kiyana ate some chocolate and waited for him to arrive.

⌒⌒⌒⌒⌒

Alistair's head pounded and he had to squint against the faint sunshine as he walked to Finn's place.

Drugging a dragon silent was never easy, but after the mental battle he'd had with his beast the previous night, his brain felt as if it were full of holes. Stringing two thoughts together was difficult.

Coffee hadn't helped, nor had breakfast. He only hoped seeing Kiyana would jumpstart his neurons. Otherwise, he'd never be able to convince her to forgive him and be his mate.

He reached Finn's cottage, took a deep breath, and knocked on the front door. Arabella answered it. She didn't waste time saying, "I hope you're the male I think you are."

"I am."

She studied him a second before bobbing her head. Arabella stepped aside and motioned down the hall. "Kiyana is in the kitchen."

"Don't you want to announce I'm here?"

"You may be a quiet man most of the time, but your voice carries enough for even a human to hear you. I'm sure she knows."

Under normal circumstances, his dragon would've teased him.

But his brain remained silent.

For all the times he'd complained about his beast, Alistair missed him when he was absent. And the only way to get him back sooner rather than later was to convince Kiyana to forgive him.

So he nodded at Arabella and went toward the kitchen. The second he entered, he instantly zeroed in on Kiyana sitting at the table. Her back was to him, but even without his dragon's lust coursing through his body, he wanted to lift her hair and kiss the back of her neck. Then he'd tug her up and against him before giving her a proper kiss.

He wanted her, pure and simple. Alistair just had to win her first.

After he cleared his throat, Kiyana whirled around, a chocolate biscuit in her hand. "Alistair."

Her voice washed over him, and in the process, wiped away the exhaustion and fog of the morning. "Kiyana. May I join you?"

She studied him a second, and he expected her to tell him to sod off. She had every right to do so.

However, she motioned to an empty chair across from her. "Sit and start explaining things. I just want the truth."

He couldn't help but smile. He loved how direct she was with him.

Once he took the proffered seat, he placed his hands on his knees under the table. Otherwise he might reach across and try to take Kiyana's hand before she was ready.

He hoped she'd be ready at some point.

Not wanting to go down that tangent, he looked into her deep brown eyes and said, "I trust Finn and Ara told you some of it?"

She swallowed the last bit of biscuit. There was a crumb at the corner of her mouth, and he wanted to lick it away.

However, he made himself focus on her words instead of her lips. "Well, I know your dragon was drugged silent temporarily. And Finn seems to think there's a bloody good reason for how you treated me last night. However, that's all I know."

What he wouldn't give to smooth away the frown between her brows. "It's true, my dragon is quiet right now. And as for the reason..." Alistair took a deep breath and forced himself to continue, "While she wasn't my true mate, I had a female I loved named Rachel. She died just over three years ago, from a disease affecting her inner dragon that no one in the UK or America knew how to treat. However, we thought maybe someone in South America might. The problem was that there was no way to reach them." He stopped a second, not wanting an image of Rachel pale and wasted away to flash into his mind. "It was on her deathbed I made the vow of no sex until I found a way for dragon clans to share information more easily, to prevent other unnecessary deaths."

He went into the finer details of the possible cure, the lack of communication, and his spending all of his free time researching ways to fulfill his vow. Then he added, "So when kissing you kicked off the mate-claim frenzy, I panicked. I was convinced that if I carried it out, broke the promise I'd made to myself and Rachel, and accepted your offer to be in the frenzy with me, I'd become someone I didn't recognize."

She asked quietly, "What changed?"

Alistair rubbed his legs under the table. "Finn. He has a way of making you see the truth when you can't see it yourself."

"And what's that truth, Alistair?"

He didn't look away. "That you're the second chance I never expected to have. And not just because of some random act of fate, either. You're bonnie, intelligent, funny, and so much more. You weren't born a dragon-shifter, yet you're not afraid of us. Not to mention I'm positive you're more interested in helping us than exploiting us. So I'm sorry. Sorry I rejected your offer when it had to be a scary thing to process so quickly. I'm sorry I made you cry. And most of all, I'm sorry I forced you into any of this in the first place."

"It's not really forcing me, though. I mean, I was all set to be your pretend mate for six months. This way, I'd at least get sex, too."

"I want to smile and make a joke, but this is more serious, Kiyana. Females who mate dragon-shifters, then decide to divorce, returning to the human world aren't treated well. Maybe one day it'll change but for now, if you still want to go through the frenzy and be my mate, then it's a serious decision. One I can wait for you to make, if you don't outright refuse me."

She searched his gaze. "And what if I said okay to the frenzy, was your mate-to-be, and then left at the end of the six months if it doesn't go well? Wouldn't that be an option?"

He shook his head. "Dragon-shifter children, even if they're only half, must stay with a dragon-shifter clan. The gene to shift is always dominant, and it's a risk to everyone to let them grow up thinking they're merely human."

"So in other words, I'd have to come back to have my child and then leave him or her here?"

"Aye."

Kiyana glanced down to her mug and traced the rim. It was one of the few times he'd seen her unsure of herself, and he didn't like it.

Especially because the decision she mulled over was related to him.

However, he wasn't going to trick her into his bed for the sake of it. The true mates who failed in the end were usually because the two people hadn't been honest.

She finally raised her head and met his eyes again. Her expression was unreadable, which made him rub his legs with his hands again.

After a few more beats, she said, "Promise me you'll be honest and as open as you can with me, and I'll say yes. I get people have secrets, we all do. But I also have the feeling not even Finn knew about what happened to you three years ago, and he's your clan leader. I can't live with a male who hides so much from me. I want more than a lover. I want a partner in life."

Hope swelled in his chest. "I will do the best I can, Kiyana. Opening up about certain things isn't easy for me, but I'll try."

She nodded. "Okay, so what happens next?"

His heart raced. Could it really be that simple? Explain things to Kiyana, and she believed him?

Maybe she had some sort of pseudo secret-power about detecting liars, or something. Regardless, he would keep telling her the truth. Lying about anything from this point forward would push her away.

And Alistair didn't want that.

He replied, "Aye, well, my dragon won't return for a few days yet. So maybe before all of the hot and sweaty sex, we try to get to know each other?"

The corner of her mouth ticked up. "Imagine that, going on a date with the future father of your child. Who would've thought?"

He chuckled. Life with Kiyana would be one full of smiles and laughter, he was sure of it.

Alistair just needed to not fuck it up.

Putting a hand on the table, palm up, he waited until Kiyana placed her palm in his. Her warm skin against his felt good, as if it had always meant to be there.

His dragon would've made a crack about becoming poetic, and Alistair snorted. Kiyana raised her brows. "What's so funny? Care to share?"

"Well, I'm thinking of what my dragon would've said to me, is all. I guess without the chatty beast there, I fill the silence myself."

She leaned forward a fraction. "Which brings up something we definitely need to discuss in more detail. Once the drugs wear off, tell me what to expect, Alistair. And don't try to shield me, or make it seem as if he'll merely say how do you do and wait patiently for me to get naked."

"I see you're a wee bit prepared already."

"That's sort of what I do."

"Me, too."

As they smiled at one another, Alistair imagined part of his future—one where he and Kiyana worked together to find the answers he needed.

It seemed as if fate had done a good job after all.

She squeezed his hand. "You still haven't answered my question."

"Aye, well, he'll be demanding. Inner dragons work mostly on instinct to begin with, but a mate-claim frenzy is the epitome of that. All they want to do is have sex, over and over again, until you carry our scent. If that happens, it means you're pregnant."

"Oh."

Oh indeed. "There is a major positive to you being my true mate, though, lass. My semen will make you orgasm."

Kiyana shifted in her seat, and he hoped it was for a good response.

She nodded. "Well, that means I won't have to think of faking it, then."

He growled. "A female shouldn't have to fake it. I can't always guarantee it during the frenzy, but without it, I will always make you come before me. Always."

Kiyana's eyes heated, and his own cock stirred. Even without his dragon's pounding need, he wanted to sit her on the table and take her right then and there.

She'd agreed to be his, and Alistair wanted to make it official.

And yet, he didn't want to be a bastard. She'd want to get to know him better first before getting naked. It was the least he could do.

Kiyana's husky voice fill the kitchen. "Kiss me again, Alistair. Just to make sure we're as good a fit as fate thinks we are."

He didn't hesitate to stand. Once she did as well, he pulled her against him and stroked her cheek. "You're so very beautiful, Kiyana. And yet, it's your mouth and what comes out of it that draws me the most."

She raised her brows. "Now you're just being over the top."

Cupping her cheek, he replied, "No, it's the truth. I've never met someone quite like you, and if I don't fuck it up, I hope you'll be around to surprise me every day."

Her lips turned upward. "You may regret those words one day."

Leaning even closer to her mouth, he whispered, "Never."

"Then—"

He cut her off with a kiss. The instant his lips pressed against hers, she opened and allowed his tongue. Her arms soon looped around the back of his neck.

Even without the frenzy, one taste of Kiyana and he couldn't hold back. He stroked, explored, nibbled, and reveled in when she made small pleasure noises into his mouth.

He wanted to rock her against his hard cock, but no. He wanted to tell her how he felt with his kiss and nothing more.

Of course when she pressed even closer against his chest, her hard nipples making him groan, he came that much closer to tossing her on a counter and ripping off her clothes.

Then he heard the noises. Fuck, he was in Finn's house.

Since someone was coming, he broke the kiss to be safe. Her breathing was as ragged as his, and a sense of contentment coursed throughout his body. She asked, "Why did you stop?"

Finn's voice filled the space. "I think because he didn't want to give us all a wee show."

Kiyana looked over her shoulder at the same sight Alistair saw, which was Finn standing in the doorway with one of his sons in his arms.

Alistair grunted. "You should've knocked or made a wee bit more noise to let the lass know of your presence."

Finn jostled his little baby. "Why? This is my house, aye? Besides, I knew you could hear me."

He was about to say Kiyana couldn't and Finn shouldn't dismiss the human so easily, but his female spoke up. "It's okay. Since things will, er, become rather busy in the near future, I should probably visit with the human women and let them know I'll be out of touch for a stretch of time."

Finn glanced at Kiyana, to Alistair, and back again. "Oh, aye? And when will you become 'rather busy' as you put it."

Alistair narrowed his eyes at his clan leader. Most of the time, he liked Finn. But there were times when he could punch the male for being obviously annoying. To keep Kiyana from answering, Alistair growled, "We'll let you know when we do. Now, can we have a few more minutes alone?"

Finn's son—Alistair could never tell the twin boys apart—patted his dad's cheek. Finn made a face before answering, "A few minutes and no more. I don't want my kitchen turning into mate-claim frenzy central."

He spit through clenched teeth, "My dragon won't wake up for at least two days."

Finn shrugged and then bounced his son. "You've always been strong-willed, so who knows, maybe you could bring him back simply because you will it."

Alistair took a step toward Finn, but Kiyana placed a hand on his chest. "Don't let him get to you. Because if you do, he wins."

Finn's gaze shot to Kiyana. "Clever lass."

She raised her brows. "Male dragon-shifters tend to be mostly predictable. If someone doesn't notice their proclivity toward alpha, stubborn, veiled challenges the first week, then they aren't looking hard enough."

Finn snorted. "Aye, you'll do fine here, lass."

Kiyana stood a little taller at his side. And even though they'd barely done more than kiss and agree to have a frenzy, a surge of pride rushed forth.

He needed to do everything he could to win her heart before some other dragonman saw how bloody fabulous she was.

Finn swung around once and then tickled his son's neck. As the bairn squirmed, he said, "I'll give you a few minutes. Before you leave, come find me, Alistair."

With that, Lochguard's leader exited the room.

Turning toward Kiyana, he kissed her quickly. She blinked. "While I'm not complaining, what was that for?"

"I couldn't help it. I just needed to."

"Hm, more likely it's so I can taste you again, giving you the chance to brand it into my memory? And as a result, I'll crave it?"

He snorted. "You're a cheeky one, aren't you?"

She grinned. "As you Scots say, aye, I am."

He chuckled. "I'd like to tease you some more, but it'll have to wait. When can I see you again?"

"Do you have to teach today?"

"Aye. Not only that, I need to coordinate with the other teachers to cover me in case we have the frenzy."

She searched his eyes. "In case?"

"I'm not going to assume anything until my dragon is back and you're naked under me, moaning my name."

"Oh."

Cupping her cheek again, he thrummed his finger over her soft skin. "Och, now you get shy."

Her lips turned upward again. "Studying dragon-shifters from afar? I know how to do that. But I don't peep through windows and watch couples going through a mate-claim frenzy. That would make me a pervert."

"That it would, so don't go peeking into windows in the next few days, aye? We don't want any rumors starting."

She stuck her tongue out at him and he laughed. The female kept making him do that, and it was brilliant, especially as it slowly kept dawning on him how serious he'd become in the last few years.

Good thing his dragon was absent or Alistair would never hear the end of his admission.

He kissed her nose. "Okay, I'll stop. Besides, Finn will be back any second. Come find me after three o'clock. I should have everything sorted at the school by then."

She bobbed her head. "What will we do after that?"

"Let me surprise you, Kiyana. Make sure to bring a jacket and wear sensible clothing."

"Right," she said slowly. "Then I'll, uh, see you later?"

The parting seemed so bland and uneventful when compared to the discussion they'd had less than ten minutes ago.

Gently tilting her head, he murmured, "This kiss will help you remember my taste."

He pressed his lips to hers. The instant she opened, he pressed his tongue into her mouth and took his time teasing, licking, and treasuring her.

While he'd said it was for her to remember him, in reality, it was to help keep Alistair going until he could do it again. Even though his dragon was silent, he wanted to claim his human.

However, kissing would have to be enough for the moment. And so he put everything into that kiss, letting Kiyana know how much he'd miss her for the day.

CHAPTER SEVEN

*K*iyana somehow managed to go through the motions until three o'clock arrived. Well, actually ten to, but it was close enough.

The receptionist of the school had directed her to Alistair's office. Apparently, each teacher had a small office inside the school since sometimes the classrooms were shared.

She didn't nose around for about twenty seconds, and then she scanned the room. There weren't any photos, just a massive corkboard with all sorts of things pinned to it. The words were written in some sort of code, though, and didn't make sense. She wondered if it had to do with Alistair's research in the archives.

Kiyana had just noticed a misshapen dragon sculpture on his desk when the door opened.

Alistair's eyes instantly found hers, and she couldn't resist a shiver. Even without his dragon, his mismatched eyes were a tad bit predatory. Not in a bad way, but more in a I'll-devour-you-and-you'll-never-get-enough sort of way.

He entered silently, closed the door, and reached out a hand. As he gently traced her forehead, his skin against hers made it harder to breathe.

Damn, the dragonman had too much power over her, and he wasn't even trying. Maybe it had something to do with being his fated mate. And as was her way, she blurted, "You mentioned how your semen would make me orgasm. Does your touch do something strange, too, to your destined mate?"

The corner of his mouth ticked up, making his handsome face that much sexier. "I don't have some sort of pheromone or oil I secrete to drive you wild. Although I rather like that I can do that to you."

"Who are you and what have you done with the serious, hermit-like Alistair Boyd?"

"Oh, he's right here. But for the first time in a long time, I have something to look forward to that doesn't involve me, an old book, and dim lighting."

"Well, I imagine dim lighting will play a part eventually with me, too."

He leaned closer. "In the archives, you mean?"

"Maybe. Although I'm talking about research. What are *you* talking about?"

Alistair chuckled, the warm sound making her insides flip. "I'll keep it a surprise for now, aye?"

She smiled. "Can I ask you something else?"

"Anything."

The way he didn't hesitate reassured her that there would be a future for them.

She asked, "You don't sound overly Scottish, compared to some of the others. Is there a reason for that?"

He raised an eyebrow, although clearly it wasn't in offense since humor danced in his eyes. "Aye, there's a reason. I spent my university days in America."

"America?"

He nodded. "I attended MIT in Massachusetts. Not just because it's a good university, but also because I wanted to learn more from the American approach to learning. I studied electrical engineering and computer science, for both my undergrad and graduate studies."

She frowned. Kiyana hadn't heard of a dragon-shifter in the UK going outside of Europe to study before. "How was that even possible? I didn't think dragon-shifters could attend university in North America."

"Oh, aye, it's difficult. But in case you haven't noticed, my mother can be rather determined. For once, her brash ways helped me to follow one of my dreams."

"But wait. I thought you were a history teacher?"

"I am. Before...before Rachel died, I was an electrical engineer for Lochguard. The work was demanding, but I loved it. However, *after*, my job was a constant reminder of Rachel since that's how we met—she also studied the same courses at MIT. So once I was able to pull myself together enough after Rachel's passing and return to Lochguard, I gave up my previous job to teach. That way I could spend more time researching in the archives and not be faced with a constant reminder of my late girlfriend."

Kiyana wanted to keep asking questions, to learn more about how he met Rachel, and then some. However, if she was to be part of a mate-claim frenzy in a matter of days, she should focus on what to expect instead. Not to mention, deep down, she wanted to have a nice evening with him without the sadness of his past.

Maybe, just maybe, she could help him achieve that.

So she packed away her questions related to Rachel, MIT, and the like for later. "So, what's this surprise you mentioned?"

The sadness vanished from his eyes. While it was only temporary and it would take more than one conversation to help Alistair move on, it made her heart lighter to see it.

He took her chin and lightly stroked the underside. "It wouldn't be a surprise if I told you, now, would it?" Glancing down, he nodded. "You wore sensible clothes, including shoes, just like I asked. Good, because you'll need them."

She hoped he didn't plan on making them walk through mud or something. Kiyana had only been allowed to bring two suitcases to Lochguard and didn't have a backup pair of trainers. "Not so much as a hint as to where we're going?"

"Aye, well, I suppose I can say we won't be flying anywhere, what with my dragon still being silent and all."

She blinked. "Wait, you fly and take humans up sometimes?"

"Not just any human. But you, lass? Aye, I would."

His words made her cheeks warm. "Then I'll remember that for later because it sounds fascinating."

He kissed her quickly. All too soon his lips were gone and he murmured, "Now, come. We can chat as we walk, but if we dally here too much longer, we might miss it."

"Okay, that hint only made me more curious."

He winked. "Good."

She shook her head. "You're awful."

His grip slackened in hers. "I hope that's a joke."

Her eyes instantly found his. "Of course. I'm only teasing you."

Alistair let out a breath. "Good. I was just afraid you wanted grumpy, hermit Alistair and not the true me. Some of my old ways are creeping back, mixed with the new, and I don't want to disappoint you."

Even if he hadn't said it, Kiyana was starting to think Alistair had been lonely in his self-imposed isolation over the last few years. While probably not as outgoing as Finn, she suspected they had been close back in the day. "I rather like the new mix. He can be fun or serious. All that matters is that it's you being honest."

He brought her hand to his lips and kissed the back of it. The light brush of skin made her belly flutter.

Alistair's deep voice rolled over her. "Now, let's go before I decide to keep you in my office and kiss you for the rest of the evening."

It was on the tip of her tongue to say do it. However, she truly did want to know more about Alistair while she had the chance. After all, she would probably soon be carrying his child.

Correction, carrying *their* child. And not just any child, but a half-dragon-shifter child. Given her research over the years, she knew the risk of her dying in childbirth, too.

No. She wouldn't ruin the evening by thinking of darkness and death. That could come later.

And so she asked Alistair to take her to his surprise, and did her best to talk about anything apart from what could happen to her in nine months' time, or what had happened to him three years ago.

⌒⌒⌒⌒

Alistair had barely managed to complete all his teaching duties during the day. Even though he was nearly thirty, he'd acted like a teenager, not wanting to think of responsibilities and duties but rather his evening with Kiyana.

However, his true mate deserved someone who was responsible and reliable. So he'd done his best to focus, arranging everything for a two or three week absence, and survived the day.

Discovering her in his office, on the other hand, had been harder to resist. The image of her straddling his lap as he claimed her in his office had turned his cock instantly hard. There was something about the possibility of being caught that made it that much more arousing.

His dragon would've said it didn't matter if someone walked in or not. They should claim Kiyana and not worry about anyone else.

Of course, his mind was silent and his beast said nothing.

During the brief absence, Alistair had slowly realized how much he relied on his dragon for acting rather than merely thinking things to death.

Soon. He'd have his dragon back soon, and then he could finally have Kiyana all to himself.

For the present, however, he focused on guiding her off Lochguard and along the shores of Loch Naver. Even though there was a human camper van site on the opposite, far side of the loch, no one was there this evening. He'd made sure to check with the Protectors earlier.

While the humans in Sutherland tended to view Lochguard as more friend than enemy, tourists from other parts didn't always do so. And he wouldn't risk Kiyana's safety, no matter how much he wanted to surprise her.

They'd made it nearly a mile, talking about minor things, before Kiyana asked, "Are you sure Finn won't have someone trailing us? Another dragon just flew overhead."

The dragon had been Cat MacAllister, probably coming back from yet another artist meeting or some such. "No, it wasn't a Protector. I have a mobile phone, as well as a special clan tracking device. If we go more than a few miles from Lochguard, everyone will know and then we'll be monitored closely."

Kiyana climbed onto a low tree stump and then jumped down. It was such an innocent action, but it made him wonder if she was also the sort of person to jump in mud puddles for the sake of it.

But she replied and he had to focus on her words. "Is that normal? I know Lochguard sometimes has dragon hunter and Dragon Knight problems, but I thought both were better under control now?"

"Aye, they are. But until we can take out the leader of the dragon hunters, they'll always be a risk."

"Then why haven't you done that?"

Her tone was merely curious. He suspected she'd always ask questions, to find out as much information as possible.

Truly, a female after his own heart. "Well, Finn has tried. So has Stonefire's leader, too. But personally, I think it's going to take every clan in the UK and Ireland working together to accomplish it."

"What about the rest of the world? I know they have dragon hunters in most countries as well, and the dragons there probably also want to get rid of them, too."

He shrugged. "They'll have to figure it out for their own countries, I suppose."

"But why? Your big project was to foster better communication between the clans, right? Why stop at medical information? You were reading a book about treaties from the eighteenth and nineteenth centuries, ones that united various dragon clans from around the world. Why can't you strive for something similar? That way, you could also work together on mutual enemies. Maybe then you can eradicate the dragon hunters once and for all."

Alistair stopped in his track and turned toward Kiyana. "That would be...difficult."

She raised her brows. "But do you think it'd be that much more difficult than taking care of the hunters in the UK, though? Besides, there are resources that could help. I'm usually based near London, so I've heard a lot about Clan Skyhunter lately. And one of their new co-leaders, Honoria Wakeham, helped improve communications in western America with great success. Why not have Finn work with her and the other Skyhunter leader, too? They might have the knowledge and technology to help reach the bigger overall goal."

He opened his mouth and promptly closed it. Kiyana Barnes may be a human, but she knew more about dragon-shifter affairs than most. Add in how bloody smart she was, and she might be able to help solve more problems than anyone could've imagined.

She tilted her head. "What? You're looking at me strangely."

Shaking his head to clear his stupor, he said, "Sorry. It's just, you lay things out so easily. And yet, I haven't heard anyone else think of something like that, something so obvious on the surface."

She smiled. "Well, to be fair, it sometimes takes an outsider to add a new perspective."

They were close to his surprise, but he couldn't help but pull her up against his body and kiss her. Each nibble, lick, and caress let her know with actions how much he thought of her.

Once he finally moved his head back a few inches, her hot breath against his lips nearly made him find some sort of cover and maybe do more than kiss his brilliant human.

Kiyana whispered, "So I guess this means you like me spouting off ideas?"

"Most definitely." He kissed her quickly again. "Don't ever hold them back."

She grinned. "What if they're ones I team up with your mother to achieve?"

He raised an eyebrow. "What, worse than when you and her thought about the pretend mate scheme?"

"Hey, to be fair, it was a good idea."

"I still think it's cute you think I would've been able to live with you and not try to kiss you."

"Only kiss me, huh?"

He growled. "Don't tempt me, lass. Because when I claim you the first time, I want not only my dragon around, but us somewhere private, where no one else can see your naked body."

She reached up and stroked his jaw. Each whisper of her fingers against his skin made his dick throb in anticipation. She murmured, "I hope that's soon."

"Aye, it should be. I'm going to talk with Layla first thing in the morning, about hurrying my dragon's return."

Her brows furrowed as she searched his eyes. "Are you sure you should do that? I don't want you to hurt him by forcing it."

The fact she so easily cared about his inner beast only reinforced how perfect she was for him. "I wouldn't do anything to harm him, don't worry. He can be bloody annoying, but he's *my* annoying dragon half and no one else's." She bit her bottom lip, and he stroked her lower back before murmuring, "Ask me anything, Kiyana. Don't ever hold back with me."

"Well, it's just I want to know what it's like to hear an inner dragon. Don't worry, I'm not going to suggest some crazy medical experiment or anything. But maybe, er, when yours returns, you can let me know more of what he talks about? How he acts?"

"I can do better than that, lass. If I let him take control, you can ask him yourself."

Her eyes widened. "I thought that only happened during sex? And then a dragon isn't exactly the most cooperative."

That statement piqued his interest. "And how do you know that? I thought you didn't peek into windows."

She shook her head. "I never have. But, well, I did sleep with a dragon-shifter before."

Alistair swore he felt some sort of stirring in his mind, almost as if his dragon was trying to communicate. No doubt his beast didn't like the idea of their true mate being with someone else.

He didn't care for it, either, but he didn't expect his true mate to be a virgin. It was the twenty-first century, after all.

His dragon, on the other hand, wouldn't worry about centuries or changing societal norms. All that mattered to him was how Kiyana was their true mate to have, hold, and protect.

Alistair needed to warn Kiyana about his beast, to maybe help prevent some sort of issue later on. "I don't care if you've been with anyone else. Okay, maybe a wee bit. However, my dragon won't like it at all. So maybe it's best not to bring it up again."

"Just the dragon-shifter, or all of the other men from my past?"

He wanted to know how many others. However, Alistair didn't ask. It wasn't as if he wanted Kiyana to know his past sexual history, either. "All. The frenzy will be intense enough. But once it's over, and even if you're pregnant, just mentioning that might set him off again."

"Set him off how?"

Damn, he was on a topic that could scare her. Alistair just had to trust his female would listen to the facts and not let fear take over. "Dragons can go rogue. Sometimes for a wee while, and sometimes for good. While I hope my beast is mature and strong enough to avoid it, merely mentioning other males trying to claim his true mate is a risk, one that could turn him rogue."

"So if I slip up and mention something from my past, it could make your dragon rogue?"

"Maybe. Although a small sentence should be fine. Just don't go on about impressive cock sizes and the like."

A small smile appeared on her face, and he wanted to breathe a sigh of relief. Maybe that meant she was secretly pissed off, but he didn't think so. "I'm sure you'll be fine in that department. After all, dragon-shifters are supposed to be...adequate in that part of their anatomy."

He growled. "Adequate?"

She laughed. "So even you need a little ego stroking, then?"

Growling louder, he took her lips in a rough kiss. Only once he needed to pull back to breathe, did he stop. "Since I can smell your arousal, my ego is doing fine."

She narrowed her eyes. "I thought you weren't supposed to mention things like that? Dragon etiquette, and all that?"

"Maybe with strangers. But if things go the way I hope, you'll be the farthest thing from a stranger." He kissed her again before adding, "I can answer more questions later. Right now, we need to hurry, or the light will fade and I can't show you my surprise before dusk."

It took every iota of strength he possessed to release her body and merely take her hand. However, he wanted to create a few memories before the frenzy. Ones that could maybe help her endure it.

Most humans enjoyed the experience, but if it took him longer than normal to impregnate her, then she might get too tired and frustrated.

He wanted her to remember there was more than just sex and attraction between them. And so he guided her the rest of the way to one of his favorite spots along the loch.

⌘

Kiyana was starting to believe she'd won the jackpot when it came to Alistair. He was smart, sexy, and even occasionally funny.

Not to mention he liked to talk about serious things as much as silly ones. He didn't dismiss her ideas, which meant maybe she could help Lochguard with more than helping them find mates, and possibly write a book.

As much as she was drawn to Alistair, it was hard to look away from the lake and its surroundings. The area was empty and peaceful. True, she knew the horrible history behind why the Highlands were empty—the Clearances had replaced the tenants with sheep, forcing the Scots to emigrate elsewhere—but while she wouldn't dismiss the past, she could enjoy the present.

Birds soared overhead, and occasionally the smooth surface of the water rippled from either a fish or bug of some sort, distorting the perfect reflection of the sky and hills.

So absorbed in her surroundings, she ran into Alistair's side when he stopped. After catching her balance, she looked up at him. "It's breathtaking here. Was that your surprise? To share this scenery with me?"

"The loch is always beautiful, but I want to go up there."

She followed his finger and made out the ruins of what had probably been a stone cottage. "Is that related to your family somehow?"

"Yes and no. Come on."

The slight incline didn't take more than a few minutes. Alistair gestured toward the remaining low stone walls of a small building. "This is where Lochguard's former leader and the British formally signed an agreement, giving Lochguard their land."

She glanced at him. "I thought Clan Lochguard has lived here for centuries?"

"Aye, they have. But it was mostly because the landowners were too afraid to tell the dragons to leave. The skirmishes here forced the government—well, and the monarch at the time, Queen Victoria—to come to a formal agreement."

"Wait, so that's after the Clearances, then? Queen Victoria reigned from 1837 to 1901."

He grinned. "You know history, too? Och, lass, you're getting more perfect by the minute."

She rolled her eyes. "I told you before, I like to know the history of an area before studying the present inhabitants. I know the basics of treaties, but there's little in human records about this supposed signing you're talking about."

Alistair shrugged. "I'm sure that's by design. From what I've read, the humans thought they were magnanimous in granting Lochguard their land. In reality, they had little choice. Lacking the weapons or biological weapons of the modern era, they had little hope in winning a war with a clan of dragon-shifters without great cost, if at all."

She gestured toward the ruins. "So then why is this one of your favorite places? Because of the historical significance?"

Alistair looked back at the piles of rocks in the middle of the walls. "Partially. However, it's been a constant reminder to me that two different factions can make an alliance work, of sorts. Aye, the DDA has put more and more restrictions on us over the years. And aye, your parliament tries to pass laws about us. However, Lochguard kept its land through determination, stubbornness, and a wee bit of dramatics. That sort of thing will be necessary for getting other dragon clans to work together, too, I think."

She studied Alistair's profile. The man constantly surprised her with how many layers and depths he possessed. "So this place became your favorite once you returned from your last visit to America, right?"

His eyes instantly found hers. "Aye."

She squeezed his hand in hers. "Because this place reminded you of what could be accomplished, even if it took some time." He nodded, but she continued before he could speak. "Then once we find a way to get the dragons to work together, we should put a small memorial nearby, to mark the achievement."

Silence fell, but it wasn't strained. Judging from his eyes, Alistair's mind whirred with who knew what thoughts.

Someday, she'd be at the point where she'd always ask what he was thinking. But considering he'd just shown her something dear to his heart, representing the past three years' inspiration for his work, she would let him speak first.

People weren't always ready to talk about certain issues with a near stranger. And no matter how much she and Alistair connected, there were still barely past the stranger phase.

Alistair eventually cleared his throat. "You're a brilliant female, Kiyana Barnes. And the more I learn about you, the more I wonder if I truly deserve you."

"Deserving isn't part of the equation. At least, not this early on. Just don't lie to me, Alistair, and we'll be on equal terms."

He gently pulled her close and nuzzled his cheek against hers. "Do you need more time to acclimate to me, lass? Or, would you be okay with me bringing my dragon back tomorrow? And not just because of the frenzy, either. He's part of who I am and the longer he's silent, the more I feel as if I'm cheating him out of the experience of getting to know you. Besides, you deserve to know what it's like to be with a male who is essentially two personalities in one body."

Wrapping her arms around his broad back, she lightly rubbed one hand up and down. "Of course I'd like to know him. And I'm positive it won't change my answer concerning the frenzy."

He pulled back a fraction and placed his forehead against hers, his breath dancing across her lips as he said, "Thank you."

She was about to say it was ridiculous to thank her for something so basic, but an older woman's Scottish voice filled the air.

One belonging to Alistair's mother, Meg.

"Och, there you are, lad. We've been looking for you."

Alistair sighed and raised his head. Since Kiyana wanted to see who constituted "we," she released Alistair and turned to find Meg, Faye MacKenzie, and Grant McFarland.

The latter two individuals were Lochguard's co-head Protectors.

Which most likely meant something had happened.

Alistair asked, "What is it?"

Faye replied first. "We wouldn't be here if it wasn't important, Alistair. I hope you know that."

Alistair grunted. "Aye, and you can save explaining why my mother is trekking out here until later, too. What's wrong?"

Faye glanced at Kiyana and back to Alistair. "Meg came to take Kiyana back to Lochguard."

Alistair took her hand. "She's to be my mate. She should stay."

Faye grimaced, and her partner grunted. "We don't have time for you to be noble and romantic. Finn says she's to return with Meg."

Kiyana jumped in. "It's okay, Alistair. It'll give me a chance to get to know your mother better." She looked at Faye and then Grant. "And I'm sure one day you'll trust me enough to say what's going on." Faye bobbed her head, and Kiyana smiled up at Alistair. "Find me when you can."

Alistair's grip on her hand tightened. Not wanting him to make things worse for himself, she murmured, "It's okay. I won't go running for the hills, I promise."

Meg placed her hands on her hips. "Och, now, come, lad. I'll take good care of Kiyana. Finn needs your help. It's the least you can do."

She tugged and Alistair let her go. Once she was at Meg's side, she waved. "Help your clan, Alistair. Because that's what good dragons do—help their clan and family."

Meg grunted her approval. But Alistair spoke before his mother. "Aye, I will, lass. Until later, then."

Even though she knew she'd see him again soon, she took a second to memorize Alistair's short hair blowing in the wind, the ruins just behind him.

Satisfied she'd burned the image into her memory, she finally turned and walked away with Meg.

Alistair's mother chatted the entire time back to Lochguard—the woman was spritely for her age, that was for sure—but Kiyana barely paid attention. Thankfully the older woman liked to talk, so she could merely think about Alistair. Both what he'd revealed, but also wondering how Lochguard needed his help.

She only hoped something dangerous wasn't happening or about to happen. Because then she had a feeling Alistair would have to go without his dragon even longer, and that would put a whole different kind of strain on him.

And Kiyana didn't want her future mate to be in any sort of pain.

⚬⚬⚬⚬⚬

Alistair waited until his mother and Kiyana were out of earshot before he grunted and demanded, "What's so bloody important that you had to ruin my first date with my true mate?"

Faye clicked her tongue. "My, my, someone's tetchy today."

He growled, and Grant sighed at Faye's words. "Don't provoke him, Faye. And if you say it's merely the baby making you do it, so help me, I won't go out on the next odd craving run you have."

Faye narrowed her eyes. "You wouldn't."

Grant raised both eyebrows. "Wouldn't I?"

Under normal circumstances, Alistair wouldn't care if the two went back and forth, their odd love playing out in a way he didn't always understand.

However, Kiyana was stuck with his mother for who knew how long, and he wanted to rescue her from that form of torture. "So what's the damn emergency?"

Grant put up a hand, the pair exchanged some sort of nonverbal communication, and then the male looked back at Alistair. After taking something out of his pocket—a mini-scrambling device by the look of it—and clicking it, the male answered, "You know how Snowridge found and raided the place being used by the Dragon Knights in Wales, aye?"

Anger rolled in his stomach. The bastards had trapped children and experimented on them. "Aye, I do."

"Well, after going through all the stuff they found with a fine-tooth comb, one of the Snowridge Protectors found something concerning, something related to what Stonefire sent us recently."

He frowned. "Wait, what did Stonefire send you?"

Faye jumped in, clearly unable to stay quiet for long. "A human showed up on their land with a flash drive full of information. Even though she's still unconscious from some kind of poison that's in her system, it appears she worked for the Dragon Knights at one point. Why she broke with them and ran, no one knows. But the flash drive contained loads of detailed information concerning ongoing projects, hideout locations, and more."

Grant spoke again. "Which brings us to why we're here. Snowridge found some tiny, weird-shaped devices they think were used to internally administer and monitor their prisoners. The information from Stonefire contained some schematics to something similar, although it doesn't say what they were used for

107

explicitly—the human must've copied what she could find, not fully understanding what she got."

He put it together. "Which means you want me to look at the schematics, compare them to what was found on Snowridge, and determine their uses. And, if possible, ways to disable them if we find anyone with one of the devices in their bodies still."

Faye bit her lip in an unusual sign of hesitation or regret. "I know you're supposed to go through the frenzy with Kiyana. And until your dragon wakes up again, I'm sure you'd rather spend the time with her. However, this is important. If these sorts of devices are being used en masse, without our knowledge, that could be dangerous."

"Just how wee are they?"

"Very. You can barely see them with the naked eye," Grant stated.

Alistair rubbed both hands through his hair. He may want to spend time with Kiyana, but the lass had been right. Clan was important to a dragon-shifter. And even worse, the mystery device could be affecting the children they'd rescued in Wales. Especially if the devices were small enough to escape notice on various medical scans.

He couldn't risk them suffering, or worse, because he wanted to joke and tease with his future mate.

The only bollocks of it all was how he couldn't share his work with her.

Faye's gentle voice filled his ears. "I know this is a lot to ask. And I know you're a teacher now, not a researcher or electrical engineer. But this is a highly sensitive task, and Finn, as well as the other two clan leaders, want someone they trust to handle it. And given your background, you're the most qualified by far, Alistair."

Lowering his hands, he sighed. "I know. I'll take a look and figure it out, provided you fulfill one request."

Grant grunted. "You can't share this information with the human. She's not your mate yet, and it's too risky."

He clenched his fingers into a fist. Rationally, he knew Grant had to be careful. However, he didn't like him dismissing Kiyana so easily.

Tamping down his irritation, he bit out, "That's not my request. Kiyana seems to get along with Arabella. So can you have Ara rescue Kiyana from my mother? If I'm busy doing this, I don't want the lass trapped in that special variety of hell for long."

Faye snorted, and Grant shot her a look with narrowed eyes. The male looked back at Alistair. "I'll talk to Ara myself."

He nodded. "Okay, then I need everything you have. And I hope you've collected one of the devices from Snowridge."

"Aye, we have. Everything is ready for you inside the Protectors main security building."

As they made their way back and Alistair wheedled out as much information as he could about the assignment, he did his best not to think of Kiyana. He'd trust Finn and Arabella with his life, and they would take good care of his human.

No, what worried him was how long this project would take. Alistair already missed his inner beast, but he couldn't let him return until it was time for the frenzy. Because once a dragon-shifter kissed their true mate, there was no stopping their inner dragons' instincts without the use of drugs for extremely long stretches of time.

He only hoped Layla and the other doctors knew how much of the dragon sleeping drug he could take before it became too much. He and his dragon had a strong bond, but drugs did odd things to inner dragons. Sometimes, it silenced them forever.

And he shuddered to think of that ever happening to him.

CHAPTER EIGHT

As one day passed, and then another, Kiyana began to worry.

She knew in her gut that Alistair would come to see her if he could. But all of the hush-hush whisperings of what he was doing and the uncertainty of how long it'd take for him to finish was getting to her.

And while yes, helping his clan was important, she didn't want him to harm his dragon in the process.

Which was why after she'd finished working with the other human women for the day, she stood in front of the door that belonged to Fergus MacKenzie and his human mate, Gina's place.

Arabella had let slip how Fergus had contained his mate-claim frenzy for months before finally letting it out. And all without any sort of drugs.

Kiyana wanted to know how, and if someone else could do it. Because another thing she'd learned was that the longer Alistair drugged his dragon silent, the greater the chance his inner beast would either turn rogue or maybe not return at all.

She knocked and soon after, a red-haired woman carrying a baby on her hip answered. She instantly smiled. "You're Kiyana. What do I owe the pleasure?"

The human's American accent was charming, and in a way, made her smile. "I'm sorry to bother you, but I have some questions about Fergus."

"Fergus isn't here right now. You're still welcome to come in, but I might not be able to help."

"No, it's you I wanted to talk to."

Gina didn't hesitate to step aside and allow Kiyana to enter. Once the door closed, Gina gently bounced her baby and spoke again. "What's on your mind?"

The best way to get through the conversation was to treat it as a professional one. After all, the more she learned about inner dragons and mate-claim frenzies, the better she could prepare the other humans. "It's about how Fergus resisted the mate-claim frenzy for so long."

Gina tilted her head. "I heard about you and Alistair. To be honest, I thought you'd be deep in the throes of the frenzy by now. It's exhausting, but also amazing at the same time."

She'd heard something similar from Arabella, but it helped to add more people to the list of those who enjoyed the frenzy. Kiyana wasn't scared, exactly, but she liked to be prepared. "He's doing something secretive at the moment, for the clan."

Gina bit her lip. Kiyana would bet everything she had the human knew about what.

But she hadn't come to interrogate Gina about Alistair's assignment. So she said, "And I know you can't talk about it. However, the drugs keeping Alistair's dragon silent should be wearing off soon, and I'm worried if he keeps taking the dragon sleeping drugs, then it'll do lasting damage."

Gina shook her head. "I wouldn't worry. Layla is careful about those things, especially since Lochguard's former doctor—Innes—mated a dragon-shifter on Stonefire who lost her dragon for twenty years before it came back again."

She blinked. "Wait, what? Her dragon came back after twenty years?"

Gina nodded toward the living room. "Let's sit so I can bounce my little chunky monkey on my knee as we talk."

Gina then tickled her son's neck, and Kiyana couldn't help but smile. She followed her to the living room and sat down in a chair opposite the sofa. Unable to wait for Gina to continue, she prodded, "How do dragons leave and come back?"

Sitting down, Gina answered, "Oh, in Sid's case— she's the Stonefire dragon-shifter I mentioned—it's complicated. Something about an overdose when Sid was younger. But that's why Layla's extra careful and keeps strict records of how much she administers and when."

"Still..."

After bouncing her son a minute, Gina studied Kiyana's eyes. "For someone who hasn't known Alistair long, you're awfully concerned about his inner dragon. Not to mention you haven't had much time to bond before learning you're his true mate, either."

Kiyana tapped her fingers against her legs. "I'm not like most other humans. I know a lot about dragon-shifters and have spent over a decade trying to learn more. And from what I've learned of Alistair, I like him. Quite a bit. It's that simple."

Gina bobbed her head. "Good. He's quiet, but nice. I've always felt sorry for how his mother went on and on about trying to find him someone."

"Meg's not so bad, once you get to know her. I think a lot of people dismiss her before they should."

Gina searched her gaze. "Okay, you definitely need to explain that statement."

Kiyana was debating how much she could tell Gina when a tall, ginger-haired dragonman burst into the room. While she wasn't good enough yet to tell the MacKenzie twins apart, she assumed it was Fergus since it was his house.

Fergus's blue eyes instantly found hers and her stomach churned at the anger there.

He ordered, "Come. We need to get you somewhere safe."

"What are you talking about?" Kiyana demanded.

Fergus shook his head. "There's no time. Something's wrong with Alistair, and Finn's afraid for your safety."

Her heart raced. "Alistair wouldn't hurt me. I'm his true mate, remember?"

"Aye, that may be so, but something is off. And until we know what, you need to be kept in hiding."

Gina stood and held her son close. "You're scaring her, Fergus."

He glanced to his mate. "Aye, and rightly so." Fergus looked back at her and gestured toward the door. "Come, lass. I won't ask again. If you're not up and walking in the next five seconds, I'll carry you out of here if I have to."

Her skin turned cold. There was true panic in Fergus's voice.

Making her body work, she stood, and Fergus gently gripped her upper arm. "This way." He threw over his shoulder, "You stay here, Gina, with the bairn. Everyone's to stay inside until Finn, Faye, or Grant give the all clear."

Gina bobbed her head, but that was all she managed before Fergus was half dragging Kiyana out of his house and down a path. The entire time, he scanned the area, both on the ground and in the sky.

Her heart raced, and she did her best to keep panic from her voice. "Why are you looking at the sky? Alistair

114

shouldn't be able to shift right now."

Fergus met her gaze. "He just might."

The secretiveness drove her crazy. While she didn't slow down her pace, she did growl out, "Just tell me what's going on. By not saying anything, you're making it worse."

"All I can say right now is that we're not exactly sure of Alistair's location."

Her heart skipped a beat. "I thought he was doing research?"

"Aye, he was. But something went wrong. Now, come on. The sooner we get you to the underground bunker of the Protector's building, the sooner you can learn what happened." He pierced her with a fierce gaze, and she nodded. He added, "Can you run for a wee while, lass?"

Despite the sudden frog in her throat, she managed, "I think so."

"Good. Then let's go."

As Kiyana ran, a dragon-shifter pulling her along, worry crept over her. Something had obviously gone very, very wrong to make the reputably level-headed MacKenzie twin so cautious and frantic.

Stop it, Kiyana. Don't worry until you have all the facts. Maybe you can help. Right, maybe she *could* help somehow. And if there was a way for her to assist Alistair, she would do her bloody best to help. The stories always had the men swooping in to rescue the women, but she wasn't the sort to sit back and let others take all the responsibility. Alistair may not be her mate-slash-husband yet, but he would be. And so if she needed to save him, she'd do whatever it took.

Twenty minutes later, Kiyana sat in a room, drumming her fingers on the table, when the door finally opened. Finn, Fergus, and the clan's head doctor, Layla, walked in. Kiyana stood and rushed to Finn. "What's going on? Is Alistair okay? I can't help unless I know the details."

A sad smile crept over Finn's face. "I'm not sure you can help, lass, but I'll tell you what we know. Sit, please."

Finn's demeanor made her wary. She'd seen both the charming and strong leader versions of him, but never the sad, gentle one.

Kiyana sat and raised her brows in question. Finn sighed and said, "Alistair was working on a secret project for us, one concerning a tiny device. Despite every precaution being taken, he was somehow exposed to a chemical compound found inside the blasted thing. His dragon woke instantly, and from what we can tell, he ran from his research lab clawing his head and shouting something about not letting his dragon win."

She froze. "Where is he now?"

Fergus jumped in. "That's the bugger of it all, we don't know. He must've tossed his phone and isn't carrying a tracking device. However, there's another piece of information one of the clan members overheard from Alistair, as he ran away. And that was him saying he wouldn't let his dragon force you, and he would fight his beast to the death rather than allow him to harm you."

She shook her head. "I don't understand. Alistair wouldn't hurt me."

Layla grimaced. "Usually, aye, he wouldn't. But the chemical compound is something the doctors on Stonefire have been studying for a wee while. The effects seem to vary from dragon-shifter to dragon-shifter. And in Alistair's case, it's probably made his dragon violent and unpredictable."

First his dragon being drugged silent, and now his beast going berserk? Alistair had suffered enough with the death of his former girlfriend and didn't need more pain.

There had to be a way to help him, there just had to. "But that's just because of the frenzy, right? If I join him and participate, then he might return to normal."

Finn shook his head. "I won't risk it, lass. From what we can tell, his dragon wants to harm you as he claims you, and I won't allow it."

She swallowed, doing her best not to let her split-second fear show on her face. "What do you mean he wants to harm me? Tell me the specifics."

Finn scowled. "Then I won't sugar-coat it, Kiyana. Alistair was shouting he'd never allow his dragon to cut you as he fucked you. And that is definitely not the Alistair Boyd I grew up with. Until we can find some sort of remedy—someone already tried what we thought was the universal cure by shooting him with a dart and it failed—you have to remain here."

Kiyana would sort through her feelings later. If she let fear or sadness creep into her mind, she'd never be able to focus. And she needed to keep relatively calm and collected. Otherwise, she'd never have her Alistair back. "But he may never return to normal. The other dragon clans don't share easily, and Alistair could die before they do."

Curiosity flared in Finn's eyes. "How do you know that?"

She replied, "Alistair mentioned it a bit, and I've been researching the topic. If we have any chance of saving him, you need to talk to Honoria Wakeham as soon as possible."

Lochguard's leader blinked. "Honoria? As in one of Skyhunter's recently appointed co-leaders? Why?"

She waved a hand. "All that matters is that Honoria found a way to reach out and communicate with other clans in the western half of America. Even if it's just a matter of asking those clans for a solution, it's a start and better than us sitting here and ho-humming about how Alistair is doomed."

Fergus studied her. "You're not acting the way I thought you would, lass."

Kiyana sat up taller. "I don't care about that. We need Honoria's help, as well as Stonefire's and any other dragon clan you can talk to." She looked at Layla. "I'm assuming you have a sample of this substance and are, or have, already analyzed it?" The doctor bobbed her head. "Good. Then we can share what we know."

No one spoke for a few beats, and it finally dawned on Kiyana that maybe she'd crossed a line. She was still a guest on Lochguard's lands, for one. And two, she was a human from the DDA, and dragons didn't always like being ordered about by DDA employees.

She was about to state her case about only wanting to help Alistair when Finn spoke once more. "I'll reach out to Skyhunter. Layla, get everything ready to share with any clans willing to help us. And Fergus, you stay with Kiyana and find out what else she knows, or suggestions that may help." He finally found her gaze again. "Once all of this is over, you and I will have a rather long chat, lass."

Kiyana didn't slump her shoulders; instead, she merely nodded. She may know a lot about dragon-shifters, but she didn't know all of Lochguard's laws or rules. If she was violating some of them, she'd face the consequences later.

However, she couldn't just abandon Alistair. Especially since if he'd found a solution to his project, about how clans could better talk with one another, he might already be in recovery.

Alistair may not be able to reach out to other clans and make suggestions to Finn, but Kiyana could.

This time, she wouldn't allow someone else to die because of a lack of cooperation between clans. Even if she had to pull every string she had inside the DDA, she'd do it. Alistair deserved to live after the tragedy he'd gone through, and Kiyana was determined to ensure he came out the other side in one piece.

CHAPTER NINE

*A*listair was losing the battle with his dragon.

Even now, his dragon roared inside his head, shouting, *I want our true mate. She should be branded, fucked, and impregnated. She is ours, no one else's. And I will find her and make sure she knows she belongs to us and only us.*

He'd long given up trying to reason with his beast and simply crouched on the floor of a cave, hoping the chains he'd grabbed on his way off the clan held.

Normal ones wouldn't, but they were strong and would hold unless a dragon-shifter was willing to shift and shatter bones in the process.

Although given the way his beast demanded to fuck and brand Kiyana with their name burned into her arm, his dragon might be willing to risk breaking bones to get to her.

I want her, now. She is ours. Stop denying us what is ours. Men have touched her before, and she must forget. Forget all about them. She will only know us, our name, and nothing else.

Images of Kiyana being strapped to a table and a hot poker to her arm made Alistair's stomach flip.

Rationally, he knew it wasn't his dragon's true nature.

The bloody drugs had messed with his beast, to the point nothing short of some sort of cure would help.

He had faith in Finn finding one, but if it came to the choice between keeping Kiyana safe or taking his own life to protect her, he would take his own life.

Fuck, his life had turned shitty all of a sudden. And all because one of his staff hadn't double-checked the seal and filter of the special case he'd been using to study the Dragon Knights' device.

His dragon roared and managed to shift their fingers into talons. Alistair forced his beast back into a mental prison, unsure of how much longer he could keep it up. It hadn't even been a day, and he was past exhaustion into some state he didn't even know how to describe.

If Finn and his clan didn't find a solution soon, Alistair would have to sacrifice himself to save everyone else, especially Kiyana. He refused to go rogue.

Even from inside the mental prison, his dragon's shouts rang in his mind. *No, no, NO.*

His beast burst from the invisible prison and slammed Alistair into a corner, turning the tables and making him the captive.

He did his best to break free—pushing, shoving, pounding with all this might—but Alistair couldn't get the walls to budge.

He'd barely tried all those methods before he could do nothing but watch in horror as his dragon shifted, not caring that the chains and cuffs broke their forelimbs and back legs as their shape changed into that of a dragon.

Because the full shift was enough force to split the metal. Which meant as soon as their bones healed in a week—even if somewhat poorly due to not being set—his dragon would hobble if need be to find Kiyana and do unspeakable things to her.

Alistair had one week, only one fucking week, to think of a plan. Because no matter what it took, even if it cost his own life, he wouldn't allow that to happen.

So as his dragon thrashed their tail and did his best to creep along the floor to the nearest water source, Alistair sat down inside his prison and started thinking of possible solutions. This time, he didn't want to fail. Yes, he'd do what needed to be done to protect Kiyana, but he'd lost one female before and he sure as hell didn't want to lose another.

There had to be a way to win over his beast. There just had to.

Kiyana tried to ignore the tall, imposing form of Iris Mahajan behind her, so she could focus on the barely legible words in the book in front of her. However, even with the woman being silent, Kiyana could feel the dragonwoman's dark eyes on the back of her head.

Play nice, Kiyana. She's just doing her job. While she didn't think Alistair would make it through the clan and into the archive building without someone catching him, Finn wanted to be prepared. Which meant Kiyana had a guard or two with her at all times.

Iris was the least of her worries, though. It'd been nearly a day, and no one had yet found Alistair.

On top of that, even with Kiyana receiving regular updates from Finn, no one had unearthed anything to help cure him, either.

Including Kiyana.

Closing her eyes for a few seconds, she tried to push down her frustration. Kiyana hated feeling powerless, unable to contribute in any way. Until she could find something meriting the attention of the DDA director—she'd already tapped all of her trusted DDA contacts to no avail—all she could do was stay safe and continue her research on more long-term methods of assistance.

Surely there had to be something she could use from one of the books to improve communication and alliances. After all, dragon-shifters hadn't always been isolated, and she was determined to find out the reason why.

Opening her eyes again, she concentrated on the page of dense text once more. Research was how she could help Alistair, even if it was only to carry out his dream. Wondering about this or that would accomplish nothing.

The book, *A History of Dragons from the fall of Rome until 1900*, had mentioned a few times how the dragon clans had once been united across the world. She had yet to read any specifics, though. Of course, she had only made it through the year 1200 C.E. and still had seven hundred more years to comb through.

Undeterred, she scanned down, looking for anything related to unity.

About twenty pages later, she paused at the section's title: "The Dettifoss Gathering, Iceland."

In the past, gatherings had been more important and played more significant roles in the daily lives of dragon-shifters. Combine that with the fact the author had yet to mention any gatherings for the last hundred or so years, and it was most likely important.

Kiyana switched to reading instead of skimming:

Many believe the Dettifoss Gathering to be one of the biggest assemblies of dragon clans in history. Representatives from every clan in the Northern Hemisphere met to discuss future ties. After six weeks of negotiations, the Dettifoss Assembly was born. The dragon clans continued to meet every two years to share information, settle intra-clan disputes, and other items that have been lost to history.

The Assembly survived for a few hundred years and eventually included clans from the Southern Hemisphere as well. However, the dawn of human European colonialism slowly destroyed the alliances as the dragon clans in the Americas, Asia, and the Pacific battled new enemies and focused on their survival above all else.

Several attempts have been made to restart a similar Assembly, but due to the overreaching rules and laws passed by the various human governments in the nineteenth and twentieth centuries, the dragon clans have been unable to accomplish it.

Kiyana stopped reading. Ideas swirled through her head, but she needed to check something first before fleshing them out. Turning in her chair, she blurted to Iris, "Have you heard of the Dettifoss Assembly?"

Iris's brows came together. "Aye, although I'm not sure why you're asking me about it."

Turning all the way around, she asked, "Does everyone learn about it in school? Or are you a special case?"

Iris shrugged one shoulder. "On Lochguard, we spent a few days learning about it as teenagers, and another day practicing our own Assembly. However, I can't speak for any of the other clans on whether they do the same or not."

Standing, Kiyana closed the distance to the dragonwoman. "Is there a way I can ask some of the other British clans if they study it, too? Maybe even the Irish one in Glenveagh National Park as well? You know, the one with the female leader."

Iris searched her gaze. "Care to tell me why? I won't waste their time without a good reason."

Kiyana burned to go and do something, anything, even if it didn't provide an instant solution for Alistair. The idea burning in her head might help him, might not. But even if not, it might help others from avoiding a similar fate.

No. She wasn't going to think about what could happen to Alistair if no cure was found. She believed in positive thoughts and wouldn't change that about herself now. Especially since the dragon-shifters in the UK had overcome great obstacles in recent years. They could do it again this time, too.

Regardless, Kiyana wanted to widen the net of potential information sources. She needed to find out how many dragon-shifters knew about the Dettifoss Assembly before she could formulate more of a plan to bring it back.

However, she couldn't force her way into the head Protectors building and then make someone reach out to other clans.

She'd have to spend a few minutes answering Iris's questions if she wanted the help. "If a good number of dragon clans have heard of the Dettifoss Assembly, it's possible they can bring it back. And I know there are barriers and roadblocks. But just listen for a second." Iris bobbed her head, and Kiyana continued, "If it turns out the Assembly is mostly common knowledge, then there's a tie of nostalgia to it. Often this is useful when it comes to public relations and negotiations, as many people think fondly back on those time. While, of course, it would be different and more modern now, it's a starting point. And having common ground to work with can go a long way in changing people's minds and slowly convincing them it could work."

"While admirable, what you propose will take too much time to help Alistair."

Her heart squeezed, and somehow Kiyana ignored it. "I know, but this is something he wanted to accomplish. And if I can possibly help others in the future, it's a good use of my time." She hesitated, and then added something she hadn't shared with any of the dragon-shifters, "Besides, if I can confirm the Dettifoss Assembly is widespread knowledge, then it gives me a reason to reach out to the DDA Director to discuss the idea with her. Whilst doing that, I can ask and see if she'll help Alistair by reaching out to other DDA directors around the world."

Iris didn't miss a beat. "I didn't think they did that."

"I can't speak for all directors, but the UK one does. The depth of her connections around the world isn't widely known, but she has them. Also, when Rosalind Abbott assumed office, she asked for ideas to help improve dragon relations. This qualifies, so she'll talk with me soon after I make the request."

Iris's expression didn't change from her cool, collected one. "Say the other clans have heard of the Dettifoss Assembly. And say the DDA director is open to supporting the idea. If I recall properly, the Assembly was ended by human interference. That hasn't gone away, so what's your solution to that? Even if the DDA Director in the UK is on board, she alone won't be enough to accomplish what you're suggesting."

For a split second, Kiyana wished Iris was less cautious and could be persuaded easily. Of course, if that were the case, she wouldn't be the skilled Protector she was.

Taking a deep breath, Kiyana replied, "I'm sure we can think of something. The DDA Director in the UK has been secretly working on deals and information exchange agreements with other countries in Europe, the Commonwealth countries, and even America. I know that doesn't include a large portion of the map, but it's a start. Why can't there be a United Nations-like institution for dragon oversight departments?" Iris opened her mouth, but Kiyana pushed on. "I know, I know, it would be better if dragons had true freedom. However, we're not there yet. So let's work with what we can do now and then address bigger issues as we go."

For almost a full minute, Iris didn't say anything. While Kiyana was still getting to know Lochguard and its people, she knew enough about the dragonwoman to know she always thought things through. Rushing her would accomplish nothing.

So when Iris finally replied, Kiyana held her breath and strained her ears for each and every word. "Let's talk with Finn. If he wants to support your idea, then I'll help you. But this isn't my decision to make."

She exhaled. It was better than a flat-out no. "Please tell me we can go to Finn straight away?"

Iris gestured toward the door. "Cooper should still be at the door. As long as there's two of us, we'll be able to protect you for the walk to Finn's house."

Kiyana scooped up the book. "And I hope you can convince the woman running the archives that we need to borrow this."

Sighing, Iris exited the room. "She won't like it, but seeing as she's my mother, I'll find a way to persuade her."

Under different circumstances, Kiyana might've smiled and thanked the universe for her good fortune.

However, instead, she read and reread the passages related to the Dettifoss agreement so she could commit them to memory. While she rather would've had more time to prepare, she'd have to use what she had. Especially since she had no idea how Alistair was doing or how much worse he already was.

No, the sooner she could talk with the DDA director about her idea and see if any of her allies had a cure to his condition, the better.

She didn't even care about receiving credit if a new Assembly was born eventually. All she wanted was to see her future mate again without strain or pain, and maybe, just maybe, the UK DDA Director could be the help they needed to accomplish her goal.

CHAPTER TEN

Kiyana sat inside Finn and Arabella's cottage, trying her best to pay attention to Meg Boyd. But she was failing miserably.

The older woman's method of coping was chatter. But her constant speech distracted Kiyana from perfecting her speech and suggestions to the DDA director.

Not that she could talk with Director Abbott until Finn finished talking with his allies. Kiyana didn't fear the woman as some might. She'd interacted with her a few times over the years, long before she was in charge of the Department of Dragon Affairs.

However, her suggestion of an international dragon oversight coalition was important, and she had to get her arguments and facts just right.

Meg reached across the table and took her hand. "Are you okay, lass?"

She blinked. Kiyana hadn't even noticed the older woman had stopped talking. "Being okay or not doesn't matter right now. I just want to stop sitting and thinking so I can do something."

Meg smiled. "Stubborn, determined, and caring. You will fit right in on Lochguard, Kiyana."

Only if Alistair returned and was still whole and not insane.

Not that she was going to mention that possibility for Alistair's mother and worry her more.

Iris, leaning against one of the kitchen counters, spoke up for the first time in a while. "Are you sure you want to be here, Meg? Maybe you should help distract your older grandchildren, so they don't worry about their Uncle Alistair."

Kiyana resisted a small smile. Guilt-tripping was one of the few ways to get Meg to do anything easily. The female Protector knew her clan members well.

Maybe once everything was settled with Alistair, she could talk more with Iris. The dragonwoman didn't talk a lot, but she often made it count when she did.

And yes, things would be okay with Alistair. Kiyana refused to think of any other outcome.

Meg released her grip on Kiyana's hand and stood. "I know when I'm being dismissed. You may be a Protector now, Iris, but I remember you when you were a wee thing always hiding up in the trees."

Iris raised an eyebrow. "I was better able to watch everyone from the trees."

Sighing, Meg turned toward her. "I'll check on you later, lass. But don't hesitate to reach out to me, aye? You're my Alistair's true mate, and that makes you nearly family."

Since Kiyana didn't have a lot of extended family, it was strange to have so many people willing to care so quickly. "I will."

"Good. Then I'm off." She pierced Iris with a look. "Tell me the second you know anything, aye? It's my son they're trying to help, after all. And I'd rather not have to chat with your mother about keeping things from me."

To her credit, Iris merely nodded and didn't say anything about the small threat.

Once Kiyana was alone with the Protector, she stood and paced the length of the kitchen. With Meg gone, she no longer needed to pretend she was cool and collected. "Shouldn't Finn be done by now? He's been in his office for at least two hours since I talked with him."

The dragonwoman opened her mouth to reply, but her phone beeped. After looking at it, Iris groaned. Kiyana asked, "What is it?"

"It's nothing to do with Alistair, don't worry. But Finn asked someone to help with the history of the Dettifoss Gathering. Although why he asked an archaeologist, I have no bloody clue."

"Archaeologist?" she echoed.

"Aye, Max Holbrook. He'll be here shortly, and you can talk with him whilst we wait for Finn."

She'd heard the name before, triggering the memory of a fedora-wearing human with a vast collection of Roman-era artifacts. "I met him once before, at the exhibition the DDA held in Glasgow."

"Then you know how bloody annoying he is." Iris checked her phone again. "Stay here. He's nearly to the door. I want to let him know some ground rules before you talk with him."

Kiyana didn't know if Iris would place restrictions on what could be shared or not. However, she didn't plan on letting that stop her from finding out as much as possible to help Alistair.

She paced a few minutes, reviewing what she knew, until a blond-haired man carrying a battered fedora and wearing clothes covered with dirt-smudges entered the room.

Max didn't waste time putting out a dried mud-covered hand. "You must be Kiyana nice to meet you. While the social side of anthropology never tickled my fancy as much as the archaeological part, it's still nice to meet someone who shares a common interest."

Deciding she could wash her hand later, she shook his and answered, "I hope you can help."

"Yes, of course. I've even been to Dettifoss a few times, although there's not much there to help fill in the gaps of the history." He lowered his voice. "It's hard to get proper permits, you see. So I have to find other ways to look into things."

Iris's voice filled the room. "Aye, you usually break the law."

He placed his hat over his heart. "All in the pursuit of knowledge. That is far more important."

"Until you end up in jail one day," Iris muttered.

Not wanting to waste time, Kiyana jumped in again. "Sit, please, and tell me everything you know. I'll need as much information as possible to convince the DDA Director to help us."

Max raised his brows. "You know the DDA Director? My, that's quite impressive, Dr. Barnes."

"Kiyana, please."

For a split second, she realized she only offered Kiyana and not Kiki as an option. Alistair always using her full name had made her agree it suited her more as an adult.

Not wanting to think of Alistair and losing focus, she leaned forward and said, "Tell me everything you know, Max. And quickly."

Iris snorted from her spot against the counter, but Kiyana ignored her and listened to everything Max could tell her.

⚬⚬⚬

Finlay Stewart had accomplished quite a bit in the short time he'd been clan leader. From forming alliances with other nearby dragon clans to helping change how the human sacrifice program worked to even supporting his cousin Faye as one of the first female head Protector in recent memory; it'd all been necessary but also had helped make his clan a more stable, welcoming place to live.

Of course, shit kept happening to prevent his clan, or even his family, from taking a breath and enjoying some peace.

Not that it was Alistair's fault by any means. Finn had asked for the dragonman's help, and a minor slip up from Alistair's staff had turned him into a vicious, unpredictable problem.

One he would solve, whatever it took.

And not just because at one time, he and Alistair had been best friends. Dr. Kiyana Barnes was trying to move mountains to save a male she barely knew, and Finn didn't want to disappoint her. His clan could use someone like her, and not just because Lochguard had so few humans living on it, either.

His dragon growled, *Why haven't you contacted Skyhunter privately about asking the American clans for information yet?*

It's been less than twenty-four hours since Alistair's accident. Working with Stonefire and their doctors was more important, as was coordinating with the Protectors to search the area for Alistair.

His dragon snarled. *This is a dragonman's life, not some diplomatic act I don't understand. You should ask them and not waste time with fancy video conferences about grander plans. It would take a matter of minutes and could've been done yesterday.*

Finn knew his beast functioned differently from his human half and often didn't understand protocols. But sometimes, it made things a lot more difficult than necessary. *I already have both the doctors here and on Stonefire analyzing the data and asking any other colleagues they can trust. We can do many things, but we're not doctors or researchers. We have to rely on others to help Alistair. Regardless of what you think, the meeting is happening now, with all the leaders in the UK. It'll save time to coordinate at once.* His dragon grunted in defeat, and Finn added, *On top of that, we can try to help shape the future at the same time. Kiyana's idea is a good one, if we can convince the others.*

His beast fell silent, a sign of tacit agreement.

Which was good, because the faces of the other leaders from Stonefire, Skyhunter, Snowridge, and Northcastle all came onto the screen, one after another in their respective boxes.

It was the first video conference with all the dragon clan leaders in the UK participating at the same time. A few months ago, it would've been unthinkable. And yet, here they all were.

He'd prefer to have Arabella with him. Not just because of the importance of the event but also because she was his partner in all ways. However, he didn't know how everyone would react to including mates for the meeting. He trusted most of the faces on the screen—especially Bram from Stonefire—but he didn't want to rock the boat. Not when he had the biggest fucking favor to ask them.

Bram was the first to speak. "We're all here. Now, tell us why."

Finn silently thanked Bram for jumpstarting the meeting, even though the Stonefire leader already knew most of what the videoconference would be about. He'd held back Kiyana's suggestion for this moment. "First, are all of you sure the lines are secure at your end?" Everyone nodded, and Finn continued, "Is everyone up-to-date with what happened in Wales not long ago?"

His dragon grunted. *Stop being so vague.*

I won't violate Snowridge or Rhydian's trust.

Rhydian was the Welsh clan leader and the only unmated leader of the bunch. Well, technically the co-leaders from Skyhunter—Honoria and Asher—weren't mated yet, but were definitely a couple.

It was the female from Skyhunter, Honoria, who spoke up. "We're still trying to catch up with everything. I know Dragon Knights kidnapped and drugged some children, and also used them for experiments. On top of that, a joint effort between clans caught the Knights and handed them over to the DDA. But there are a lot of details we don't have since the former leader here didn't share or receive information."

Finn replied, "Aye, well, Marcus King was a bastard. You both understand."

The former Skyhunter leader had tortured his own clan members, executed a few, and had even worked with the former corrupt DDA Director. Overall, Skyhunter had been a right fucking mess for years.

However, Finn and Bram had spent some time with the new leaders recently and were hopeful for Skyhunter's future.

His dragon growled. *Just tell them what's going on already. This is just wasting time.*

The Welsh leader, Rhydian, beat him to the explanation. "Yes, that's correct. But we also searched every inch and dismantled their hideout, confiscating everything we found. One of the most recent discoveries was a tiny microchip-looking device that can be injected into a person's body. Alistair was studying how one such device was constructed."

Finn jumped back in. "Aye, whilst studying it, the chemical from inside the device escaped and caused his current madness." Finn quickly explained Alistair's symptoms. Before any of the leaders could interrupt with questions, he continued, "And that brings me to why I asked for this video conference. I want to help Alistair, but it requires more than just my clan to do it. I'll cut to the chase to save us time—we need to reach out to as many of our dragon allies as we can and see if they have any suggestions on how to cure Alistair."

Lorcan, the Northern Irish clan leader and oldest of them all, grunted. "That's all well and good, but how do you plan to get around the various dragon oversight committees? I have a bloody hard enough time coordinating with clans in the Republic of Ireland, and we're on the same damn island. I bet it's nearly impossible to reach out to any clan you like and not get into trouble."

Finn put up a hand, to stop anyone else for speaking for a moment. "We all know the difficulties, aye. And it won't be easy. But we've all heard of the Dettifoss Assembly, right?"

Bram frowned. "As in the long-dead gathering of dragon-shifters that met every other year? What does that have to do with your clan member, Finn?"

Finn was closest to Bram out of all the clan leaders. And while most of the time he made it his mission to annoy the Stonefire leader, now wasn't the time to do so. Not when Alistair's life was at stake. "I think we should bring something similar back. It's impossible right at the moment, but we can do the best we can with reaching out to other clans on our own for the time being." Bram's frown meant he'd object, so Finn added quickly, "And before you protest, just know that one of the humans here knows the DDA Director and thinks she can convince her to help us with this. My best guess is that Director Abbott will overlook us contacting other dragon clans if we're caught somehow."

Lorcan grunted. "You say that, but if you don't have it in writing, I won't hold my breath."

The Welsh leader nodded. "I hate to admit it, but I agree. Abbott is better than recent directors, but she hasn't earned my trust yet."

Finn inwardly frowned. He was usually better at persuading others to his way of thinking.

His dragon said gently, *Each day, you take on more and more. You need help.*

Before he could tell his beast to be quiet—even if it was speaking the truth—Bram jumped in. "Forget the director for a minute. There's something important you're not telling us, Finn. Who is this mysterious person with connections to the DDA and why do they want to help Alistair so badly?"

He shrugged. There was little point in delaying the information. "I wasn't hiding it. I just hadn't gotten to that bit yet." Bram sighed, and Finn ignored it. "The human is Dr. Kiyana Barnes. She's an anthropologist that works for the DDA. She's also Alistair's true mate."

Lorcan whistled. "Please tell me he's already gone through the frenzy before being exposed to the mysterious drug?"

Finn shook his head. "I'm afraid not."

Skyhunter's other leader, Asher, spoke for the first time. "Let me guess—you don't even know where he is at the moment, do you?"

"No," Finn answered.

Everyone talked at once, even his dragon. *You need to take better control of the meeting. At this rate, we'll never find a way to help Alistair.*

Human halves complicate things. You know this.

His beast grunted. *And it's annoying.*

Finn clapped his hands until everyone fell silent. "No, it's not ideal. But this is a clan member and my friend we're talking about. And a female who barely knows him is doing everything she can to find a way to help him. We can at least do the same, given as we're supposed to all be allies."

The Skyhunter pair glanced at each other, and for a moment, he wished Arabella was with him. She was far better at sorting out alpha, stubborn dragonmen than he was.

But she wasn't, and he'd do his job. He looked at the Northern Irish leader. "Lorcan, I'll have my head doctor send over her analysis of the drug to yours. You can also see what Teagan and the other clans in Ireland may or may not know about a cure. And before you say it's tricky with the two DDAs, we all know your mate should be helpful enough to reach out to Glenlough."

Lorcan had recently mated the mother of Teagan O'Shea, Glenlough's clan leader, which meant there was a direct line of communication open between the dragon clans in Northern Ireland and the Republic of Ireland. Not even Lorcan could deny the connection.

Lorcan grunted. "I'll ask."

"Good." Finn moved to Rhydian. "Do the same with any connections you have with other dragon clans. I believe you know some in Australia."

Rhydian bobbed his head. "My grandfather's family is there. And since you were helping us out to begin with, Snowridge will do whatever it can to save Alistair."

At the beginning of their acquaintance, Finn had doubted the Welsh leader. However, with time, he'd learned more about him and thought one day he might be a closer ally. "Good." Finn glanced to the Skyhunter pair. "I know a lot has happened recently and you two haven't been leading Skyhunter for long, but I know you have ties to America, Honoria. I need you to reach out to them. And if there are any others you trust there, ask them to do the same with as many clans as possible."

The male Skyhunter leader frowned and spoke first. "We have a long list of things to do to get Skyhunter where it needs to be, Finn. And you bloody well know it, too."

"Aye, but do this, and it goes a long way toward me trusting you two. Besides, I've agreed to foster your sister, Asher. You can at least do this for me."

Asher's sister had a silent dragon. The backstory was long, but all that mattered was Arabella wanted to help the lass. Finn would've taken her in regardless, but it was useful to nudge the new leaders a wee bit, too.

The female Skyhunter leader replied, "I'll do it. And not just because you're taking Aimee, either. If one day we need a favor, I'm hoping you'll help, too."

"I'll try, although I can't promise miracles." Finn looked at the last leader and one he called friend, Bram. "I already know you'll help. Just keep me updated, aye?"

"Of course."

Finn looked at each leader in turn. "One last thing. Once this problem is solved, I want to talk more about a Dettifoss-like Assembly. Maybe we should start fortnightly meetings, to better know each other and strengthen alliances."

The move was something he'd discussed with Bram before, but not the others. Finn didn't know what to expect.

The Welsh leader nodded. "Fine by me. I may need some help with something soon, too. And the more allies my clan has, the better." Finn opened his mouth to ask what, but Rhydian continued. "No need to worry about it now. I wouldn't classify it as an emergency by any means. Let's find a way to find and hopefully save Alistair first."

Lorcan chimed in next. "As soon as my mate hears what's going on, she'll want to help. Just don't assume things again, aye? I know you and Bram are trying to change things, but I have a lot more experience with certain things. Don't forget that."

Lorcan had ruled Northcastle for decades. While Finn knew Lorcan was thinking of retiring soon, he wasn't going to bring that up. "Understood." He glanced at the Skyhunter pair. "And you two? Ready to show your first piece of goodwill toward a future alliance?"

The female spoke up. "As I said, we'll help. Although I can't promise anything since I don't know all the clans in America."

"I wouldn't expect you to, Honoria. Thank you." He looked at each leader again as he said, "I'll have my mobile with me at all times. Ring me whenever needed, even with the smallest update. And in all seriousness, I appreciate your cooperation."

The leaders murmured their goodbyes, and the screen went dark.

Finn let out a sigh and stood. However, by the time he turned around, Arabella was already standing in the doorway. "You're amazing, Finn. And no, don't brush it off."

He closed the distance and cupped Arabella's cheek. "Let's hope it's enough to help Alistair."

She kissed him quickly and then murmured, "Kiyana is ready to talk with the DDA Director. She wants you nearby, so she can pull you into the meeting if it goes well."

After stroking Arabella's cheek a few times, he nodded. "Aye, that's fine. Although I'll need you to keep my mobile with you, in case anyone calls. I don't want to miss anything."

"No worries. My dad is helping to watch the children, along with Aunt Lorna and Ross. So we don't have to worry about little baby dragons trying to jump out of windows for a bit."

He smiled. "I actually look forward to that again, though. So let's solve this problem, aye? And then I can spoil our daughter and have you scold me for it."

She lightly hit his chest. "You're the worst."

"Aye, but you love me anyway."

After giving his mate one more quick kiss, Finn followed Arabella out into the kitchen. It was time to tackle the next item on his never-ending list of duties.

CHAPTER ELEVEN

*A*listair had long ago stopped trying to escape his mental prison and instead had spent countless hours reviewing everything he knew about inner dragons, frenzies, and even rogue dragons. While there was a slim chance the effects of the drug would wear off on their own, he couldn't bank on it. In a little over five days, his bones would heal, and his beast would go searching for Kiyana.

Aye, Finn would do his best to protect the female. But with a rogue dragon made even more dangerous by the influence of an unknown substance, it may not be enough.

Thanks to the extra walls he'd constructed around his own mental presence, Alistair could think without his dragon hearing. Every once in a while, his beast's emotions of lust and dominance would seep through, but not enough to drive him crazy.

For the first time since his dragon had spoken to him at six years old, Alistair would have to think and plan on his own.

It was weird and gave him a glimpse of what humans had to contend with. But still, he would somehow make it work as best as he could.

There had to be something he'd read over the years that could help him. Ever since the Dragon Knights had started using various drugs on dragon-shifters, Alistair had gone out of his way to track the effects and remedies. While he wasn't a biologist or chemist, he'd studied enough of it earning his degrees to understand the basics and form his own theories about what might help.

The moss from Wales had cured the female dragon, and there was something else taken from the Amazon rainforest that had helped with the children in Wales. He tried, and failed, to remember the chemical makeups and what was similar about them.

His beast's latest round of lust and need filtered inside his mental space, and Alistair did his best to patch up any cracks. Doing so made him remember something about how the drugs had worked before, with regards to how they invaded a person's cells.

Or, rather, specific types of cells. Since the Dragon Knight drugs hadn't worked on humans, the effect was limited to dragon-shifter specific genes and markers.

He stilled. What if introducing human blood into a dragon-shifter helped to dilute the effects of the drug?

Alistair didn't recall ever hearing about such a type of blood transfusion. Usually humans wanted dragon-shifter blood to help cure illnesses. However, if anyone had tried it the other way round before, it would have no doubt been in the field of war when there hadn't been any other option but to try a human-to-dragon blood transfusion.

Which meant he needed to talk with Rafe Hartley and Nikki Gray on Stonefire. Both had served in the army— one human and one dragon-shifter—and would probably know others who had, too, and could reach out to their contacts. They might be able to shed light on the matter.

Of course he couldn't just fly to Stonefire and have a nice, long chat. He needed to think of a way to get his information out so Finn and the others could investigate it.

The only question was how.

Even if he managed to wrestle control long enough to make a phone call, his legs were broken, and he couldn't walk or jump to fly in the air.

The only option—and it was a slim one—was to save up his strength and devise a way to take control when his wounds healed. Well, healed as best as they could without a doctor setting his bones back in place.

Alistair was fairly sure he'd limp for the rest of his life.

But he'd take limping over having to kill himself. He only hoped Kiyana wasn't the type of female to easily change her mind over such a transformation.

No. He didn't think she would be.

To get to her, he needed to refine his plan. Focusing back on what he needed to do the day he could walk again, he ran through every technique he knew when it came to containing an inner dragon.

After all, with his dragon's current temperament, Alistair wouldn't be able to take control for long. He didn't need hours, but just long enough to place a call to Lochguard before finding a way to knock himself unconscious until the others could find him.

Find him to either administer some sort of cure, or kill him to protect everyone.

Alistair hated all the variables in his solution, but for the moment, it was all he had.

He'd keep thinking on it, of course. However, he was going to do it from his wee corner of their mind, using as little energy as possible. That way, the day he could walk again, he'd be ready.

⌒⌒⌒⌒⌒

Kiyana did her best to breathe evenly when the UK Director of the DDA, Rosalind Abbott, appeared on the screen.

The dark-haired female smiled often, but much like Lochguard's leader, it was usually there to create a false sense of security and ease. Oh, neither of them wanted to hurt someone, but they both understood how power plays worked, especially when it came to having others underestimate you. That way no one would suspect the person pouncing when they did.

Pushing aside all her years of studying the fascinating topic of power and control, Kiyana did her best to smile at Director Abbott. The older woman finally spoke. "Given the content of your message, we both know this isn't a routine update. So what's this idea you hinted about?"

"It has to do with cooperation on a worldwide scale."

"You don't aim small, do you, Dr. Barnes?"

"Neither do you, Director."

Rosalind smiled genuinely for a few seconds. "That is true. So tell me this idea of yours in detail, and why it was so important for me to hear it now instead of a few days from now."

Kiyana had decided before the meeting to be straightforward with the DDA director. "The urgency is because I want to help one of Lochguard's clan members." She did her best to recount events, leaving out a few of the details about how bad Alistair's condition really was—she didn't want the DDA to go tracking and eradicate a threat until absolutely necessary.

When she finished her rundown, she added, "So you see, to help him, we need knowledge no one on Lochguard seems to possess."

"While I appreciate a dramatic, drawn-out tease as much as the next person, I can only keep this quiet for a short while, and the clock's ticking. Spit out your idea, Dr. Barnes."

A small shot of relief flooded her body at the director still wanting to hear her request, but Kiyana knew she wasn't out of the woods yet. "We're trying to find a cure to help him, as I mentioned. However, reaching out to as many people as we can for possible remedies would greatly increase the chance of a happy ending to this. Which is where you come in, with your connections to other dragon-shifter oversight committees."

"I don't really work for happy endings, but rather agreeable solutions. I think I know what you want, but ask me clearly, Dr. Barnes. I don't want any ambiguity to cloud my judgment or actions, which then could do more harm to the dragon-shifters, even if unintentionally."

The media always painted Rosalind Abbott as a politician who cared more about formal relations than the dragon-shifters in particular. However, Kiyana knew better. The woman secretly was fascinated by them. Few would ever connect the dots, but Kiyana had a shrewd eye for such things.

If Rosalind Abbott were twenty-five years younger, she'd want to be part of the sacrifice system, for certain.

If she wanted the woman's help, now was the time to be clear. "I know you've been working with other dragon oversight departments in various countries. I'm hoping you can reach out to them, quietly of course, and see if they can help find a cure."

Director Abbott searched her eyes. "There's no law that allows me to do such a thing, as you well know."

She nodded. "Yes, I do. And I even have an idea of how to maybe fix that once all of this is over with an international organization of oversight officials—that's the idea I hinted at to obtain this meeting. But for now, I need your help. And it's me, Kiyana the DDA employee asking. Not a dragon-shifter, which means you're not currying favor to one over the other."

The director raised an eyebrow. "You could be a politician if you wanted, Dr. Barnes."

"I'll leave that to you. So, will you help me?"

For fifteen seconds, the DDA director didn't say a word. And with each passing second, Kiyana's heart thudded harder.

The director finally replied, "I will see about helping you, Dr. Barnes, a human and fellow employee. I'll call back when I have something to report or request from you." She expected the screen to go blank, but the director added quietly, "And I want a more in-depth report on the idea you mentioned, about an international organization, as soon as you can manage it."

The screen went dark, and Kiyana slumped in her chair. She hadn't been a hundred percent certain the director would lend a hand, but it seemed she would.

Finn's voice came from the door. "I guess you didn't need me, after all."

She looked at Lochguard's leader. "Sorry. It only dawned on me as I was talking that if you asked for help, it would be showing favor to one clan over the other. If it had been something minor, it wouldn't have mattered. But she's right—there's no law allowing her to communicate freely, let alone secretly, with other oversight departments. This way she's merely helping me. That shouldn't cause as much of a headache if someone discovers her actions."

And given the things Kiyana had learned about the DDA Director over the last few months, she didn't think it would be a problem. Other sections of the British government barely paid her any attention, and not even MI5 was aware of everything that went on in the Department of Dragon Affairs due to various laws passed over the years.

Laws that may change soon, given the former director's scandal, but not yet.

Finn replied, "No, you did well, lass. The more people we have looking for a solution, the better odds of saving Alistair." He gestured out the door. "Now, let's get some food into you before you pass out. Ara said you only had some chocolate for breakfast, and you'll need your strength to keep fighting this hard."

She gave a small smile. "It's certainly been a different experience from what I had expected for my six months here."

"Aye, well, Lochguard is never dull. But my end goal is to make life so boring here people will be begging for a commotion."

Kiyana knew Lochguard and Stonefire had had their fair share of trouble. And she hoped they found some peace in the near future. They both deserved it.

She stood and followed Finn out of the room. "Given your daughter's, er, unique circumstances, I don't think you'll ever have a boring life."

Finn chuckled. "I suspect you're right. But if the only trouble I have to wrestle with is my family, I will be a happy male indeed." He pulled out a chair at the table inside the kitchen. "Now, sit. As you eat, we'll bring Max back here. He can assist in researching what you need whilst the rest of us scour every connection we have for information to save Alistair. Because if it exists, we'll find it, lass. That, I promise you."

Nodding, Kiyana sat down and closed her eyes for a moment. Not because she was tired, but rather because Finn's words had caused tears to prickle her eyes.

While it hadn't been deliberate, he'd said "if it exists," meaning despite all their hard work and effort, Alistair could still be hunted and shot down in the end.

And even though she'd always wanted to live with the dragons and study them better, her current situation wasn't what she'd had in mind. She, too, wanted the boring life Finn spoke of. A routine one with Alistair, and the new friends she was making.

Taking a deep breath, she blinked her eyes open and willed her tears away. She had work to do, and crying wouldn't help any of it.

CHAPTER TWELVE

After six days of thinking, planning, and doing his best to ignore the lightheadedness brought on by lack of food and little water, it was time for Alistair to act.

He'd been storing up what energy he could for this moment, the moment when his dragon had tested out their legs, moved enough to catch and eat a sheep, and sleep to recover his strength. His beast hadn't been as skilled at keeping his thoughts to himself. And if his dragon followed the plan he'd made to ensure he could claim their mate properly, he would hunt one more time before heading back to Lochguard.

Or, wherever Kiyana had ended up.

Given his situation, he wouldn't blame her for moving continents to stay away from him.

Regardless if Kiyana was still on Lochguard or not, Alistair wanted to try one last thing to keep living before resorting to the last possible solution. And to do that meant wrestling control away from his dragon.

Aye, it may have been better to wait until they'd eaten again, but he couldn't risk it. His beast had long thought Alistair had given in and wouldn't fight him.

He was wrong.

While dragon-shifters didn't have any sort of super mental abilities, the one arsenal they could use were invisible forces in the mind. It was how his dragon had corralled him into the corner in the first place. All Alistair had to do was turn the tables and contain his dragon for a wee while.

No more stalling; it was time.

Thinking of Kiyana and his family and friends back on Lochguard, he pushed out against his mental wall with everything he had. His beast hadn't expected the force—more so because he was sleeping—and Alistair managed to flip their positions and force his dragon into a corner of his mind.

Now fully awake, his beast roared, clawed, and threw himself against the barrier. While his words were faint, Alistair easily heard them. *No, no, we're so close. I need her, she needs us, the world will take her away. I must have her. Now, don't wait, don't let the others fuck her in our absence.*

Arguing would accomplish nothing. While his beast was slightly less savage than a week ago, the mystery substance still made his dragon unstable and crave violence in a way he'd never done before.

Alistair stood in their dragon form, tested out his legs—they held but there was an instant twinge that shot up his spine—and he slightly limped out of the cave into the clearing. There was a village nearby, one that still had a red phone box. If he could reach it, he could place a reverse charge call to the Lochguard Protectors, who still had ordinary line phones.

He jumped into the sky, barely making it high enough to flap his wings, and headed toward the village. Since it was night and they were in the country, there weren't as many lights to bounce off his red scales.

Nearly to the village, Alistair landed and struggled to shift back. His beast's protests only intensified as he imagined his snout shrinking into a nose, his wings retreating into his back, and his limbs morphing back into human ones.

When finished, he did his best to ignore the jolts of pain as he ran as best as he could manage. He may hurt himself further, but that didn't matter. This was his one and only chance to help his dragon and escape being hunted down.

He reached the phone box, still grateful no one was about to see his naked body, and went through the tedious process of placing a reverse charge call. Each second that passed only made his dragon more erratic, and it wouldn't be long before his beast took control and ensured Alistair would never be able to escape again.

The phone rang and someone finally answered. It was hard to concentrate as his beast's roar became more frantic, but he said quickly, "This is Alistair Boyd. I'm at Tongue village." The Protector tried to speak, but he didn't let him. "I don't have much time. You need to see if there's ever been a human-to-dragon blood transfusion. It may be a way to save me. Check with Nikki and Rafe. Hurry, I'll be here unconscious for you."

His dragon's forearm burst through the prison, meaning Alistair had less than a minute left.

Dropping the phone, he searched until he found a streetlamp. He needed to complete the last part of his plan.

Even if it could end up killing him.

His dragon's other forelimb broke free. Alistair pushed aside his trepidation and ran toward the pole. He needed to smack his head hard enough to knock himself out but not do lasting damage.

However, he wasn't a doctor. It was quite possible he could die.

Just as his dragon broke through, he stopped at the pole, turned his head for what he thought was a good angle, took a few steps back, and then rammed his head against the streetlamp.

The world went blissfully silent. And his last waking thought was how he hoped it wasn't for the last time.

⁓⁓⁓

Kiyana sat with Dr. Layla MacFie as they listened to the Stonefire doctors report their latest findings.

Most of the medical science went over Kiyana's head, but she was desperate to hear anything.

Even with sending the chemical makeup and data of the substance which had affected Alistair to as many clan doctors as they'd been able to reach, no one had yet found a cure. There was something related in the recently acquired Dragon Knights information, but all of the formulas had been written in some sort of code.

One the Stonefire doctors and their associates hadn't been able to break yet.

Finn burst into the room, glanced between Layla and the Stonefire doctors, and blurted, "Blood transfusions. Have there ever been ones from humans to dragons?"

Dr. Sid, the female head doctor on Stonefire, replied instantly. "I've never heard of one. Which makes sense, given how human blood usually doesn't mix well inside our bodies despite how it's fine the other way around. It's become sort of taboo over the centuries, but it's also illegal in some countries."

Finn didn't miss a beat. "Ask Rafe and Nikki if the army ever attempted it in the field. Alistair called the

Protectors and said a transfusion might help since the drugs don't affect humans. Probably something specific he didn't have time to say, and I couldn't guess what it'd be."

Layla jumped in. "While just hearsay, I thought doing that could affect a dragon-shifter's inner beast?"

Finn shook his head. "That's not a good enough reason to avoid looking into it. Especially since I have people going to the village where Alistair called from, to see if they can find him. I'll need you to come, Layla, and have some dragon silence drugs on hand in case they bring him in."

Layla stood. "We don't know how that'll affect him, though, given his current state."

Finn grunted. "It's a risk we're going to have to take. It's been a week, and if his beast was canny enough to break the restraints and his bones, they'll be healed or nearly so. This may be our only chance to save him from the DDA's special dragon operations team."

A million thoughts whirred through Kiyana's head. However, Dr. Sid spoke before she could make her mouth work. "I'll talk with Rafe and Nikki. My guess is that if it's been done before, it'll have been in the army during wartime when there was no other choice. Alistair's clever to have thought of that. And...wait a second." Sid looked at something, probably on a tablet in front of her, and then back at the screen. "That could account for why we couldn't break the code used for the formulas, if it's referencing human blood as part of the antidote. Let me and the other doctors take a look, but don't do anything until you hear from me again. I know I'm not your clan's doctor, but Lochguard is Gregor's family, and I want to save Alistair."

Gregor was Sid's mate and a former Lochguard doctor. Kiyana finally made her mouth work. "Do you really think it could help?"

"I don't know," Sid stated firmly. "I'll ring back as soon as I do."

The screen went blank, and Kiyana tried her best to ignore the pounding of her heart.

Leave it to Alistair to think outside the box and maybe find a way to save himself.

And the rest of Finn's statement, about him being brought to Lochguard, sunk it. She turned toward Lochguard's leader. "Can I see him?"

"Sorry, lass, but no. We can't risk his dragon waking or fighting the drugs to claim you. I need you to stay here and wait for any incoming video calls since this is one of two secure stations. Any number of people may contact us now, and if they do, you ring my mobile." Finn motioned toward the door. "Come on, Layla. We need to go."

The pair left, and Kiyana clenched her fingers. She wanted to do something, anything, to help. And yet, she knew she wasn't a physician or medical researcher and would only get in the way.

Arabella's voice reached her ears, along with a squeaky roar. "We're here to keep you company."

Little Freya rushed over in her tiny dragon form and jumped up. Used to the move, Kiyana caught her with ease and then sat down so Freya could settle in her lap. As she stroked the baby dragon's back, she looked at Arabella. She fell back on humor to help deal with the enormity of the situation. "You just want a place without a big enough window for Freya to jump out of."

Arabella glanced around Finn's office and smiled. "That's true enough, but that's not the reason. I know what

155

it's like to worry about your male and if something will or won't happen to him. Finn may never have suffered any of the drugs manufactured by the Dragon Knights, but he's been in dangerous situations before. And it took me a while to realize how much having someone else around made the wait a little better."

Kiyana focused on Freya, watching as she turned her head up for a chin scratch. As she complied, she murmured, "Thank you."

And even though they sat in silence, with only the occasional squeak from Freya, Arabella was right. It helped make the wait about their future a little more bearable. Not much, but enough to keep her strong and from breaking down.

⁂

Layla MacFie had long ago learned to focus on what she could do to solve a situation instead of focusing on the person she worked on.

So as monitors beeped and Alistair's heart stopped working at one point, she did what she needed to revive him and get back to work on relieving the pressure around his brain from the swelling.

Asking for instruments, using them, asking for the nurse's help to clean the area, and using the knowledge she'd amassed in medical school and from her experience working on Lochguard to try and save one of her clan members—those were the only things that mattered.

Hours went by as she worked, adrenaline fueling her. When she finished, she murmured her usual, "There you go," and went to clean up. The words were more for her benefit than the patient's, but somehow helped her walk away to tackle the next stages of work.

Namely, talking with friends and family about the surgery and what the outcomes could be.

As she washed up, she ran through what she'd say. Since Lochguard was a close-knit community, reporting on her patients was harder than if she were working in a big, public hospital. She had to be more careful about her word choices, especially so as to not trigger anyone's inner dragon.

Once she changed and quickly downed a coffee, she went into the private waiting room. Finn was there, as was Alistair's mother and brothers. Meg Boyd stood. "Well? How is he?"

"The surgery went well, although it's too early to tell if there's any permanent brain damage." Meg opened her mouth, but Layla beat her to it. "As soon as I know anything, you'll know, too, Meg."

"When can I see him?" the older dragonwoman demanded.

Layla replied calmly, "In the morning. He's being monitored overnight."

Because if he survived the night, Alistair would live. In that aspect, dragon-shifters were fortunate. They healed quickly but also died quickly. There was no lingering gray area.

She looked at Finn. "Is there anything from Stonefire I need to look over?"

Finn placed a hand on her shoulder and turned her around. "Not yet. So go take a wee nap, Layla. You've been on your feet for more than twelve hours today. Go home."

If she hadn't been working long hours over the past week, trying to help the Stonefire doctors and others find a cure, she might've protested.

But Finn was correct—she needed the sleep. Otherwise, she wouldn't be of use to anyone.

Her dragon woke from her usual slumber—her beast didn't care about surgeries and became bored—and said, *We'd sleep deeper if you found a male and rode him hard.*

There are more important things to worry about.

I think not. Besides, there's a male who'd like to share our bed. Let him in.

No.

Ignoring her dragon, she answered a few more technical questions from Meg and her sons and then trudged out of the waiting room to the back rooms.

Once her junior doctor had all the information she needed, Layla exited the building and headed toward her cottage.

She debated stopping at the clan's restaurant for food, but didn't. Sleep was more important.

Layla entered her cottage and froze. Some rustlings came from her kitchen.

Her family never entered without her there, so she tiptoed quietly to see who it was. The Protectors watched the clan's lands closely, so it was most likely a child or teen looking for food, fulfilling a dare, or some other such thing.

She poked her head around the doorway and blinked.

Her table in the little dining nook was set, and food was being dished out onto a plate by a male she knew.

Chase McFarland.

"What are you doing in my kitchen?" she demanded.

Chase turned, flashed her a grin with dimples that made her stomach flip, and gestured toward the food. "This is compliments of your staff."

Her dragon perked up. *He's in our kitchen. Kiss him, fuck him, eat, and then we'll have a good nap.*

She was good at ignoring her dragon. All doctors perfected that skill early on. "I didn't think you did restaurant deliveries."

He shrugged. "Normally, no, I don't. But Logan's a friend of mine, and I owed him."

Logan was one of her best nurses. And if not for the fact Chase always showed up at the surgery bearing food or drink, she might've believed him. "More like you and Logan have some scheme that I don't want to know about."

He shrugged a shoulder, and she did her best to ignore his toned biceps or broad shoulders.

Shoulders she shouldn't notice given he was over a decade younger than her.

Chase replied, "Someone has to take care of you, Layla, since you don't seem to take care of yourself."

If she had more energy, she'd argue. Or, maybe even scold. She'd let his infatuation go on long enough.

However, with the scents of pasta and bread wafting through the air, all she could think about was how hungry she was. "Thank you for the food. You can leave now."

Shaking his head, he sat across from her. "I promised Logan I'd stay and ensure you ate first."

She drawled, "This is my house, you know."

"I know, but you also deal with dragonmen every day. If one makes a promise, do you think they break it easily?"

"No," she muttered. "Never would I think it a negative trait."

She slid into the chair and picked up a fork. The faster she ate, the sooner Chase would leave.

Her dragon jumped in again. *Why? His eyes flashed. He's interested. Why not take what he offers?*

Because he probably wants more than I can give him, and you know it. Clan doctors rarely have mates, unless their mate is also a doctor who understands the long hours. Chase is an electrician, and it would never work.

How do you know?

Right now, I'm too tired to talk. Leave me alone.

With a huff, her dragon curled up into a ball and ignored her.

After a few bites, she glanced up. Chase watched her.

He said, "Even with pasta sauce on your chin, you're beautiful, lass."

Grabbing a napkin, she wiped her face. *Enough.* She handled the most stubborn of dragonmen on a daily basis. She would deal with the one currently in her kitchen. "Chase, you're not getting laid tonight, so save your time and go home."

His pupils turned to slits and back. "Aye, well, I can wait. You're worth it."

For the first time, she didn't think of Chase as the younger, easily impressionable male. No, his words were full of promise and determination.

Time slowed as they stared at one another, and a rush of desire flooded her body at the image of Chase looking at her like that when he claimed her.

Her dragon spoke up. *You've never had a wild night in your life. Take it. He wants us. It'll be good.*

Her beast's words made her stand and back away. *No, I can't. There's Alistair who might need us, and Finn is also counting on us.*

That's an excuse, and you know it.

Chase moved to stand in front of her. She had to look up a few inches to meet his gaze, and did her best to ignore the heat radiating from his body. "I'm patient, Layla. Remember that."

She half expected for him to kiss her, or touch her, or maybe even press her against the counter and lift her up.

But all he did was wink and head out the door.

When she heard the front door click closed, she slowly slid to the floor and rested her head on her knees.

Not because she was sad Chase had left, although that was a wee bit true. No, more because for a split second, she'd envied the females who didn't have to dedicate sixty, eighty, or more hours a week to keep the clan healthy. Females who had time for males, dating, and even families.

But Layla would most likely never be one of those females.

Medicine had been her life for so long, and she could never abandon it. And since dragon-shifter doctors were in short supply, she would forever be a workaholic.

Fifteen minutes ago, that hadn't mattered. However, now was a different story.

Now it made her want to cry.

Taking a deep breath, she forced herself to eat what was left of her dinner and head upstairs. She was exhausted, that was all. A solid four hours of sleep would do wonders for her mental state, and she'd stop being so silly.

Layla was a doctor and would always be one. Clan came first, no matter what. That was the life she'd signed up for, and she'd best remember that.

Chapter Thirteen

A familiar cadence filtered into Alistair's ears, one he both loved and dreaded.

His mother's.

He couldn't quite make out the words. A fog settled over him, one that seemed to keep his eyelids or any other part of his body from working.

Although the silence inside his head meant something had happened to his dragon.

His first instinct was panic—as much as his dragon could be annoying, the thought of never talking with him again was unthinkable.

Some part of his body must've moved because someone grabbed his hand and lightly squeezed. The words were fuzzy, but slowly he could understand them. "Alistair, lad, are you awake? Come on, open your eyes, even if just a wee bit, and let your mother know you're okay. You don't want to take more years off my life, aye?"

Leave it to his mother to both worry about him and guilt trip him.

However, that comforted him in a way. Enough to help push down his panic until he heard an explanation. Because surely there was one, otherwise he wouldn't be alive.

Another familiar voice filled the room, that of Dr. Layla MacFie. "Alistair, if you're awake, either grunt or move a finger."

His bloody finger wouldn't move, so he did his best to grunt. While it was barely audible, it was enough for Layla to order, "Meg, I need you to wait outside. Logan, good, you're here. Be at the ready, in case we need to tame his dragon again."

He wanted to ask what could go wrong, and what be at the ready meant. While Alistair had been prepared to die earlier to protect Kiyana, he was alive now and didn't have it in him to sacrifice himself again.

Kiyana. He wanted to ask where she was, but no matter how hard he tried, he couldn't speak.

Layla continued, "I know you probably have questions, Alistair. Who wouldn't? But right now, I need to assess your situation. And to do that, I want you to try something simple, such as opening your eyes. If you're willing to try, make a noise again."

Since he trusted Layla, he did as she asked because she would do everything to make him better as soon as possible, even if he didn't want to take it slow and easy.

After attempting to grunt again, he focused on his eyelids. They were so bloody heavy, it was as if they were made out of concrete instead of flesh.

But if he wanted answers, he needed to try.

After what seemed like hours, he managed to squint a bit. The light blinded him at first, but Layla's face slowly came into focus. Good doctor that she was, she kept her expression welcoming and free of anything negative.

Sometimes he wondered if Layla should've been a Protector instead of a doctor since she could keep her thoughts to herself better than almost anyone else he'd known.

She did something with his eyes and a small torch. Normally, he'd know what it was called, but he was exhausted and not at his best.

Putting her torch away, Layla nodded. "You're coming around. The initial danger has passed, but I'm going to be honest—I don't know what, if any, side effects will show up once you're healed.

He croaked, "Why?"

"Aye, well, the surgery was only the first step. Once you've recovered from that, we'll have to discuss your options."

Doing the best he could, he asked, "Kiyana?"

"She's safe. And no, you can't see her. I need you to recover your health a wee bit more, and then we can talk more about your future. Depending on what path you choose will determine if you see her or not."

He did his best to frown. All Alistair wanted was the full truth, and yet speaking two words had worn him out.

Regardless, he needed to say one more. "Dragon?"

Layla's expression didn't change, which meant he couldn't gauge her feelings or thoughts. "Another thing that will have to wait. He's silent for now, but most likely not forever. I wish I could give you a clearer answer, but that's the best I can do right now."

His eyelids grew heavy again, but Alistair fought it. "Truth."

"I have only spoken the truth, Alistair. The quicker you heal, the sooner we can discuss options and see about your future. And since you'll try to fight it, I'm going to force you to sleep a wee while longer." She looked away and back again. "We'll talk more when you wake up again."

A heaviness settled over Alistair, and keeping his eyelids open was too much work. As they slid closed, he wanted to ask for the full truth, including the negative outcomes Layla was avoiding. Not to mention he needed to know what had happened to Kiyana.

And then there was the most important issue—if it was possible to have his dragon back for good once he was better.

However, none of those questions had been answered, nor could he ask them. Instead, darkness crept over him yet again, and the world fell silent.

Kiyana was helping to change Finn and Arabella's twin boys' nappies when there was a knock on the front door.

Arabella, who was breastfeeding Freya in her human baby form, looked at her. "Can you get it? I'm afraid if I move at all, Freya will stop eating, shift, and run away. And she needs to eat in her human form at least twice today."

Finishing Declan's nappy, she placed him in his bouncy seat and fastened the strap. "No worries."

Since Kiyana was only allowed in Finn's house or the archives, interacting with anyone else would help distract her from thinking about Alistair. Again.

Or, worrying about her upcoming pitch to the DDA director about her dragon Assembly idea. She may not have brought up the Assembly just yet, but she was hoping to sneak it into the next video conference she had with the DDA director.

Opening the door revealed Layla on the front stoop. Kiyana's stomach lurched upward. "Is everything okay?"

"The best news is that he's still alive. However, there's something I want to talk with you about straight away, in private."

Kiyana had interacted enough with Layla to know she wouldn't divulge any details until they were alone, so she guided her toward Finn's office, which had gradually become hers over the last few days.

She shouted toward the kitchen, "I'll be with Layla in the office for a bit, Ara," before shutting the door.

The room was soundproofed so no one would know what happened inside it apart from her and Layla. "Right, then tell me what's going on. And the more to the point you are, the better."

Layla nodded. "I like how the first thing you brought up wasn't about asking to see him again. So I'll bypass that bit and get to the point. Alistair woke up for a wee while."

Kiyana gasped. "Is he okay?"

"As far as we can tell, his human half is intact. It was for a matter of minutes, though, so I couldn't fully gauge his mental state. But given his questions, I think he didn't suffer any significant brain damage."

Kiyana's heart rate ticked up. Alistair had woken up once, and from what everyone had told her, that was the most important step for a dragon-shifter. It almost always meant they'd survive.

Still, she wouldn't get her hopes up too much. Layla's face was still set in a neutral expression, and she sensed there was more to the story. "While that makes me happier than you know, I sense that's not what you came here to tell me."

Layla shook her head. "No, it's not. Sid and the other doctors have been researching blood transfusions and doing their best to decode the data swiped from the Dragon Knights. While it's mostly anecdotal at this point about what happens to a dragon-shifter who receives a human blood transfusion, there is one single common factor amongst them all I can't dismiss. One that makes everything complicated."

She sighed. "Layla, my entire situation here is complicated. That's not new, and can hardly scare me."

"Maybe, maybe not. But the commonality? Every dragon-shifter who's received a human blood transfusion had become sterile."

"Sterile?" she echoed. Of all the possibilities, that hadn't been one she'd thought of.

Layla bobbed her head. "Aye. Further research is needed to ensure it's universally true, but it's a big enough concern that I need to discuss that outcome with you."

She started to put things together. "Meaning if Alistair's dragon wakes up and still wants a frenzy, he'll never be able to complete it and will probably end up rogue."

"Unfortunately, that's a real possibility. However, there is one way to maybe avoid that situation."

"If you say send me away and drug Alistair until the frenzy can pass, then so help me, I may start yelling a little."

Layla smiled. "No, it's not that." Her face returned to its calm, collected demeanor. "You may or may not know that dragon-shifter sperm doesn't survive freezing. So if you wish to stay and be with Alistair, we'll have to artificially inseminate you until you're pregnant. Correction, if you can become so because artificial insemination has a very, very low success rate amongst dragons."

Kiyana recalled hearing that in her early days at the Department of Dragon Affairs, and it was the reason why humans had to actually have sex with a dragon-shifter in the sacrifice program instead of being impregnated off the clan's lands. "And if it takes, then what happens after?"

"After, if successful and we can be sure his dragon

167

will be calm if returned, we can try saving Alistair using what data we've managed to find. There is a ticking clock here, though. Because of the foreign chemicals in his body, ones that don't seem to go away through normal metabolic processes, each shot of the dragon sleeping drug is dangerous. It could, possibly, make his dragon silent forever."

Kiyana crossed her arms over her chest. "So I have to decide soon, is what you're saying?"

Layla nodded. "Aye, I'm afraid so."

To think, Kiyana had pictured a few lazy days getting to know Alistair before participating in the frenzy. She'd already prepared herself for becoming pregnant and all the risks—including death—that came with it for humans carrying half-dragon-shifter children.

But now, she couldn't even talk with Alistair. And if she didn't agree to a possibly long, drawn-out artificial insemination process, she may never be able to do so.

Some might think her crazy given how long she'd know the dragonman, but she hadn't given up yet and wouldn't do so now.

Still, she needed as much information as she could gather. "My main question is whether me being pregnant will be enough to satisfy his dragon's need to claim? Because that seems to be where the problem lies, in that Alistair will hurt me if awake, with his dragon present, to complete the frenzy."

Layla placed her hands into the pockets of her lab coat. "If I were a betting person, I think it should be enough. After all, you'll carry Alistair's scent, and that should appease his inner beast." Layla reached out a hand and gently squeezed Kiyana's bicep. "I know it's not ideal, and probably not how you pictured being Alistair's true mate would turn out, but it's the best I can do."

She wanted to laugh nervously, but bit her lip instead. Kiyana's rosy dreams of Alistair carrying her off to bed, her being able to see his dragon in the frenzy, and better getting to know the dragonman before getting pregnant, were gone.

And yet, after spending nearly two weeks on Lochguard, it was fast becoming her home. Some might say she was rash when it came to her feelings concerning Alistair, but she'd never felt the same connection with any other man than she'd had with Alistair.

Even if they hadn't fallen in love with each other, she believed they could someday.

And Layla's proposition could be the only way she ever had a child with the dragonman she wanted a future with.

Uncrossing her arms, she stood tall. "I'm fine with the artificial insemination. But Alistair should have a say as well. This is too important a decision to make without him."

"Aye, I know. And I plan on asking him. However, I wanted to talk to you first. Not only will this change your life forever, but it also sets you on a path you can't change, Kiyana. Once you bear a dragon-shifter's child, there will always be a stigma attached to you in the human world, meaning that if things don't work out with Alistair, you might not get a second happy ending."

She put up a hand. "Don't say that. True mates are supposed to be a dragon-shifter's best chance at happiness, right? Besides, Alistair is kind, caring, and more honest than many people I've known in the past. Add him wanting to protect me—no matter how much I wished he'd have asked for my help with his problem—it all points to a man I want."

"Aye, well, then I'll talk with him. We'll also have to put you on hormones, to hopefully help the pregnancy take. It won't be easy, though, so prepare yourself."

She ignored the flicker of worry in her belly. "I can handle it."

"Then I'll be off to get things ready. As soon as Alistair's awake, I'll talk to him about it."

Layla moved toward the door, but Kiyana asked, "Can I see him at least once? You know, before I try to conceive his child?"

"I won't lie to you—I don't know. I can't risk his dragon waking up and taking control."

Her heart sunk a little. "I understand."

"Sorry, Kiyana. I wish it didn't have to be this way. But know this—I will fight for whatever support you need, and will even convince Finn to expand your list of safe places so that you can see some of the other humans on Lochguard until Alistair is whole and sane again. Especially since talking with Gina and Holly will help you, I think, as they've both survived the pregnancies and births of their half-dragon-shifter children."

Human mortality was more common than anyone liked when it came to a human bearing a dragon-shifter's child. However, Kiyana knew Lochguard had much fewer complications in the last year or so than the other clans. She suspected there was a reason, but one she would ask about later, once Alistair was past the danger zone.

She motioned toward the door. "Then go and get everything set up. I'll be here if you need me."

After giving her a sympathetic look, Layla exited the office.

Kiyana immediately sat into the chair and took a deep breath. Without ever doing more than kiss Alistair, Kiyana might soon be carrying his baby.

It shouldn't make tears prickle her eyes, but it did. Not because she'd soon be pregnant. No, because she could still lose Alistair—or part of him, if his dragon went eternally silent.

She'd been strong for nearly two weeks, but right then and there, she wanted her mother to come up from the South and comfort her.

However, she didn't think that would be possible. So she'd merely have to take Layla up on her offer to speak with the other humans mated to dragon-shifters on Lochguard.

CHAPTER FOURTEEN

Several days later Alistair lay in his bed still inside the surgery, staring at Finn's face, and tried to think of how to reply to what he'd just heard.

A human blood transfusion was most likely his best chance at recovery, but by doing so, he'd probably end up sterile.

And the doctors weren't completely sure the solution would work.

Alistair asked, "Why would Kiyana agree to this?"

Finn shrugged. "The lass cares for you. Aye, it's not love. But I think it can be, one day. And this may be the only chance for you to have a child, Alistair. Even then, it's not a guarantee."

If he had the strength, he would've lifted his hands and rubbed his face. However, merely staying awake still drained his energy, so he settled for a sigh. "And I can't even talk with her before making a decision, aye?"

"No, Layla thinks it'll trigger your inner beast, and she doesn't want to use any more drugs than strictly necessary."

It was a reasonable decision. However, Alistair was at an important fork in his life, and he wanted not only to talk with the possible mother of his future child, but he also wanted his dragon's opinion as well.

And yet, he wouldn't be able to get either. Which meant he needed to decide for himself what to do.

Humans definitely had a harder time, he understood now, when it came to living life on their own.

Alistair had more questions than he could ever have answered, but he focused on the more important ones. "Does Kiyana understand the dangers, if she does conceive?"

"Aye, of course. She's been talking with both Layla and Fraser and Fergus's mates."

The MacKenzie twins' mates were humans, too. "That may give her a false sense of security about bearing a dragon-shifter child, Finn, and you know it. They both survived easily."

"And you know the reason why, too. Dragon-shifter blood injections seem to improve a human's chance of surviving childbirth. Kiyana will receive the same. Not yours, I'm afraid, as it's too diluted with drugs. But both of your brothers have volunteered, to ensure it'll come from the same gene pool as your child, which has provided the best results so far."

He loved his brothers most of the time but hated the thought that they could possibly save Kiyana when he couldn't.

Not wanting to dwell on negative thoughts, he focused on the question at hand. Would he allow Kiyana to try to conceive his child via artificial insemination or not?

Even without his beast, the image of Kiyana holding their baby, smiling down at the bairn, sent a course of want through his body. For years, he'd put off thinking of a family or the future. However, Kiyana had made him want it all, and more, once again.

If this was the only way he could achieve it, then it'd have to be so.

"Aye, I agree. However, I want to know as soon as she's pregnant. I don't want to hear excuses about it setting off my beast, or some other bloody excuse."

Finn reached out to squeeze his shoulder. "You have my word, Alistair." The dragonman released his grip. "I hope you're strong enough for the task of getting the seed your female will need. Otherwise I'll be teasing you for decades about how you needed help. Asking for help in most things is okay, but a random male nurse rubbing my dick? Och, that I don't want."

Alistair knew Finn was trying to lighten the mood, but his teasing wasn't going to work this time. "I'll be fine. Send the doctor as soon as you can. I don't want to keep Kiyana waiting and guessing."

Finn moved toward the door. "I know you can't see or talk with her, but do you want me to pass along a message?"

What was someone supposed to say to a female who had tried so hard to save you, to the point she was trying to change how the entire world worked, and was even willing to bear your child without even a kiss or caress to make it all more enjoyable? Alistair had no bloody idea.

So he merely replied, "Tell her thank you."

Finn studied him a second before nodding. "Aye, I will. But I hope you know that's not the way to woo a lass's heart. You're going to have to try harder once you're out and well."

Alistair grunted. He didn't want wooing advice from Finn at the moment. "Aye, I know that."

It was all he could say, really. Although if he ended up surviving without his dragon, Alistair might not be in the best frame of mind to woo anyone.

No. He couldn't think like that. Kiyana deserved better. Even without his beast, he'd have to try his hardest to make her happy. Not just because he was grateful, but because he wanted to be the male Kiyana deserved.

Finn murmured, "It'll all be fine, Alistair. You'll see."

He grunted louder this time, and Finn left him alone.

Everything may not be fine in the end—Alistair knew pain and tragedy better than most—but he wouldn't give up on a life he wanted simply because he could end up half the male he'd been.

No, even if he had to live as a human, never being able to shift again, he'd do it. Because soon more than himself would depend upon him. Soon, if he for once had a break in his life, he'd have a mate and child, too.

And to a dragon-shifter with any sense of honor, that was worth fighting against any obstacle for.

CHAPTER FIFTEEN

Kiyana sat in a chair inside one of the rooms of Lochguard's surgery and couldn't help but tap her fingers against her thigh.

After three long months, this was it. If her pregnancy test came back negative, there weren't any more chances. Alistair's health had deteriorated to the point he'd had his blood transfusion the day before. While there was a slim chance he didn't end up sterile, no one was pinning their hopes on it.

Not that she would've had it any other way. She wanted Alistair alive more than his ability to give her a child. The doctors didn't want to risk anything if the procedure hadn't been successful, and had banned all visitors. Otherwise, she would be at his side instead of in an empty room.

However, the silent space only made her more anxious.

Layla entered the room, and Kiyana sat up straighter. This was it—part of her future would be decided here.

Layla sat across from her. As usual, the doctor's face was calm and mostly unreadable. Her first instinct said the pregnancy hadn't taken. Again.

However, she didn't want to jinx herself. "Well? What does the result say?"

Layla smiled, and the churning in her stomach eased a little. "Congratulations, you're pregnant."

Kiyana stared down at her lower belly. After three long months of hormone injections and two failures, she'd done it. She carried her and Alistair's baby.

There was a flood of relief and a little happiness. However, after so long without more than a few words with Alistair, it was harder to be excited than she'd have thought.

No, she didn't think it was a mistake. After all, she'd talked it over endlessly for weeks with her mother, who'd been allowed to come to Lochguard and stay with her.

But she and Alistair were basically strangers.

It wasn't the way she'd pictured having a baby.

Layla reached over and touched her hand. Kiyana met the doctor's gaze again, Layla's smile helping to wash away a little bit of her trepidation. Layla said softly, "It'll be all right, so don't try to worry. As long as you receive your scheduled dragon's blood injections from the Boyd brothers, you should survive. No matter what happens, I will always be fighting for you, Kiyana."

Tears prickled her eyes. "It's not that. I, well, what if my memory of Alistair is just that—a memory? Maybe he'll regret this."

The dragonwoman answered firmly, "No, he won't. He's brightened with every scrap of news about you. He wants to be your mate, Kiyana. He's a good male. Once he wakes up, I'll do my final check to ensure you can see him. And then I'll make sure you have some privacy, even if I have to tie Meg Boyd to a chair myself."

Her lips twitched at the image. "I think everyone would pay to see that."

Layla snorted. "There's the Kiyana I know. I suspect all the hormones have played havoc with your emotions, not to mention your body. Talk with Alistair before going down the rabbit hole of what ifs, aye?"

Taking a deep breath, Kiyana nodded. "But don't tell anyone else until after I've told Alistair, okay? He deserves to know first."

After squeezing her hand, Layla withdrew it and sat up straight. "Aye, of course." Something beeped in Layla's pocket. The doctor took out her phone, checked it, and slid it back. "Alistair's awake, so you may have that meeting sooner than you think. Stay here, aye? I'll have Logan check on you and let you know one way or the other if you can see Alistair."

She hoped with everything in her being, she could. Her life had been incomplete for the past three months. Sure, she'd made friends and had even watched one of the human women mate one of the Lochguard dragonmen. Not to mention she'd tried her best to help the other women, who hadn't found a dragon of their own yet. However, it was hard trying to make a future when the one person who was supposed to be in it was locked away from you.

Not that it was done to harm her. But still.

Kiyana nodded. "I'll wait here. Although some tea and chocolate would be nice, to help settle my nerves."

Layla stood. "Logan will bring some right away, then. He's the only other one who knows about your pregnancy, which will work in your favor. Well, for now. Dragon-shifter males become even more overprotective when a female is pregnant. Ask for the moon, and any of them will fetch it."

She smiled. "That is some power right there."

Layla winked. "That it is. Until you get tired of it and have to yell at them to leave you alone. Which, don't be afraid to do." The doctor moved to the door. "I'll let you know about Alistair as soon as I can."

And then Kiyana was alone again. Not truly, as she placed a hand on her lower belly, remembering the baby growing there.

My child. Even if things didn't turn out perfectly in the end for her, she'd still have her baby. And since he or she was half dragon-shifter, it only made her more determined to bridge the knowledge gap between humans and dragons. After all, she didn't want people to fear her baby. And ideally, she wanted him or her to have both human and dragon-shifter friends and family.

Of course the child wasn't solely hers. And she needed to tell the father soon.

She started thinking of ways to break the news to Alistair when Logan rushed in with a cuppa and three different kinds of chocolate. As the male rambled on about getting anything else she needed, Kiyana sipped her tea and smiled at how Logan was bending over backward to make her happy.

She might tire of the extra attention eventually, but for the moment, it was exactly what she needed to forget about all the negative possibilities for her future and focus on the positive ones.

⌒⌒⌒⌒

Alistair had learned to both love and hate the white ceiling above his bed.

For three long months, he'd had to stare at it. Aye, they'd brought in a telly, and cards made by his students as well as his nephews plastered the walls. However, the ceiling was blank.

And sometimes he liked the sereneness of it. Other times, it only reminded him of what was missing—

namely, changing into a dragon and jumping into the sky.

He hadn't gone mad yet, which was a good thing. But being alone inside his mind for weeks on end was lonely. So much lonelier than he ever could've imagined.

Lonelier still since he hadn't spoken with Kiyana for the same time period.

At least he'd woken up from the transfusion feeling stronger. The massive doses of various drugs had taken its toll—not to mention the surgery he'd had to repair his broken bones as best as Layla could do—and his health had nearly failed a few days before. While he'd love to be happy about finally being on the road to recovery, the procedure likely meant he was sterile now.

If the last attempt with Kiyana failed, that was it. Alistair would never have children of his own. And given how hard it was for dragon-shifters to have large numbers of children in the first place, he may never be able to adopt, either.

He almost filled the silence with what he thought his dragon would say, but the door opened, and Layla walked over to his bedside. "Leave out the bits about being bored or restless and tell me how you're feeling."

As anxious as she to cut to the chase, he replied, "Not as tired as before. However, my dragon hasn't returned."

"I wouldn't worry about that yet. He may have been put into a sort of coma from the long-term use of the dragon-sleeping drug. The effects should wear off in a matter of days, and we'll know for sure how he's doing."

No comforting words from Layla. It was one of the things he both hated and loved about her, as did all the clan members. "And Kiyana? Can I finally see her?"

"I need to check a few things first, aye? Then I can tell you."

As Layla conducted her examination and he answered her questions honestly, he resisted the urge to ask if she was fine. It'd been over three fucking months since he'd seen, let alone talked with, the female who was his true mate. Even though he hadn't known her long before all the difficulties crashed into his life, he missed her. Missed her humor, her intelligence, hell, how she just felt like the lover and friend he'd always been meant to have.

He'd never forget Rachel and would always love her, but Kiyana was his future now.

Or, so he hoped. If the pregnancy didn't take, then she could leave at any time.

And if his dragon didn't return, then maybe she would, unable to deal with the changes that would no doubt come because of the absence.

His thoughts drifted to what he could do to ensure Kiyana stayed when Layla finished and placed her hands into the pockets of her lab coat. "All of your vital signs are stronger, and your mind seems to be fine, too."

Hope bubbled in his chest and blurted, "So does that mean I can finally see her?"

"On one condition—I want to be here when you first see and talk with her, just to ensure your dragon doesn't act out."

His happiness deflated. Her words had to mean one thing. "Then the pregnancy didn't take?"

Layla raised her brows. "And if it didn't?"

Alistair growled. "Don't toy with me, Layla."

"Answer the question."

He wanted to curse stubborn doctors. If she wasn't such a bloody good one, he might have.

Instead, he answered, "I still want to see her, hear her voice, and feel her hand in mine. With or without a bairn, she's my true mate, Layla. Even without my dragon, the world feels brighter when she's near. I want, no...need her."

Layla bobbed her head. "Good answer." He opened his mouth, but she beat him to it. "Let me help you sit up and then I'll fetch her."

Even though maybe a minute passed, Layla helping him to sit up and place pillows behind his back seemed like hours.

Then she left, and Alistair's heart rate ticked up. After so long, he was finally going to see Kiyana again. He hoped it wouldn't be awkward.

But even if it was, he'd start over and work toward getting back to where they'd been.

The door opened, revealing Kiyana's dark eyes and curly hair. The second her eyes met his, he forgot about his worry and all the bloody awful things that had transpired over the past three months.

His true mate was here, and the world felt brighter.

Aye, it was poetic but true. He murmured, "Kiyana."

She smiled, and Alistair felt stronger than he had for days. Each step she took toward him happened in slow motion, but she finally reached his side. He took her hand, brought it to his lips, and kissed it. Inhaling her scent—the one that had visited him so many times in his dreams—he froze. It wasn't just her scent. No, it was his, too.

Which meant only one thing.

Meeting her gaze, he asked, "Is it true? Are you pregnant?"

As soon as the words were out, he felt a stirring in the back of his mind. It seemed he might learn about both his child and the state of his dragon before too much longer.

Kiyana didn't remember the walk to Alistair's room. But as she laid her eyes on his pale face and a body much leaner than it'd been before, her heart squeezed. Her strong, healthy dragonman looked weak.

But then his gaze found hers and the happiness in his mismatched eyes washed away her concerns. Alistair had a difficult recovery ahead of him, but he was still here. And all she wanted to do was rush to him and jump into his arms.

However, Layla had warned about taking the initial meeting slowly. Only once the doctor was certain Alistair's dragon wouldn't act up would she leave them alone.

Making her feet work, she crossed the room, never taking her gaze from Alistair's. When she finally reached him, and he took her hand, a jolt of electricity raced up her arm at his touch. And then he kissed her hand, and she sighed in happiness. His touch made most of her anxiety and fears melt away.

However, Alistair looked up at her with curiosity, his pupils flashing for a split second. "Is it true? Are you pregnant?"

Before she could answer, Layla was there and demanded, "Is your dragon awake? Is he acting up?"

Alistair never looked away as he answered, "He's there, but he hasn't said anything. Now, if you don't mind, I want to know if my mate is pregnant."

Kiyana jumped in. "Future mate, remember?"

Worry crossed his face, and Kiyana felt three inches tall. She didn't want to toy with Alistair, only tease him.

It seemed teasing would only become natural again with time.

She quickly continued, "Don't worry, I'm not retreating. I'm still here, aren't I?"

He never released her hand. "And is there a bairn?"

Unsure of how to say it, she nodded.

Alistair kissed her hand again and closed his eyes. "Thank you, Kiyana. I know it must've been hell, but thank you. I'll be the best father in the world, aye? I vow it."

She should be happy, but anger shot through her. "Me going through hell? We almost lost you, Alistair, and more than once. You nearly died for the chance to maybe have a child. Just be glad you didn't die because I would've brought you back to kill you myself."

He met her gaze again. "I'm still here, aye?"

She couldn't help but smile at him echoing her own words. "I think going forward, we need to work on communication. Since there are no longer restrictions on me seeing you, we should do fine."

Layla chimed in. "I'm still determining that, to be fair."

Frowning, Kiyana finally looked away from Alistair to the female doctor. "What do you mean?"

Layla motioned toward Alistair with her hand. "His dragon is still stirring, aye? His pupils aren't changing completely, but they flicker every once in a while. I'm not sure I want to leave you alone with him until I'm certain his inner beast isn't a threat."

Alistair growled, and she looked back at his face as her dragonman said, "I would never put Kiyana in danger."

Layla replied, "Not intentionally. However, it's still a possibility. I'm just doing my job, as you bloody well know."

Afraid to release his hand lest she be forced to leave, Kiyana gripped Alistair's hand tighter. "Others can come in, but I want to stay. I've followed every order and done as you said for three long months, Layla. But I'm not going to abandon Alistair again unless he's a concrete threat. I think I've earned that much."

Alistair murmured, "Kiyana..."

She moved a little closer to Alistair's bed. "I know this will sound crazy, but I've missed you. Who else will discuss centuries-old events with me and not get bored?"

"There's Max," Layla pointed out.

Kiyana resisted a sigh at the overly enthusiastic archaeologist. "It's not so much a discussion with Max as me listening to his latest lecture. Don't get me wrong, I appreciate his excitement. However, not many seem to get a word in edgewise with him."

Layla snorted. "True."

Alistair spoke again. "Fetch whoever is waiting to see me, but return slowly. I want a minute or two alone with Kiyana. And before you protest, you can station a nurse outside the door, and Kiyana can put her hand near the call button. But give us a few minutes, aye?"

Layla looked between them before shrugging. "Fine, a few minutes, but no more. I'm not setting restrictions simply to be spiteful, you know. But I'm not about to risk a pregnant female simply because you think you're okay when it's still a bit uncertain, aye?"

Alistair grunted, and Kiyana decided she could better hurry the doctor along than Alistair's growly reply. "We appreciate all your help, Layla." She moved her hand near the call button. "See? I'll keep it here. Can we have a few minutes now?"

"Aye, but I'll be back in less than five minutes."

Layla left, and Kiyana stared into Alistair's eyes. There was so much she wanted to tell him, and yet, she didn't know where to start. So much had happened in the last three months.

And after all the fighting, and crying, and frustration, she should be relieved things had calmed down. However, everything going forward would be real, would shape her life, and she didn't want to mess up the second chance.

Before she could say anything, Alistair whispered, "Kiss me, Kiyana. It's been far too long, and I'm tired of my memory."

Seizing the chance to express herself without words, Kiyana didn't hesitate to lower her head and press her lips to Alistair's. The instant his warm skin touched hers, she sighed, and Alistair gently swiped his tongue between her lips.

The past three months of worry, frustration, and anger melted away as he licked and nibbled, each caress stoking a fire in her lower belly.

He may be thinner and weaker, but she still wanted him with every fiber of her being.

Lifting a hand to his head, she lightly scratched her nails against his scalp. His growl deepened, and his movements became more desperate, more demanding, simply more everything.

She wanted to lay next to him, wrap her leg around his waist, and feel his tall body pressed to hers.

However, Alistair broke the kiss but kept a light grip on her neck to keep her face close to his. His breath danced across her wet lips as he said, "If you keep kissing me like that, I'm not going to be able to follow the doctor's orders about not taking you right here on this hospital bed."

The corner of her lips ticked upward. "I haven't been a rule breaker for years, but you're tempting me to become one again, Alistair Boyd." His warm chuckle reverberated through her body, making her heart lighter. She couldn't help but blurt out, "It's good to hear you laugh."

He gently squeezed her neck. "I can't wait to hear yours again, too, lass."

They stared at one another, saying nothing and yet everything.

It was a strange situation, both awkward and familiar. But she was determined to kick awkwardness to the curb as soon as she could. "It should be easy to do since I'm going to be living with you as soon as you can leave the surgery."

He searched her gaze. "Are you sure, Kiyana? Some might wax on about no time passing, and we're like one soul or some such shite. But it'll take a wee bit of time to get back to where we were, and I don't want to pressure you."

She traced his jaw. "I made the decision myself. And it's not entirely selfless, I promise you. My mum had strange cravings when she carried me, and we'll see if it's genetic. And if so, once you're in full health, I will be making all sorts of weird requests at odd hours."

"So I'm to be your delivery lad? As long as you tip me well, I won't mind." His voice turned husky. "And I prefer my tips to be given in the bedroom."

She snorted. "That's such a man thing to say. It almost makes me think of a really bad porno. A man shows up with a pizza, and the woman doesn't have any money. So they negotiate another way for her to pay him..."

Alistair grinned—complete with his dimple—and she sucked in a breath. Even recovering from three months of hell, he was still sexy. "I'll bring better food than pizza. So I hope the payment will match the quality."

She lightly smacked his shoulder. "Someone is getting ahead of himself."

His face turned a little more somber. "The future can be taken away at any moment, lass. I'm not about to forget that again."

"Alistair," she murmured.

Kiyana had barely pressed her lips against his again when Finn's voice filled the room. "Och, that didn't take long, did it? The pair of you may need chaperones until Alistair's health is fully cleared."

Alistair sighed, and she bit her lip to keep from laughing. After a second, she turned around to see Finn, Arabella, Meg, Kiyana's mother, and Alistair's two brothers.

From somewhere behind them came Layla's voice. "I'll be back in ten minutes, and then you lot will leave. Those were the conditions, so don't forget them. And yes, I'm talking to you, Meg Boyd."

Meg waved a hand. "Aye, aye, we'll follow your rules." The older dragonwoman smiled at her and Alistair. "It's good to see the pair of you together again."

Meg had been kind to Kiyana over the last few months. While Meg still hadn't shared the details of her assignment with the Department of Dragon Affairs, Kiyana was fine with that. After all, it wasn't as if Meg were an undercover assassin.

Kiyana's mother walked past the dragon-shifters who were all at least six or more inches taller than her without so much as a blink and stood next to Kiyana. "It's about time to introduce us, don't you think?"

Finn snorted from the side, but Kiyana focused on her mother. "You've been here less than a minute, Mum. Give me some time, okay?"

Her mother merely raised a barely-there blonde eyebrow and waited. With a sigh, she gestured toward Alistair. "Mum, this is Alistair Boyd. Alistair, this is my mother, Carol Barnes."

Despite it all, Alistair smiled at her mother. "I see where Kiyana gets her strong will from."

Her mother smiled. "Good thing, too. Both her father and I were rather stubborn, and a complacent child may not have survived childhood so well."

"Mum," she muttered.

Alistair never looked away from Kiyana's mother. "You'll have to tell me more later. I'm curious about Kiyana as a wee child."

Her mother bobbed her head. "Once you're better, I will. And in case you're wondering, I'm staying with your mother at the moment so I won't have to bother you two once Alistair is free to leave this place."

Her mum and Meg shared a look. Kiyana resisted a sigh. The pair had bonded rather well, too well in Kiyana's opinion, and who knew what shenanigans would follow once Alistair wasn't bedridden.

And for a second, she wished her father was still alive. He'd have given the Boyds a run for their money, and not just because he was as tall as any of them. Her father had been a manager most of his life and knew how to handle people well. No doubt, he would've had Meg doing things without her even realizing it.

But he was gone several years now, and nothing would bring him back.

Alistair took her hand, and she met his gaze again. He raised his brows in question, but she gave a small shake of her head. Now wasn't the time to tell him more about her father. Especially since while her mother was strong in public, she would sometimes still cry at home, missing the love of her life.

Arabella spoke, breaking into Kiyana's thoughts. And even though the dragonwoman's voice wasn't the loudest, it somehow carried over everyone else's. "Layla will be back any minute now, so if you want to hug your son, Meg, do so now."

Meg didn't waste time moving to the opposite side of the bed and kissing Alistair's cheek. "Don't ever scare me like that again, aye? My hair is already gray, but you could always make it fall out."

"Yes, Mum," Alistair murmured.

Kiyana did her best not to smile as Meg fussed over her nearly thirty-year-old son. She was watching them so intensely that Kiyana nearly jumped when her mum whispered into her ear, "So everything seems fine?"

She bobbed her head and met her mother's hazel eyes. "I think so."

Her mum smiled. "I'm glad, Kiki. Your worries were for nothing."

She yearned to tell her mother her secret, about the baby, but hadn't discussed with Alistair about when they should say something.

Then she noticed Hamish Boyd's face near her shoulder, sniffing her. She blinked. "Hamish, what are you doing?"

He took one more deep inhale and then smiled. His gaze found his brother's. "Well done, Alistair."

Alistair sighed. "You couldn't wait and let us tell everyone?"

Her mother jumped in. "Tell us what?"

Hamish didn't miss a beat. "Kiyana's pregnant."

Everyone talked at once, but it was Finn's whistle that finally silenced everyone. "I'm all for celebrating as much as the next person, but Alistair went through a difficult procedure just yesterday. Dragon-shifters heal fast, but maybe not quite that fast. Let's try to keep the commotion down, aye?"

Hamish shook his head. "And here I thought you were the fun one, Finn. Our brother will soon have a mate and a bairn. If that's not something to celebrate, I don't know what is."

Layla's voice came from the doorway. "You lot can celebrate later. It's time for everyone but Kiyana to leave for the day." Meg opened her mouth, but Layla beat her to it. "And no protests, either. You promised, and unless you're going to break it and show dragon-shifters in a poor light to Kiyana's mother, it's time to go."

While Kiyana's mum usually didn't fret about trying to convince someone of something, even she had learned that when Layla put dominance into her voice, a person obeyed.

Finn motioned toward the exit. "Aye, let's leave. We can start planning the big celebration for Alistair and Kiyana, once he's well."

After Kiyana hugged her mother, everyone left except Layla. She performed a few more tests before turning to Kiyana again. "You can stay here as long as you like, provided you let me know of any changes and don't overexcite Alistair until I give the all clear."

Kiyana was glad her cheeks didn't show blushes very well. "Of course."

"Right, then Logan will bring you a cot in a wee while and some dinner for you both. We'll check back every so often, but you two will mostly have some time to simply talk again. You both deserve that, and so much more."

Layla was gone before Kiyana could do more than murmur her thanks.

Once the door clicked closed, she sat on the edge of Alistair's bed. Just as she touched his cheek again, his pupils turned to slits and stayed that way. She was torn between calling Layla and waiting to see what happened.

191

Alistair needed to talk with his dragon, or he'd never be able to test the waters.

So Kiyana watched him closely and waited to see what happened.

CHAPTER SIXTEEN

When he and Kiyana were alone once more, she'd barely touched Alistair's cheek before the stirring presence emerged into a full-blown one, complete with speaking. His dragon grunted. *Where are we? What happened? Why does Kiyana smell of us?*

Considering the last time his beast had been conscious, his questions were a vast improvement. *What do you remember?*

I-I don't remember much. Kissing Kiyana, and then the rest is blank. Tell me what happened. I don't like this.

With his dragon back in his head, there was so much he wanted to tell him, ask him, discuss with him. However, Alistair needed to be cautious. No one knew what affects the human blood mixing with his own would cause, not to mention they still didn't know if he'd been completely cured.

He answered carefully, *Do you remember the lab and working on the wee device?*

Yes. No. His beast hissed. *I don't know. What the fuck is going on?*

Before I tell you anything, are you in control? I won't risk Kiyana.

I'd never hurt her. How dare you think I would.

193

Keeping his thoughts tightly shielded, he mulled over his dragon's reactions. How could his beast not remember anything? Especially when at one point, his dragon had wanted to strap their human down and brand her.

Alistair wanted to test his dragon and push his boundaries a bit, but he needed to ensure Kiyana remained safe. So he said aloud, "Kiyana stand near the door."

She frowned. "Is your dragon okay? Should I get the doctor?"

"Not yet. But stand over there as a precaution."

She moved as she replied, "I will for now, but only because I want to be close to the door to call for help if you need it. Not because I want to flee at the first sight of your dragon."

His mate was a fierce one, and he loved her for it.

Alistair nearly blinked. He couldn't love her yet. They'd barely known each other long.

However, as his dragon growled and paced inside his mind, he had to push aside the feelings and focus on his inner beast. He could never truly have Kiyana as his mate as long as his dragon was unpredictable.

Turning his thoughts to his beast, he said, *What about this? Do you remember this?*

Alistair raised his arm and showed the jagged scar. While his arms worked nearly perfectly again thanks to Layla's surgery, nothing would erase the scars.

His legs, on the other hand, were a different story. But not one he wanted to dwell on just yet.

After a few beats, his dragon asked, *When did that happen? Stop these games and tell me the truth. You aren't supposed to hide anything from me.*

Alistair decided to be honest and test his beast further. *You turned mad after we were exposed to*

194

some chemicals. So dangerous that we had to run and I chained us up. He gestured toward the scar on his arm. *This is a result of you breaking the chains and our legs, as well as them healing improperly.*

No, no, no. I would never do that. You lie. Why would you lie to me? I don't understand.

His dragon thrashed about, roaring and hissing, not comprehending what happened.

Apparently, his dragon truly didn't remember the events of the past few months.

Engrossed with his thoughts, he hadn't noticed Kiyana return to his bedside. He was about to tell her to go back, but she placed a hand on his cheek, and his dragon instantly calmed down to say, *Kiyana. I don't know why, but I've missed her.*

Kiyana's voice prevented Alistair from replying. "Tell me what's going on inside your head, Alistair. And why your pupils only turned round again after I touched you."

His mate was observant, even under pressure. Yet another reason to want her at his side, always.

Alistair shook his head. "I'm not sure I understand myself. But my dragon has amnesia for the last three months and wasn't handling it well. At least, until you touched me and then he calmed."

Of course I did. She is our mate. She carries our bairn. I will always calm for her and try to protect her.

He wanted to believe his dragon, he truly did. But for the first time in his life, Alistair doubted his beast's words. *For a time, you wanted to hurt her.*

Liar! I would never hurt her. Try to claim her, yes. But hurt her? No. His dragon paused before asking, *Why don't you trust me? I don't understand. Something happened, but you aren't telling me. You aren't supposed to keep secrets from me.*

He sensed his dragon's hurt and confusion. *Maybe we should send Kiyana away and discuss this in private.*

No, I want Kiyana to stay. I don't remember claiming her, but her touch soothes me, as does her scent. She should always be by our side.

"Alistair?"

He blinked and met Kiyana's eyes once more. "Sorry. It's hard trying to break the news whilst not worrying about you."

She shook her head, her dark curls bouncing. "Don't worry about me. The call button is right there, and at the first sign of trouble, I'll run." She paused and bit her lip before adding, "Does he need to claim me to remain stable? I know the doctor said not to overstrain you, but if I'm on top, I can do the work."

His human was fighting for him yet again. He was a lucky dragonman, and he would never forget it. "No, the first time I claim you, it should be good for you. Not a quick attempt to please a dragon."

She quirked an eyebrow. "It can be good for me in many different ways, Alistair Boyd." Her voice turned husky, and each syllable sent a rush of desire through his body straight to his cock. "So tell me, what does your dragon want?" She ran a finger down his chest. "Because I'm not a woman to sit back and let the man do all the work, no matter what it's about. We're partners in all ways, including this."

His dragon hummed. *Yes, yes, I want her. Let her ride us. I want to remember claiming her. It will help.*

Alistair had no bloody idea if it would help his beast or not. He should say no. That would be the honorable thing to do. Kiyana should be screaming as he made her come many times over before he finally slid between her thighs and filled her sweet pussy with his cock.

But his dragon was unpredictable. He couldn't risk his female's life yet again. Maybe allowing her to claim him would stabilize his beast long-term.

However, before he could say anything, Kiyana kissed him as her hand found his cock under the sheet. As she tangled her tongue with his, her soft, warm fingers tickled, lightly scraped, and gripped him.

His dragon hummed the entire time, sending thoughts of them taking her from behind, with Kiyana on her back, and even with her sitting on their face.

Alistair was noble, but as Kiyana pumped his dick, it faded bit by bit until he gently pulled her on top of him.

He nearly roared as her hand left his cock and she broke the kiss. But as she raised herself up, tossed back his blanket, and reached under her skirt, he couldn't look away as he heard fabric tear.

Holy fuck, his mate was tearing off her own pants.

His mate was a bloody dream come true. What he would give to rip off her skirt and finally see her plump pussy, tease it, and rub her clit until she came.

Her voice filled his ears again, and he forced himself to look up. "The one good thing from all of this is that I'm already pregnant, so no worries there."

She removed her hand from between her legs, her fingers glistening in the light. He lightly grabbed her wrist and ordered, "Let me taste you first."

His dragon hummed. *Yes, yes, I want to savor her, too. Maybe it'll help my memory. She can fuck us as many times as she likes until it returns.*

He didn't want to ruin the moment with the truth, so instead, he ignored his beast and took the hand Kiyana offered. He drew her two fingers in deep, licking and laving every last drop of her sweet nectar from her skin.

When she removed her hand, he wanted to order her back. However, her fingers moved to lightly caress his rock-hard dick, and he hissed.

Kiyana scooted back a little, looked down, and smiled. "Now that's almost worth all the bloody trouble we've been through."

His cock pulsed at her gaze and let out a drop of precum.

For a split second, he remembered how he could be sterile and unable to father any more children.

But he pushed it back. All of his attention should be on Kiyana. She was his future, nothing else.

He ran a hand up her waist, to her breast, and lightly tweaked her already hard nipple through her top. She sucked in a breath, and he grunted in approval. "You should be naked."

"No." He played with her nipple, and Kiyana's head fell back. It took a second for her to say more. "We can't, in case someone walks in."

His dragon growled. *She's right. No one should see her but us. She is our mate, ours. No one else's.*

Alistair waited for his dragon to turn dark, like before, but only images of fucking Kiyana so hard her tits bounced as she screamed and clutched their cock filled his mind.

What he wouldn't give to be able to do that right at that moment.

Kiyana moved forward again, her hips raised, and her fingers wrapped around his cock as she guided him to her hot, wet entrance.

"Kiyana," he uttered somewhere between a curse and praise.

Her heat was so close, he wanted to buck his hips and take her to the hilt.

And yet, he was already rushing his first time claiming her. Alistair would let Kiyana take him how she wished. He'd have many decades to fulfill every fantasy he had featuring his beautiful mate.

"Ready?" Kiyana asked.

"I've been ready since the first time I saw you, love. And I always will be."

"Alistair," she murmured.

"It's true. I fought it, but now I can see how useless that was. I want you, Kiyana. And I will thank the universe every fucking day that you were strong enough to stay and fight for me."

Without another word, Kiyana sank down on him and leaned over to take his lips.

He pulled her head closer as he nibbled, sucked, and tasted her mouth. Simultaneously being inside her mouth and her cunt was paradise, and one he hoped was never taken away from him.

Kiyana was his female, and he'd do everything to keep her.

Then she moved her hips, and he couldn't help but moan. She was so bloody tight, and each movement of her hips drove him a little closer to the edge.

His dragon roared. *She is perfect, will always be perfect, and she is ours. Brand her, quickly, so no one will snatch her away from us.*

The words tickled a memory, but as Kiyana moved her hips faster, he forgot about everything except her sweet, hot pussy gripping and stroking him.

His balls tightened, and he knew it wouldn't be long. However, his female hadn't come yet. She should come first. She always should.

He snaked a hand down and rubbed her hard little clit in circles, loving how her hips bucked when he found the combination of pressure and movement she liked best.

But then Kiyana gripped him even tighter, and it took every bit of strength he possessed not to let go and brand her with his seed.

Sweat trailed down his neck from the strain, and he wondered how much longer he could hold out.

However, Kiyana's pussy gripped and released his cock as she cried out into his mouth. Alistair finally let go, exploding into his female with such force he couldn't do more than lay there and let it happen.

When she'd milked every last drop from him, Alistair pulled her down and held her against his chest. His dragon hummed in the background, for once too tired to say anything.

He and Kiyana lay there, breathing heavily until her delicious voice filled the room. "I should probably clean up before Logan stops by with the cot."

Alistair pulled Kiyana tighter against his chest. "No. I don't want you to leave."

She snorted. "If I stay like this for days, that can't be sanitary."

Moving a hand down, he lightly slapped her arse. "I didn't say days."

"Are you sure? Dragon-shifters tend to want to keep their mates close, from what I've seen."

"Aye, but we all have lives to lead. And the sooner I can leave this hospital room and start my life with you, the better."

Kiyana raised her head to meet his gaze. "Does the true-mate thing make you so sure?"

He brushed some hair off her cheek. "Recognizing a fated mate is just the first step. It's up to me and my dragon to make it work."

"And what about me? I can't imagine doing whatever I please and not driving you away screaming."

He slowly stroked her lower back. "I somehow doubt even your worst would be all that bad. You spent the last three months trying to help me. And not just me, but I heard a little from the nurses about your idea with the DDA Director."

She shrugged. "There wasn't much for me to do to help you, so I merely focused on carrying out your dream."

As he stared into Kiyana's dark eyes, he wondered how she'd come to mean so much to him so quickly.

His dragon finally awoke from his dozing. *You pushed people away for so long. Once you stopped doing that, it's easy to care and love someone.*

What he wouldn't give to tell Kiyana how he felt.

However, it was much too soon.

Before he could think of how to change the topic, she stated, "Your pupils changed again. Tell me what your dragon said."

Just as he opened his mouth to do so, Logan walked into the room. The dragonman clicked his tongue and said, "Och, and now I'm going to have to separate you two. Alistair can't be getting excited just yet."

He didn't release Kiyana. "She's my mate and she's not going anywhere."

Logan raised his brows. "So does that mean I need to fetch a chastity belt of some sort for you to wear, Alistair?" He glared and Logan grinned. "That's a yes, aye?"

Kiyana laughed and sat up. It was probably the only time in his life Alistair was glad she was still dressed. Kiyana said, "No, no, we'll behave. I was just helping his dragon, is all."

Logan's gaze shot straight to his. "Your dragon is awake and you didn't call us?"

Kiyana pulled his sheet up and gracefully dismounted him and the bed. The second her weight and heat vanished from his body, he wanted to bring her back and have her hot pussy hold him again.

However, his mate shook her head. "No more for now. Tell Logan about your dragon whilst I clean up."

Logan looked like he wanted to laugh, but thankfully didn't. A good thing, too, because Alistair may have tried to punch him for it.

As soon as the bathroom door clicked closed, Logan spoke again. "I'd heard about you when you were younger, Alistair, about how you were a lot more charming and mischievous. But I never believed it. Now, however, I do. You're not as straight-laced as you make out to be."

The changes were because of Kiyana, but he didn't want to discuss that with Logan and have it end up filtering to the entire staff. "Can you just hurry up and ask me medically-related questions? I fully intend to have my mate sleep at my side tonight."

Logan's pupils flashed. "Do you now? One word from me, and she goes home."

"Don't even think about it."

"Answer my questions in full, leaving nothing out, and maybe I won't. However, if your health was affected, no amount of growling will change my mind. Too many people fought to save your life, Alistair Boyd. And I won't let your cock risk it out of stupidity."

At that, Alistair fell silent. He'd claimed Kiyana once, and she already carried his bairn. A few more days of not having his mate as he wanted wouldn't kill him.

It might come close, but not quite.

So Alistair answered everything Logan asked and was content to merely hold his mate at his side as he fell asleep.

CHAPTER SEVENTEEN

About a week later, Kiyana matched her pace to Alistair's, clenching her fingers to keep from offering him help.

Her dragonman was still adjusting to using a cane, and sometimes it would slip on the ground, and it'd take a moment for him to right himself. After the first few hours out of the surgery earlier in the day, Kiyana had learned not to try to help him. To say dragon-shifter males had pride was an understatement.

Alistair finally cursed. "I'm not sure how I'm supposed to get anywhere with the blasted thing."

She shrugged. "Layla said you'd learn soon enough. And if you keep up with your physical therapy, you shouldn't need it at all before too much longer."

He grunted. "Aye, well, I don't like it."

She shook her head. Even supposedly fierce male dragon-shifters turned into children when sick or injured. "Oh, stop it. You can still shift into a ferocious dragon. And even without being able to breathe fire, that's quite impressive."

Alistair's pupils flashed to slits and back. The phenomenon was more common compared to when his dragon had first started speaking to him again.

His beast still hadn't come out during their rather long nap that hadn't been a nap, though. She sensed Alistair's memories of his rogue dragon still haunted him to a degree. It'd take time to make her dragonman whole again, but she was confident it would happen.

He hadn't held back earlier when they'd finally had some time alone, and the lingering soreness between her thighs made her smile.

Alistair grunted again. "If we could breathe fire, the humans would've either killed us off or would have become our subjects."

"Perhaps. But who's to say dragons couldn't have breathed fire thousands of years ago? Max suggested it was possible."

Alistair sighed. "Not bloody Max again. Please tell me he's gone back down south. All I want is a few peaceful days with my female."

Kiyana didn't see Max quite as annoying as many of the Lochguard people did, just eccentric. "He left, so don't worry about him. However, I'm not sure attending dinner at your mother's house is what I'd call peaceful."

Alistair raised an eyebrow. "Not going would've been heaps worse."

Meg Boyd's cottage came into view. "Perhaps, but I've gotten to know your mother well over the last few months. If I'd asked her to give us a day, she would have done so. Especially if I suggested for Archie and Cal to distract her."

"No, no, no. Don't talk about my mum's beaus. I have enough madness in my life without that."

She didn't tease him about that comment. It was true—Alistair was forever being tested, questioned, and even consulted on some of the findings from the data cache Stonefire had acquired concerning the Dragon Knights.

"The craziness will die down soon enough. Remember, they've been working for months with all that data and you're just playing catch-up right now."

"Aye, I know that. But I'd rather go back to teaching." He met her gaze. "It's safer and means I can be there for you and the bairn."

Even with a week to get used to the idea, Kiyana sometimes forgot a little half-dragon-shifter was growing inside of her. Especially since she had zero pregnancy symptoms so far. Layla suggested maybe it had to do with the dragon blood injections Kiyana was receiving every few days. Regardless, the doctor had assured her many times over she was still pregnant.

Kiyana touched Alistair's bicep. "I know. And Finn promised you could go back to teaching once you were fully recovered. But having the knowledge and not using it, well, that seems a waste."

"I know, I know." He stopped to take her hand. "I just missed so much whilst I was unconscious, and I want to get up to speed as quickly as possible, especially when it concerns you, love."

She squeezed his hand in hers. "And I'm here, willingly going to dinner with your entire family. I think that's a fairly good way to get to know my mate."

Even though they still hadn't had a formal mating ceremony, they had both accepted it in their hearts.

No, Alistair hadn't said he loved her yet, but she was sure it would come with time. Especially since she was more than halfway there herself.

And while some might think dinner with his family would do the opposite, Kiyana was sure it'd bring her even closer to her dragonman.

The only lingering question she had concerned her mother. Kiyana wasn't yet sure if she wanted her mum to try to stay on Lochguard permanently or go back down South. And as much as she wanted her mother to stay, Kiyana wouldn't decide it for her. Even though Kiyana's childhood home reminded her mother of her late husband, her friends and family lived there. Uprooting her life would be a massive step.

Meg's voice drifted into the air, interrupting her thoughts. "Och, now, hurry yourselves up. Everyone's here already, and the food will go cold if you dally much longer."

Alistair muttered, "We're fifteen minutes early."

Meg replied as if he'd shouted it on the wind. "And in our house, that's as good as late. Now, come on. Your poor mother is waiting to spend some quality time with her youngest son."

Kiyana did her best not to laugh. Meg had visited her son every day, without fail.

She lightly squeezed Alistair's hand and released it. "We're coming, Meg."

"Don't encourage her," Alistair murmured low enough that only Kiyana should be able to hear it.

"Hey, I'm the human entering the dragon's den. I have to pick my battles, and this is one where I can side with your mother. Hamish told me that dinners at your mum's house are entertaining, and I'm looking forward to seeing if he's right or not."

Alistair grunted as he walked once more. Or, hobbled might be a better way to describe it. "You talk about Hamish quite a bit, and my dragon doesn't like it."

She rolled her eyes. "He's kind enough to donate blood to help me and the baby. Not to mention he's happily mated. Stop being silly."

Alistair fell silent, and she mentally kicked herself. The tests were still inconclusive as to whether Alistair could father more children or not—his body was still adjusting to the foreign human's blood, and Layla didn't know exactly what to expect. However, the one thing the doctor knew for certain was that Alistair's blood was still too tainted to give to Kiyana and improve her chances of surviving childbirth.

Sensing her dragonman was going to turn moody if she didn't intervene, she continued, "I picked you, Alistair Boyd, and no one else. Can't that be enough?"

He met her gaze and his pupils flashed. Merely picking him wasn't quite enough, even for her, but she wasn't going to force love from him. Bloody hell, Alistair had nearly died a few times over the last three months. His health was more important than her dreams of a solid, stable relationship with a clear happy ending in sight.

They reached the front door, which was still open, and entered. Noises came from the dining room, but after closing the door, Kiyana stopped Alistair and pulled his head down for a kiss.

Soon enough she retreated and whispered, "That should motivate you. Because if the dinner goes well, I may have a few surprises for you later."

He kept his voice low as well. "But you're sore, love."

"Only a little, but not enough to keep me from craving more."

His pupils flashed and he kissed her again. "I would capture the moon for you, lass, to claim your reward. But I can't make promises about being on my best behavior. My eldest brother knows how to get under my skin at times, not to mention my mother."

"Ah, but remember, my mum is there too. Between her and I, it changes the dynamics. Maybe even to your favor."

He smiled slowly. "I like that possibility."

She laughed. "I thought you would. Now, let's go."

❧❧❧

Alistair guided Kiyana into the dining room and was instantly accosted by his eldest nephew, Hugh. Despite being nine years old and more than two feet shorter, he nearly knocked Alistair off his feet.

Somehow he managed to maintain his balance with his cane and lightly pat Hugh's back with his free hand. "You're getting stronger every day, aye? Before you know it, you'll be towering over your mum and soaring in the skies."

Hugh's brown eyes met his, disappointment plain. "You know I can't start flying until I'm ten." He lowered his voice. "Maybe you can talk with my mum to let me try earlier?"

Hugh's mother and Graham's mate, Lesley, clicked her tongue. "You'll be doing no such thing, lad. Dragons who fly before they're ready sometimes end up missing or at the bottom of a lake, and we don't want that to happen to you. Isn't that right, Graham?"

Alistair's older brother never said much and settled for a grunt.

Hugh went to his mother's side and tried persuading her. Not that Alistair could hear what happened because his mother spoke loudly, to ensure everyone heard her. "Sit yourselves down round the table. And no more tackling your Uncle Alistair, aye? His muscles are a wee bit out of practice, and anyone who sends him flying to the ground won't be getting any dessert for at least two dinners, maybe even three. Understood?"

Since Alistair's brothers all had sons—five in total—the

three who were old enough to understand and respond muttered, "Yes, Grannie."

His mother nodded curtly. "Aye, then let's sit down and have a proper dinner. It's the first one with everyone for some time, not to mention the first full family dinner to include our human guest, Grannie Carol."

Alistair waited to see if Kiyana's mother would object to being called a grannie, but she merely smiled and said something to Hamish's mate, Alba.

As he and Kiyana sat down, Hamish said, "You just want to hold wee Roman some more, Mum."

His mother's gaze shot to Hamish. "Of course I do. I need to start spoiling him more to catch up to the other wee rascals sitting round my table."

Alistair watched as his mother took the newest Boyd, not even six months old, and wondered if he and Kiyana would have a son or daughter. Statistics said they'd have a son since dragon-shifter populations skewed male, but having a human mate meant anything was possible.

Not that he'd care one way or the other. He'd love his child, end of story.

His dragon muttered, *You say that, but I know you want a wee girl.*

Kiyana took his hand under the table and squeezed. He met her gaze, and she motioned for him to come closer. She whispered as low as she could into his ear, "Whilst they probably all know about the baby thanks to Hamish, we should tell them formally, too, I think."

He raised a brow, asking if she was sure, and Kiyana nodded.

He whispered back. "In a bit. At the news, the other mates will probably whisk you away and start offering nonstop advice. And I don't know about you, but I'm starving. My mum made shepherd's pie, which is one of my favorites."

His mother harrumphed. "Aye, your favorite. So start eating." Little Roman waved his arms, and she took one of his tiny hands. "You just ate, lad. And trust me, I'm long past the age of giving you what you want in that department."

Hamish choked on his food. After his mate thumped his back, Hamish said, "Och, Mum, don't bring that up at the table when I'm trying to eat."

His mother shrugged. "Why not? A little humor never hurt anyone."

"If it were only humor..." Hamish started and didn't finish.

Kiyana jumped in. "I've met all of the boys at one point, but let's see if I remember all of your names."

Leave it to his mate to try and smooth things over. She might help stabilize family dinners.

His dragon snorted. *For now. I doubt it'll last.*

I'll take it for as long as I can.

Cody, Hamish's eldest son, grinned and asked, "What about me?"

Kiyana tapped her chin. "Wasn't it Nigel?"

"No!"

"Hm, Neville?"

Cody made a face. "That's really not my name."

"Ah, I've got it! Cody."

Graham's second son waved his fork. "And me?"

"Jumbalaya?"

"No, silly, I'm Justin."

"Oh, of course!"

Kiyana glanced at him and winked.

His dragon spoke up. *She'll be an amazing mother.*

Of course she will.

And no matter what you say, you've missed our

family.

Alistair glanced around the dinner table, all of his nephews—apart from wee Roman—kept playing with their food and shouting words or making noises when Kiyana asked questions.

He replied, *Aye, I have. More than just the last few months, too. I don't regret trying to fulfill my vow to Rachel, but if Kiyana hadn't come along, I might've missed out on life for a lot longer.*

In that, we agree.

He nearly told his dragon how much he'd missed their normal conversations. Everything pointed to his dragon remaining normal. Well, apart from the memory lapse right after they'd been driven crazy by the drugs.

In a way, he was grateful. Yet at the same time, it worried him that his beast might become the darker version again someday.

Wee Bruce, who was barely two, somehow toddled over to him and lightly slapped Alistair's side. "Up, Ali. Up."

Alistair was not the easiest of names for a toddler, and so he was often Uncle Ali, although it sounded more like Ah-ree.

He scooted back enough and placed Bruce into his lap. After tickling his side a second, Alistair noticed the silence from the adults. Scanning the room, he raised his brows. "What?"

Hamish cleared his throat. "It's been years since you so easily played with the lads, Alistair. It's nice to have you back, in more ways than one."

As he glanced from person to person, he finally stopped at Kiyana. Holding his nephew in place with one arm, he took Kiyana's hand with his free one and brought it to his lips. "Kiyana brought me back to life. You should thank her."

She beamed at him, and his heart lifted. Bloody hell, he loved her so much. He wouldn't be the male he was without her, and that was only the tip of the iceberg of things he owed her for.

Maybe it was too soon, and maybe his brothers would say he was an idiot, but once he and Kiyana were alone later, he was going to tell her how he felt.

She didn't have to love him back just yet, but he wanted her to know she was more than just a mate randomly chosen by fate.

As if on cue, his mother broke the silence. "Aye, well, I've been telling Carol how lovely her daughter is. Now someone else can do it, too."

Carol smiled and shared a glance with Kiyana as she said, "I wouldn't go so far as to call her an angel, but I do love her."

Kiyana snorted. "If I were an angel, you wouldn't have known what to do with me."

"I suppose so."

His mother chimed in. "Aye, well, none of my lot are angels, either. Although sometimes Graham fools everyone because he hardly ever talks. But enough of that. I want to know when Kiyana and Alistair are going to have their mating ceremony."

His dragon grunted. *We should've already done so.*

I didn't want to rush it, and Kiyana deserves a nice one.

Kiyana's reply prevented his beast from saying anything more. "Not until Alistair's further along with his physical therapy. It wouldn't bother me if he walked with a cane for the rest of his life, but dragonmen have a bit more pride than most, and I know he'd like to walk on his own in front of everyone."

It was true, although he hadn't said as much.

Kiyana already knew him so well, he couldn't imagine what their lives would be like ten years down the line.

His brother Hamish jumped in. "Aye, well, our father used a cane toward the end. So maybe it has more to do with that, even though our dad was strong and stubborn to his last breath."

Alistair hadn't talked about his father in years. They all still loved him, but he'd been severely injured and poisoned by some humans. The dragon hunters hadn't been as organized ten years ago, but the internet had allowed like-minded individuals to gather and carry out their bloody deeds.

His mother huffed. "Of course he was. Try putting the three of you together, and you'd start to get an idea of your dad's stubbornness. He probably could've been clan leader if he'd aimed for it, but he'd wanted to spend more time with you three and settled on being a builder." His mother stared down at the bairn in her arms and said softly, "He was a good male, the best. And he would've been proud of you all."

Silence fell, and Alistair tried to think of what to say. His mother hadn't been so forlorn over his father in over a year, thanks to the old nutters courting her.

He may think the two males were both a wee off in the head, but Archie and Cal had made his mother happy again. And for that, he was grateful.

Kiyana's mother spoke up. "I know how that goes, too. I think your husband and mine would've gotten along well."

His mum met Carol Barnes's eyes. "Probably, unless they were trying to outdo the other when it came to stubbornness."

The two older females smiled at each other, showing

Alistair something else he'd missed over the last few months. Kiyana had said their mothers were friends, but maybe they were closer friends than he'd thought.

His dragon said, *That's a good thing. She and Lorna MacKenzie used to be this close until something happened. Mum needed a new friend who understood the pain of losing a mate and found it in Carol.*

Wee Roman cried, and his mother handed him back to Alba. Once the lad was nursing, he quieted right down.

The sight reminded him of what he'd be soon himself—a father.

And he couldn't be more impatient if he tried.

Kiyana cleared her throat. "Since small silences are rare here—and I'm not complaining, just stating the facts—there's something Alistair and I want to share officially." She glanced around the table. "Although I think everyone already knows, given how Hamish likes to talk."

Hamish looked sheepish, but Alistair couldn't be mad at his brother.

After sharing a glance with him, Kiyana said, "Alistair and I are having a baby in just over eight months' time."

Graham's son Hugh grimaced. "*Another* cousin? We aren't going to fit around the table soon. And I don't want to babysit it."

Everyone chuckled, but it was Hamish's son Cody who jumped up in his chair and did a little dance. "I want another cousin. They'll be younger, and smaller, and I can be in charge."

Cody's mother tried to get him to sit down, but since she still nursed wee Roman, Cody easily jumped off the chair and raced over to him and Kiyana. The lad tried to whisper but didn't quite manage it. "Although if it's a girl, I'll be her protector. She'll be safe with me. No one will ever be able to hurt her."

Since Bruce on his lap was trying to mimic his cousin's earlier dancing, Alistair first had to get a better hold on the lad before he managed to grip Cody's shoulder and squeeze lightly. "I know you'll do a fine job, Cody. Lad or lassie, you'll be a good protector."

Cody looked at Kiyana. "But don't name him Nigel. Or Neville. Or Jumba-something. Maybe I should help name it. I could pick a better one."

Kiyana laughed. "We'll see, Cody. We'll see."

Alistair's mother clicked her tongue. "Get back in your seat, lad, and finish your dinner. Us adults want to celebrate Kiyana and Alistair's news, but first you need to eat and go to bed."

Cody's shoulders slumped. "But I don't want to go to bed. I want to celebrate, too."

Hamish motioned for his son to go to his seat. "Go on, Cody. Sit down as your grannie asked."

The boy trudged his feet but eventually made it. And as chatter filled the table, Alistair tried his best to keep smiling and hide his impatience. Because he'd wanted to whisk his mate away as soon as possible to not only talk with her, but claim her again.

However, if his mother was serious about celebrating, he may not get to do it for hours yet.

His beast spoke up. *Let her celebrate. It'll give our mate time to rest before we take her again.*

Kiyana laughed at something someone said, and he studied her. He couldn't help but smile as his family continued to entertain her. After everything that had transpired over the last few months, his female deserved the levity. They had their whole lives to look forward to, and he could afford to spare a few more hours with his family.

CHAPTER EIGHTEEN

Kiyana had a slight sugar high from the juice she'd had to drink in place of wine—Meg only had extremely large glasses, and she'd ended up drinking every last drop—and resisted tagging Alistair's side and running ahead. "I think we should take moonlight walks as often as possible. It's quite a bit calmer than I ever imagined Lochguard could be."

The corner of Alistair's mouth ticked up. "It's not always the case, although if things ever become safe and free of worry from our enemies, then I'll take you on a walk along the loch at night. It's even more beautiful. Nearly as beautiful as you."

She stopped and turned to face Alistair. "The wine has made you a bit more poetic than normal, hasn't it?"

"Maybe a wee bit, but it's all you, Kiyana." He searched her gaze and then added softly, "I love you, lass. And that changes a male."

Her heart skipped a beat. "You love me?"

He raised a hand to her cheek and lightly caressed it with his thumb. "Aye, I do. I've been bursting to tell you for days, and always held back. But after dinner with my family, I can't keep it in anymore. I love you, Kiyana. And I hope I can be the male you deserve."

Tears prickled her eyes. "You already are, Alistair. You've done so much to try and protect me, even when it meant running away from your home and everything you knew. Not to mention you fought to the end to keep me safe, even when you could've killed yourself in that village." She stepped closer, placing a hand on his chest. "You already are a man others should look up to." She paused, debating if she should say the words back.

But at the thought of not saying them, her mind screamed, "Say it!"

Kiyana had come a long way from arriving on Lochguard with a goal of keeping her distance so she could observe everyone as objectively as possible.

She was all but mated to a dragon-shifter she admired and loved, not to mention she cared deeply for his family. On top of that, she'd become good friends with Arabella, Holly, and Gina.

Her life and future were on Lochguard, and all because of the dragonman in front of her.

Leaning closer, she tilted her head up. "I love you, too, Alistair Boyd."

With a growl, he closed the distance between them and took her lips in an urgent kiss. She opened immediately, stroking her tongue against his, wanting to be as close to him as possible.

This was her mate, her friend, and the father of her child. And currently, the clothes on her skin felt like concrete blocks, keeping her from the closeness she craved.

Breaking the kiss, she said, "Our cottage. Let's get there as soon as possible."

His hand traveled to her arse and lightly squeezed. "Someone's as impatient as me, I see."

"Alistair," she half-heartedly scolded.

He chuckled. "Aye, lass, I agree with you. I want to show the female I love just how much she means to me. And your naked body should most definitely be for my eyes only."

She glanced down. "Can you attempt to run with that cane?"

"I'm going to bloody try, even if I look like an idiot doing so."

As he took her hand and started moving as fast as he could manage, Kiyana couldn't stop smiling. Alistair loved her, and she couldn't wait to see how he told her with his body.

And maybe, just maybe, he'd let his dragon come out to play, too.

❧

Alistair would feel the aftereffects of his attempt at running in the morning, but he didn't care. Kiyana loved him, and every fiber of his being urged him to strip her down, torture her slowly with his mouth, and then claim her.

His dragon paced inside his head. *Yes, I want to claim her, too. You haven't let me. She's mine, yours, ours.*

He hesitated, keeping his worry tightly concealed from his dragon. *Maybe. You're still recovering from the drugs. Kiyana carries our bairn. We can't take risks.*

His beast growled. *I would never hurt her, ever. I want her. I don't remember the mate-claim frenzy. I need to make her ours, too.*

Their cottage came into view. *Maybe. Let me tease her slowly first, and then we'll see.*

That's not much of an answer.

But it's the one I have.

218

Not wanting to do it, he constructed a complex maze inside his head. Alistair had never had the need to do it before, but Finn and the others had taught him during his recovery in the surgery, just in case.

His beast roared, but the walls held.

Alistair released Kiyana's hand to better climb up the three steps and open the door. He'd barely stepped inside when Kiyana slammed the door and closed the distance between them. "I love you."

The words released his pent-up desire, and he hauled her against him, taking her lips in a rough kiss.

He licked and nibbled until she parted her lips for him. Alistair didn't wait to dive in and twirl his tongue with hers.

No shy, reluctant lass, Kiyana battled her tongue against his, the both of them trying to dominate the other. As her tongue tried to win, he moved a hand to her arse and rocked her against his hard cock.

She moaned into his mouth, and he did it again, wishing the material under his fingers would instantly disappear.

Since he'd promised not to rip any more of her clothes without asking, he broke the kiss and growled, "I want you naked. Either you do it, or I'm tempted to break my promise to ask before shredding your dress."

She smiled, the sight sending even more blood to his cock. "I like this dress too much. So sit on the couch and I'll take it off."

He growled even louder, but she stepped back and walked into the living room, her hips swaying seductively, beckoning him to follow.

More than eager to see every inch of her delicious skin, he made his way to the sofa and sat down. Kiyana kept her back to him and slowly dropped her dress, letting it

JESSIE DONOVAN

pool at her feet.

Holy fuck, she was wearing a thong, showcasing almost every inch of her lovely brown skin. Alistair drunk it in, positive he'd never get his fill, and itched to nibble his way around to her front. "More, show me more. I need to see all of you, love."

She slid down the straps of her bra, turned it around to undo it, and the lace floated down to join the dress on the floor. Glancing over her shoulder, her voice was husky as she said, "Should I keep the heels on or take them off?"

"On, most definitely on. But if you don't remove that thong in the next few seconds, I'm going to tear it off with my teeth."

He expected some sort of warning or retort. However, Kiyana slowly shimmied out of her thong, blessing him with every soft curve and gentle valley of her body, and he did his best to commit it to memory.

Not that he hoped to ever need to rely on memory. Kiyana was his female, and he would treasure her every day as she deserved. Still, he wanted the images to hold on to for when he couldn't be at her side.

She kicked away the scraps of material and turned around. He met her eyes before pursuing down to her already-hard nipples, her soft belly, and down to the apex of her thighs.

His mouth watered as the scent of her arousal grew stronger. "Come, love. Let me slake your itch."

Her fingers moved between her thighs, and as she began to play with her pussy and clit, his cock pulsed.

Fuck, his female was perfect.

As she increased her pace and bit her lip, he couldn't sit and watch any longer. Alistair lowered onto the ground and crawled over, loving how she spread her legs wider for him as he reached her. Gently taking her hand, he pushed it away and looked up. "My turn."

Her molten gaze made his dragon roar even louder, but the maze held. She nodded. "Make me scream, Alistair."

With a growl, he settled into the best position to lap at her pussy, her sweet honey driving him even madder.

As he continued to lick, lap, and tease, he would only barely brush her clit with his thumb every few seconds. Some males may want to hurry her orgasm, but Alistair knew building up made her come harder.

And he wanted her to come harder than ever before, screaming his name, and later saying she loved him again.

Just remembering the words from earlier made him thrust deeper. Her hands went to his hair, and she said, "Yes, there. I'm so close. Alistair. Please."

Never wanting to ever disappoint his mate, he rubbed her clit in fast, hard circles, her little moans and groans growing louder as her nails dug deeper into his scalp.

He pressed her hips more against his mouth with his free hand while he also pressed hard against her sensitive bud. She yelled out his name as her nails dug deeper, her pussy convulsing around his tongue.

Even when she relaxed against him, he slowly lapped his fill, loving the taste of her orgasm in his mouth.

His dragon rammed harder against the walls of the maze, reminding him that Alistair didn't have an unlimited amount of time before his beast could take control.

He gave one last lick and began his journey to her face. Alistair kissed Kiyana's belly—his lips staying a few extra seconds to honor the child growing inside—between her breasts, where her neck met her shoulders, and finally took her lips in a slow, lingering kiss. She sighed into his mouth as her hand ran between them, to stroke his hard cock through the fabric of his trousers.

He groaned at the pressure of her fingers and Kiyana broke the kiss to murmur, "Now it's your turn. I need to see you, feel you, have you inside me." She searched his eyes for a second before adding, "I want all of you, this time, Alistair. Show me your dragon. I'm not afraid."

His beast roared, and Alistair hesitated a second.

And yet, he knew if he kept hiding his dragon away and never allowing him out, it'd not only put strain on him and his beast; on top of that, it might even push Kiyana away.

Cupping her cheek, he kissed her nose before replying, "We'll try. But if anything happens, you promise me that you'll run to safety."

"I believe in your dragon, Alistair." He grunted, and she raised her brows. "I do. I love all of you, but if a promise is what it takes, then yes, I promise to run if I feel threatened."

Nodding, he brushed her cheek one last time before stepping back and stripping off his clothes. He created a small opening in the maze and spoke over his dragon's roars. *We'll share. But first, calm the fuck down.*

To his surprise, his dragon settled down and grunted. *Hurry up. I want her, I need her, she is ours.*

Since he didn't sense any malice, Alistair slowly took down the maze and let his dragon out.

He hoped with everything he had that he wasn't making a fucking mistake. Alistair retreated to the back of his mind and waited to see how his beast would react.

⌒⌒⌒

Kiyana's lust-haze cleared a fraction when Alistair's pupils turned to slits and stayed that way.

His dragon had finally come out to play.

Alistair's voice was a bit deeper as he said, "You're my mate. I want you. Now."

The orders didn't faze her, and Kiyana closed the distance between them. However, instead of kissing him, she took his cock in her hand and lightly squeezed. "Then take me."

With a growl, Alistair's dragon batted away her hand, turned her around, and placed her hands on the back of the sofa. "Like this. I want you like this."

The human half of Alistair would've kissed her back, lightly caressed her skin, and took his time in entering her.

However, his dragon spread her legs, pressed his cock at her entrance, and thrust deep.

Still sensitive from her orgasm, Kiyana moaned. Not wanting to scare Alistair's human half, she arched her back slightly, and his dragon took the hint, pulling out and slamming back in, over and over, making her boobs bounce in time to his movements.

He placed one of his hands over her belly. But whether it was to steady her or to acknowledge their baby, she had no idea. Alistair's dragon-laced voice kept murmuring, "Mine, you're mine. My mate. Always. Always."

"Yes, yours. Both of yours. I love you."

At her final three words, Alistair's dragon roared and moved faster at the same time his fingers found her clit. She dropped her head, each stroke building tension.

Somewhere in her hazy mind, she knew this was important. Because Alistair's semen made her orgasm automatically, and yet his dragon was trying to make her come beforehand.

Surely his dragon had returned to his normal self.

Then Alistair's warm fingers pressed harder, and lights exploded in front of her eyes as Alistair's dragon stilled inside her. She could tell the instant he came because her orgasm crested back up, sending wave after wave of pleasure throughout her body.

By the time her body finally calmed down, Kiyana's knees threaten to buckle.

However, before she could say anything, Alistair's dragon pulled out, spun her around, and guided her to the nearest wall. Hitching her leg around his waist, he positioned his cock at her entrance and stated, "Again."

Alistair's dragon had threaded dominance into his voice, but she wasn't going to let it sway her. Especially since she'd read how the first interaction with a dragon could dictate how the relationship could go for the rest of time. "Once more and then it's Alistair's turn again."

"But I want you many times. You're our mate. I don't remember the frenzy, so I need to make new memories."

Alistair still hadn't told his dragon the full truth. Maybe there was a reason for it, and she'd have to ask him later.

For the moment, she never looked away from Alistair's slitted pupils and said, "Once more and then it's Alistair's turn. You can play again tomorrow."

His pupils flashed a second and then remained slits again. Alistair's dragon nodded. "Once more. Alistair promised we can share every night. Tomorrow, I will be first."

She nodded, wanting to show she embraced both the human and dragon halves of Alistair.

His dragon didn't wait, positioned his cock, and thrust.

Kiyana groaned and dug her nails into Alistair's back. His dragon ordered, "Harder. Hold me harder."

She didn't need any more encouragement and hung onto her dragonman as the dragon half took her again, just as fast and hard as the first time.

And after she'd screamed his name and slumped against his chest, Alistair's normal voice filled her ears, "You're such a brave lass. I love you."

Snuggling against his chest, she smiled. "I'm not sure brave is the word I'd use. After all, this woman enjoys a quick, hard shag sometimes."

He snorted and tilted her head up until she met his eyes again, his pupils round. "That's only going to encourage him."

Raising a hand, she traced his firm jaw. "Is that such a bad thing? I love and want all of you, Alistair Boyd. That means your dragon, too."

His pupils flashed again before he replied, "I'm still not sure how I deserve you, but selfish bastard that I am, I'm keeping you."

"Keeping me, huh?"

He hugged her tighter against his body. "As best I can. But it works both ways—you can keep me, too."

"Then let's seal that deal with another kiss, and then it's bedtime."

Worry filled his eyes. "Are you okay? Is it the bairn?"

She shook her head. "I'm fine, just tired. Your family is brilliant, but it takes a lot of energy to keep up with them all."

"More than keeping up with my dragon?"

The corner of her mouth kicked up. "That, my dragonman, is something we'll have to determine after I've gathered more data."

He growled. "Don't tempt me, love. It's going to be hard enough to not claim you again straightaway."

She winked. "Don't worry, I see a lot of data-gathering sessions in our future. But tonight, you'll have to subsist on cuddles."

He kissed her softly. "Good, because I plan on holding you close and never letting go."

Before she could mention how his romantic side had come out again, he managed to scoop her up in his arms and slowly make their way to the bedroom.

She really should scold him for it, considering he was still recovering. However, she sensed that in that moment, Alistair needed to carry her to their bed. And so she let him, content to listen to his heartbeat underneath her ear, never caring about how long it took him.

And once they were in bed, Alistair spooning her back, Kiyana fell fast asleep with a smile on her face.

CHAPTER NINETEEN

few days later, Kiyana was writing up her final report for the Department of Dragon Affairs when someone knocked on the front door. Since Alistair was out helping with something at the Protectors' main security building, she went to answer it and blinked at Meg Boyd. "I thought you were coming over for dinner later?"

The older dragonwoman waved a hand in dismissal and waltzed inside. Kiyana closed the door and followed her into the kitchen. Meg replied, "Aye, I still am. But there's a matter for you and me to discuss, one that I don't want Alistair around to hear."

Those words piqued her interest. "I don't keep secrets from Alistair, Meg. So don't ask me to do it, unless it's something on the level of a surprise party or something."

Meg knew the cottage well and went about making some tea. "This has to do with the director of the DDA, as well as my role here. The fewer people who know about what I'm doing, the better, aye? And since you're still technically an employee of the DDA, you have to keep this confidential."

Kiyana didn't like how Meg was spouting off DDA protocols, and yet her curiosity burned to know what exactly Meg did for the DDA.

It was true, she didn't keep secrets from Alistair. However, he had things he worked on that she couldn't know about yet, either. So using that rationale, she bobbed her head. "Okay, I can keep a DDA secret, provided it doesn't involve Alistair himself."

"Och, no, it doesn't involve my lad. I wouldn't ask that of you." The kettle clicked off and she poured the water. "To be honest, this is more about you than anyone else, even me."

She resisted growling, although she was starting to understand why Alistair did it sometimes around his mother. "Then tell me already what you came here to say. You don't like people beating around the bush, and you should give me the same courtesy."

Meg snorted. "You'll do well here, lass. Aye, you'll do." Kiyana raised her brows to remind of her question, and Meg continued, "First, I'll tell you what I do, and then I'll get to the bit about what you can do to help, too."

She resisted a sigh. No amount of browbeating would hurry Meg up, so Kiyana sat at the table in the dining nook. "Then tell me. At this rate, Alistair will be back, and you'll lose your chance."

The older dragonwoman took her mug of tea and sat across from Kiyana. "I mostly watch over the humans living here now, and report back to the DDA director about how they're doing."

Kiyana frowned. "I'm not sure Holly, Gina, or let alone Ross, would appreciate you spying on them."

"Maybe not, but Rosalind Abbott isn't about to let any of the humans suffer quietly, as too many have done in the past. And since I already know almost everything that's going on inside the clan, Finn put me up to it."

"Finn?"

"Aye. You'd think he'd have nominated his own aunt, given how she always claims to know more than I do. However, for whatever reason, he approached me. And since I want to help the clan as much as anyone, I agreed."

Kiyana didn't think Finn's Aunt Lorna would love hearing the truth, but it wasn't Kiyana's place to object. After all, she'd only spent a few months on Lochguard and Finn had lived his whole life here. He would know what was best.

She asked, "So then how am I supposed to help? I'm not big on clandestinely spying on people, or sorting through rumors. No offense, but that's just not who I am. If I'm observing someone, they know it and are usually a participant to a degree."

"No offense taken, lass. No, the director has bigger things planned for you—mainly she wants you to keep researching the Dettifoss Gathering and continue to develop plans and ideas to create a new one within the next few years."

For a few seconds, Kiyana merely stared at Meg. To many, a few years might seem a long time to put together an event. However, it had taken decades or even a century to finally get the dragon-shifters to agree the first time around.

Not to mention she'd have her baby before long, and her free time would be quite a bit less than what she had now.

As if sensing her thoughts, Meg spoke again. "Don't worry, you won't be working alone. That Max lad will help, as will others. Rosalind is testing the waters with her contacts, asking them to also nominate candidates to help research and plan the event."

While normally Kiyana would ask why Meg referred to the DDA director so casually, there were bigger things to worry about. "So she's serious about putting together a similar gathering, then. I didn't think it would rank so highly in her priorities."

Meg sipped her tea. "Aye, it's one of her top priorities. She vowed to change things for the better when she assumed her position, and she's doing her best to fulfill it, even taking steps to ensure her vision can continue if something happens to her. So, will you help, lass? I'm sure if you agree and fill out all the necessary paperwork, you can convince her to let a few select Lochguard people know about your project, including Alistair."

The request was massive. It would take a lot of work and coordination, not to mention Kiyana would have to abandon any other projects, such as writing books or papers.

And yet, to help something so historic become a reality would have a longer lasting effect than anything she could do on her own. It was impossible for her to refuse.

She answered, "Provided I can negotiate Alistair into helping me sometimes, then yes, I'm up for it."

Meg reached across and took her hand. "I knew you would be, lass. Mothers, even mothers-to-be, often do whatever they can to make the future brighter for their children."

While she knew not all mothers were as dedicated as Meg or even her own, Kiyana was determined to be one. Her little half-dragon-shifter baby deserved the best chance at happiness, which meant living a life with less fear. After all, if the dragon-shifters worked together, they might be able to almost eradicate the dragon hunters and Dragon Knights. Sure, the internet would always exist and give dragon haters a place to gather, but they would cause a lot less damage and pain with fewer resources.

Not to mention that without a fully fledged organization with strong leaders, most plans and threats would never see the light of day.

Kiyana placed her free hand over her lower belly. "It'll not only help my baby, but it'll help so many others, as well."

Alistair had yet to tell his family the details surrounding Rachel and her sickness, let alone his vow to strengthen communication ties between the clans, but it was also true a gathering similar to the one in Dettifoss could help every dragon-shifter on the planet.

Just thinking of the amount of information that could be exchanged made her giddy. "When will the paperwork arrive? I'll have more time before the baby comes, so I want to get started right away."

Meg clicked her tongue. "I'll have it after your mating ceremony. Rosalind wants to ensure you're legally connected to Alistair before pushing any more boundaries."

Her and Alistair's mating ceremony was a week away. Disappointment flickered, but she forced it aside. Seven days wasn't very long. Not to mention she still had to finish her final report on the group of humans who had come to Lochguard as potential mates.

She bobbed her head. "I'll be ready a few days after, as I promised Alistair we'd spend a few days alone together."

Many people went to Lochguard's piece of land on the Isle of Skye after a mating ceremony, but Alistair had refused. His dragon hadn't acted up, but he wanted to be careful. So they were staying on the clan's lands and hoping they could keep unwanted visitors away.

Meg finished her tea. "Aye, aye, I know. I'm not to visit for at least two days after the ceremony. It'll be hard, as I only want to get to know my new daughter-in-law, but

I'll somehow find the strength."

Kiyana did her best not to smile at Meg's guilt-tripping. "I'm sure you will."

Meg stood and placed her mug in the sink. "Well, I'd best be off and let Rosalind know of your decision." She took a step and then paused. "It'll be a thankless job, so let me be the first to say I'll appreciate your efforts. If we're lucky, the gathering will happen in my lifetime."

"You'll outlive us all, Meg, so I'm sure you will."

"Such a flatterer."

It wasn't flattery so much as the truth. Kiyana only hoped she could be as spritely as Meg Boyd when she reached her age.

The dragonwoman's eyes widened. "Oh, and I almost forgot. As part of the deal, an offer will always be open for your mother to live here permanently. I know she's still deciding, but it should put you at ease to know she can live here if she wants."

She wondered if Meg had been instrumental in that condition, given that she was friends with Kiyana's mother. "Thank you."

Meg waved a hand in dismissal. "Don't thank me. You can thank Rosalind by working your hardest and keeping that Max lad in line."

She sighed. "It will be quite the task, but I know someone who can help with it. And no, I won't tell anyone who doesn't have the clearance to know, but keeping an eye on a visitor is still standard protocol after all."

"Do what you must, just keep him occupied. I'm not sure I can take his lectures every day for as long as it takes to make the important gathering a reality."

"I'll try."

"Good." Meg faced the door again. "Then I'll be off. I'll send you all the details once I have them."

The older dragonwoman was nearly out of the kitchen when Kiyana blurted, "Why don't you want to tell everyone what you're doing? Watching over the humans isn't that scandalous."

"No, but Rosalind is afraid enemies still reside within the clan. So keeping my identity secret means I can watch and be myself without anyone acting differently."

She blinked. "Enemies?"

"Ask Finn, as he has his own suspicions as well."

With that, Meg left, leaving Kiyana to wonder what other dangers existed, ones she'd have to protect her baby from.

She wouldn't worry to the point of being afraid to live life, but she'd be cautious going forward. One of the best things was to focus on her upcoming project. After all, who knew what information other clans possessed about enemies or potential threats.

Yes, the more information they could obtain, the better. However, she needed to finish her current work first. And so Kiyana went back to work.

○～○～○～○

Layla MacFie frowned as she double-checked her supplies for the third time. However, no amount of recounting was going to change the fact some of her dearest drugs—one specifically used for helping inner dragons—were missing.

It wasn't the first time it had happened, either. Over the last six months, various things had gone missing, from drugs to medical instruments to even some of the older vital-signs monitors.

Her dragon huffed. *Will you listen to me now and install a security camera?*

We already did that, but whoever is stealing knows where they are.

Then put in a secret one.

I don't have the faintest idea of how to install one.

You don't, but Chase does.

Chase McFarland had only earned his full electrician certification in the last year, but by all accounts, he knew what he was doing and did it well.

Of course, thinking of Chase brought back the evening when he'd told her he was patient, and that she was worth waiting for.

Not wanting to remember the heat in his eyes or how she'd ended up slumped on the floor afterward, she answered her beast, *I'd have to ask him in private, and promise secrecy, and that's not a good idea.*

Only because you're afraid of being alone with him.

I'm not afraid.

Liar. We share the same dreams. And you want him.

Her dragon was correct. Layla's dreams tended to center around Chase more than any other male. And to see him again after some of the rather explicit fantasies, well, they might finally break her resolve.

Her dragon growled. *Then do it.*

He'll want more, and we can't give it. Especially if we have a thief here at the surgery, one that'll be handed over to Finn once we catch them. Because I have a feeling it's an internal job, and then we'll be even more short-staffed.

Stop coming up with excuses. Tell him plainly you don't want a relationship. It's that simple.

Aye, because you'll settle for that so quickly.

Her dragon fell silent, telling Layla everything she wanted to know.

Which meant her inner beast wanted Chase for more than for a night, too.

That was mad, considering they barely knew the male. Sure, he was attentive, charming, and had even made her laugh once or twice. But that wasn't enough to make a relationship work, especially in her profession.

He needed to remain off-limits, no matter what.

With a sigh, Layla exited the supply room and went to her office. She'd have to find a time to ask Chase to install the hidden camera as a personal favor and hope he could keep a secret. The best time to ask would be when they could be alone, and yet weren't inside either of their cottages.

Then it hit her—Alistair and Kiyana's mating ceremony was soon. She could find him then, talk with him alone in a room, and then go back to the gathering.

Satisfied with her plan and how she'd be able to carry it out without her ending up naked and Chase inside her, Layla jotted down the supply discrepancies in her little notebook she kept on her, and went to the mound of paperwork she needed to complete before she could leave for the day.

Chapter Twenty

*A*listair readjusted the dark-blue material tossed over his shoulder and then turned toward the door.

It was time. He would finally take Kiyana as his mate in front of the whole clan.

His dragon spoke up. *I don't understand why it's necessary. She is ours, and we are hers. A few words won't matter.*

You say that, but of course it matters. And not just because it provides a legal contract, one the DDA will recognize so that Kiyana can live here permanently.

I'd like to see them try to force her away from our side.

He smiled. *True, but I'd rather she save her fire and stubbornness for something more worthwhile. Especially since one ceremony will save all of us the trouble of yet another fight.*

His dragon grunted. *I suppose. But let's hurry. The sooner we start, the sooner we can greet everyone and then take our female home.*

Alistair opened the door and blinked as he came face-to-face with his mother. "Mum, can't it wait? You can see me after the ceremony."

"Nonsense." She gently pushed him back into the room. "I have a wee gift for you."

Doing his best not to grimace, Alistair shut the door and asked, "What is it?"

His mother retrieved something from her bag, wrapped in a white material. "It's something from your father. He left wee presents for each of his sons, ones he wanted me to give you on your mating day. To be honest, I wasn't sure if I'd ever have the chance to give it to you."

He kept his voice light and free from irritation. "Aye, well, I'm being mated shortly, so you can give it to me now."

"I'll ignore your tone for the moment, and put it down to your eagerness to see your female again."

His mother had insisted they spend the night apart, as was tradition for many dragon-shifter families. "Aye, I am, so let's not keep Kiyana waiting."

His mum unwrapped the material to reveal a silver brooch, the type his clan pinned to the strap thrown over the shoulder for their traditional dress outfits.

The woven circle had a dragon wing intersecting the middle.

A memory from his childhood danced at the edge of his memory, but he couldn't quite place it.

His dragon spoke up. *Dad wore it for our first flight performance.*

The first time a young dragon-shifter showed off their new flying skills was celebrated on Lochguard. And while not everyone dressed to the nines for the event, his parents had done so.

Even if it had embarrassed ten-year-old Alistair at the time, he remembered it fondly now.

His mother pinned it on the material over his pectoral. "You always eyed it as a lad, and your dad remembered."

She gently patted the brooch. "And it suits you, Alistair. Make sure to wear it to your own child's first flight performance, to carry on the tradition."

While he dismissed many of his mother's requests, this one he agreed with. "Aye, of course. Thank you, Mum."

He hugged his mother, and she replied, "I was worried about you for so many years, Alistair. But now you have a fine lass, and I know you'll be happy." She pulled back. "Just try to give me a granddaughter, aye?"

The corner of his mouth ticked up. "I'm not sure I can guarantee that."

"Then keep trying until you do."

All of Alistair's tests pointed to him not being completely infertile, but merely having a low sperm count. It was possible—although extremely difficult—for him to have more children.

Not that it mattered. He and Kiyana would always love the child currently growing inside his mate's womb. If that was their only bairn, he would still be grateful. "We'll see, Mum. Now, unless you want to keep Kiyana waiting, I need to go."

She patted his cheek one last time before stepping back. "Aye, go and claim your mate, Alistair. She's not one you want to let slip away."

"No, never."

As he exited the room, his dragon chimed in again. *Walk faster. We're late.*

I'm doing the best I can, dragon.

He'd decided to go sans cane for at least the initial ceremony.

However, he did his best to reach the door leading to the dais of the great hall in record time.

He was lucky to have found a female like Kiyana— especially given how he'd thought he'd never find another female to love a few short years ago—and he wanted the world to know she was his mate.

⚬⚬⚬⚬⚬

Kiyana stood next to Finn, who was waiting for Alistair to arrive before he went on stage to introduce them.

It was strange for Lochguard's leader to be so quiet, and yet she understood the reason why behind it. Finn had some sort of announcement to make after their mating ceremony, one that Arabella had hinted about being huge but one she had refused to share.

Kiyana should care more about what it could be considering Lochguard was her home now. However, she merely kept tapping her hand against her side, impatient to get started with her mating ceremony.

Not that she was worried about Alistair having cold feet or some such thing. No, she wanted to make their connection official. Because once she did, she could share her new DDA assignment with him without violating any of the rules.

She had a feeling he wouldn't like Max being around Lochguard more often. However, Alistair would be eager to help her, considering it aligned with his previous dream of improving communications between the dragon clans.

Finn's voice interrupted her thoughts. "Aye, well, it's time to start."

After smiling at her, he left, and Kiyana tried to pay attention to what he said. However, his words didn't reach her brain, and she barely paid attention to the crowd. She could barely hear anything over her thumping heart.

Calm down, Kiyana. He'll do fine.

Alistair had wanted to come out without his cane, even though he should still be using it. While a more spiteful person would want him to fall on his face to learn his lesson, she didn't want that this time. If walking by himself made him feel more of a dragonman for their special day, then so be it.

Finn called her and Alistair's names, garnering her attention once more. Kiyana walked out onto the dais. She'd barely glimpsed the crowded hall before her eyes fell on Alistair's tall form, dressed in dark blue, his defined chest muscles making her mouth dry.

Even though she'd seen him naked more times than she could count, it still made her brain stop working for a few beats.

As if reading her thoughts, he winked. The action broke the spell, and she shook her head before walking out to join him in the center of the dais. From the corner of her eye, she watched to make sure he didn't stumble or trip, but while a tad slow, he made it just fine.

Finn descended the steps to sit in the front row, next to Arabella and the rest of the Boyds. A mating ceremony was always between two people and no one else.

Kiyana had always thought that lovely, but had never imagined she'd be experiencing it herself.

Alistair took one of her hands, and her eyes instantly found his once more. Since she'd never been to a dragon mating ceremony before, they'd agreed he should go first.

However, for a few seconds, they merely stared into one another's eyes, the rest of the world melting away.

Even in a crowded hall, he would always catch her eye.

His pupils flickered, reminding her there were three personalities involved in this relationship. And she was glad his dragon was here, too, even if he wouldn't be speaking.

Alistair's deep voice finally filled the room. "Dr. Kiyana Barnes, you are everything I admire in a female.

Intelligent, devoted, determined, and always ready with a smile or a retort. Of course, you being the most beautiful female in the world is the greatest bonus." He took her hand and brought it to his lips before continuing, "You brought me back to not only life but to my family and the clan as well. After losing a female I loved three years ago, I never thought I'd be happy again. But you have made me not only happy but a better male than I ever would've been without you. I love you, Kiyana. Will you allow me to claim you as my mate?"

She nodded, trying her best not to cry. The tears would be of joy, but still. She wanted to be strong enough to fight them off.

Alistair reached behind them to retrieve a silver arm cuff, one engraved with his name in the old language. He kissed her bicep before sliding the cool material around her skin.

Even though it was all in her head, the metal seemed to be charged with something, making her heart even fuller of love for Alistair than a few seconds ago.

Once he finished, she took a deep breath. The last thing she needed was to let her voice crack or waver. She wanted her claim to be perfect.

Kiyana took Alistair's hand and mimicked him, kissing the back of it before raising her voice for all to hear. "Alistair Boyd, you are smart, loving, intelligent, and occasionally funny." A few people laughed before she added, "But you are also kind, and will risk everything to try to keep me safe. I've never met a man like you before, and I doubt I ever will. However, if you can try not to die in the next few months—or maybe even years—that would be even better." He smiled, and the rest of her words flowed forth. "I love you and can't wait to see what life holds for us and our child in the future. Will you allow me to claim you as my mate?"

"Aye, I do."

Reaching behind her to the small box, Kiyana took the bigger arm cuff out, the one engraved with her name in the old language. After placing it on his bicep—which wasn't as easy as one might think, given how much taller he was than her—she placed her hands on his chest. She tilted her head up, and he took her lips in a slow, gentle kiss, one of his hands covering her belly, too.

He ensured that even their unborn child was part of the ceremony, which made her love him all the more.

When he finally pulled away, she searched his gaze and watched his pupils flicker. Maybe they could find a way to sneak out of the hall sooner than expected so that Alistair's dragon could claim her as well.

However, Finn's whistle quieted the hall and garnered her attention. Alistair held her close, but they both kept their gazes on Finn.

Once Lochguard's leader was back up on the dais, he spoke up. "We'll be having our celebration for Alistair and Kiyana soon enough, but first there's something I wanted to share with you. Something that can't wait."

Finn gestured toward someone, and the door at the rear of the hall opened. A second later, a small group of tall, tattooed dragon-shifters Kiyana had never seen before entered.

Murmurs rose immediately, but Finn whistled again, and everyone listened. "Aye, those are lads and lassies from Clan Seahaven. While they haven't agreed to move back to Lochguard—which I can't blame them, given how they were shunned a few decades ago—their leader and I have decided to start reconnecting again. And so as a first step, they've come to celebrate with us. My greatest hope is that this is the first of many things to help our clan and theirs become better allies. After all, all dragon-shifters in the Highlands should be able to rely on one another."

More chatter rose up, and Kiyana did her best to remember what she knew about Seahaven.

At one point, a former Lochguard leader had banished anyone mated to a human. As a result, they'd formed their own, much smaller clan near the northern Scottish coast.

However, she didn't think the two clans had even been talking with one another. She whispered to Alistair, "Is this a good or bad thing?"

"I don't know, love. We could use their help when fighting our enemies—not to mention they have as many doctors as we do, and Layla would love a few extra sets of hands—but they're also unknown in many ways, too."

Finn spoke again, silencing the hall once more. "Aye, well, let's get this celebration started. And the more who can introduce themselves to the Seahaven folks, the better. We're known for being a welcoming clan and let's not change that now."

The Lochguard leader turned and faced Kiyana and Alistair. "Come, it's time to start your greetings."

Alistair took her hand, and they carefully descended the stairs to the main floor. She took one last glance at the Seahaven group before both her mother and Alistair's rushed them. In the whirlwind of hugs, congratulations, and chitchat, she temporarily forgot about the other dragon-shifters.

⚬⚬⚬

As soon as Kiyana and Alistair reached the main floor of the hall, Layla MacFie became torn. She should seek out Chase to ask her favor, and yet she wanted to talk with Dr. Daniel Keith from Seahaven. While there were many reasons the two clans should work together, Layla was most interested in Seahaven's medical staff. After all, she'd worked with Dr. Keith before and would love to discuss future collaborations.

However, before she could take more than a few steps toward the Seahaven group, a familiar male voice filled her ear. "I've come to claim your first dance, Layla."

She resisted a shiver, instantly aware of Chase's heat at her side. Her dragon rose her head from sleep and said, *It's him. We should do more than talk inside a room tonight.*

Ignoring her beast, she turned to face Chase, and her heart skipped a beat. He was wearing one of the traditional outfits, with material wrapped around his waist like plaids of old, complete with a length of dark-blue material thrown over his shoulder. Her eyes drifted to his toned, lean body, lingering on his chest and arms, before Chase chuckled. At the sound, she forced her gaze upward. "What?"

"Nothing. You kept glancing toward me earlier, so I thought I'd come see what it was about."

She'd tried her best to be inconspicuous, but she must've failed. Lying or covering up things wasn't her strong suit. "It's just a minor matter, but I need to talk with Seahaven first so you and the dance will have to wait."

He shrugged. "Why? According to my brother, they'll be here all evening. So there's no rush. Besides, it'll probably be best to wait until the eager ones finish talking their ears off before you try to get a word in edgewise."

Chase's older brother was Grant, one of the co-head Protectors of the clan. Which meant his information was credible.

And yet, she didn't want to miss her chance of talking with Seahaven's doctor.

Her dragon sighed. *Chase is here, so ask your favor. Besides, it'll be easier to slip away now, when everyone is distracted with both Seahaven and Kiyana and Alistair.*

She hated when her dragon's logic made sense. *Fine. But you behave, aye?*

Her dragon said nothing, and the silence worried her.

Still, she focused back on Chase. "I have a favor to ask you."

"Oh, aye? And what might that be?"

She leaned forward and instantly regretted it. Every time she inhaled Chase's spicy male sent, it sent a rush of heat through her body.

However, she wasn't going to back away and show signs of nervousness. A dragon doctor couldn't be nervous, after all. Inner dragons were reactive in stressful situations, such as when injured, and a good dragon-shifter doctor had to learn to control emotions in order to do their jobs.

She whispered, "Not here. I need to talk with you privately."

Curiosity flared in his brown eyes before he bowed his head. "Then lead the way, my lady, and I'll follow."

Rolling her eyes, she whispered back, "Try to tone it down, aye? My favor is delicate, and I don't want people noticing us."

"Sorry to break it to you, but I'm sure both Meg Boyd and Lorna MacKenzie will notice."

She waved a hand in dismissal. "I can deal with them if need be. But let's try to keep others from talking, aye? I don't want them to get the wrong idea."

He tilted his head. "You care far too much about your image. This is Lochguard, which is your home. It's okay to be yourself from time to time, lass."

Layla was more than a decade older than Chase, meaning she wasn't really a "lass." But she wasn't going to waste time arguing about it. "Do you want to help me or not?"

"Color me intrigued. I'll follow your lead."

Her dragon chuckled. *I wonder if that includes you kissing him, and then him kissing us back.*

Shut it, dragon. That's not going to happen.

Hmph. Everyone needs a little break sometimes. He could be our break, and given his age, he won't tire out easily, either. Aye, that would be loads of fun.

Not wanting to deal with her beast hinting and pressing for the next wee bit, Layla quickly constructed a mental prison. The instant silence made it easier for her to pack away her emotions and desires during the walk to one of the side rooms.

However, as she tried one door and then another, they were locked. The only one she could find open was a storage closet that would barely fit two people.

She took a deep breath. *It's fine, Layla. Your dragon's contained and you can control yourself.* She gestured inside the closet. "This will have to do."

Chase's lips twitched as he entered. Layla followed suit. While she did her best to avoid skin-to-skin contact, she didn't succeed completely. Her arm pressed against Chase's, and a small jolt of electricity raced throughout her body, straight between her thighs.

A beat later, Chase's pupils flashed to slits and back. Damn. He'd smelled her arousal.

Chase's voice was husky as he asked, "What's the favor you want, Layla?"

His face was a few inches from hers, and it would be easy to close the distance and kiss him.

No. She didn't have time for males, not even for a short fling. Clearing her throat, she focused on the list of missing items. Every one was precious, and each missing one meant someone from her clan might not get the treatment they needed.

Thinking of Lochguard's welfare cooled her hormones, and she said, "Someone is stealing from the surgery."

Chase's eyes widened. "Does my brother or Faye know? While I'd like to think I can help you with anything, they're much better at security than me."

She shook her head. "No. I want to keep it quiet and try to catch the thief myself. That's where you come in. I need you to install some hidden security cameras after hours, and make sure no one sees you do it."

Layla expected him to smile and make some innuendo about how he'd be rewarded. However, Chase merely nodded and asked, "When do you want it done?"

She blinked. It seemed Chase had a more serious side, one she'd never really seen before. "Barring any unforeseen circumstances, how about next week?"

"Aye, I'll do it. We can coordinate the best time tomorrow."

She searched his gaze. "Just like that?"

"You dedicated your entire life to helping Lochguard. It's time for someone else to start helping you more."

She sensed there was a hidden meaning to his words, but before she could ask, Chase continued, "Let's return to the hall, aye? The longer we stay here, the more the old biddies will notice."

Layla could do nothing but open the door, retreat, and watch as Chase waved and walked away.

It was almost as if something had instantly changed with him. Maybe, just maybe, she'd finally been able to stop his wee infatuation with her.

Although why that made her heart squeeze, she had no idea.

Brushing it aside, Layla went back to the great hall and busied herself with talking to the Seahaven doctor. Work was her refuge and always provided the distraction she needed. Tonight would be no exception.

⤢⤢⤢

After several hours of talking, dancing, and stealing kisses, Alistair was finally able to sneak Kiyana outside to a side garden, one not used often anymore since it was overgrown. The cool night air felt good. The great hall had been overly hot, to the point he'd worried about Kiyana fainting.

However, as he guided his mate to a stone bench almost completely hidden from the view of the hall, he couldn't help but stare at her bright eyes and glowing skin. "You're so bloody beautiful."

She grinned as she sat down, which only made his cock turn instantly hard. "Well, I hope you think I'm somewhat attractive, given that you're now mine for life."

"Good you recognize it's for life, love. Because I'm never giving you up."

He sat next to her and lifted her onto his lap. Alistair barely noticed the slight twinge in his leg from the extra weight. His entire body was on fire in a good way, and he wanted more than just the weight of his mate on his body. No, he wanted every inch of her skin pressed against his.

His dragon spoke up. *We can slip away now and no one would be the wiser.*

Maybe so, but I promised Kiyana we'd stay until she wanted to leave. This is a special night, one to treasure by making new memories, and it's not like the days of old when a couple couldn't sleep together until they were mated. We've had her before and we'll have her many more times again.

His beast grunted. *I don't care. I want my turn to claim her since I couldn't do it in the ceremony.*

Dragons never come out for the ceremonies. Besides you never said you wanted to participate. But no matter, you'll get to claim our mate soon enough.

His beast huffed and curled into a ball. Maybe before everything that had happened with his dragon over the last few months, he might've been somewhat irritated at the response. However, it only reinforced what he wanted more than anything—for his dragon to be fully recovered from the effects of the drugs.

Kiyana placed a hand on his cheek, garnering his full attention. "What did your dragon say?"

"What he usually bangs on about—wanting to have sex with you again."

She chuckled. "Will that ever tone down, his wanting?"

He raised his brows. "Why? Do you need a break? I can deny him for as long as you need, love."

She shook her head. "No, it's just usually marriages turn more familiar with time, and more than a few coworkers of mine have complained about lack of sex."

Placing his hand over hers on his face, he lightly squeezed her fingers. "Never. Once a dragon-shifter is committed, it stays that way. That's why it's so devastating when one leaves and the other is still devoted."

"Although that pain can heal with time, I think."

Alistair felt like an idiot. He hadn't been talking about Rachel recently, and yet she'd invaded their mating day. He would always love her, but she was gone.

And he didn't want any sadness on his mating day for either him or his mate.

249

Kiyana continued, "Don't worry, I'm not jealous. In the end, Rachel brought me to you, Alistair. If you hadn't become a teacher after she died, you probably never would've been assigned to instruct the group of humans, and we never would've met properly. Even if I didn't know her, I'm sure she would approve that you're happy again."

His lips turned up slightly. "Aye, she wanted that for me. But I doubt anyone but you could've broken through my excuses, let alone seen how I hid behind a vow."

She bit her lip, and he knew something was on her mind. He prodded, "Tell me anything, Kiyana."

"Well, I was going to save it for later, but I should tell you now."

Alistair's heart skipped a beat. He had no idea what would make her hesitate. Surely there wasn't some other obstacle for them to overcome so soon after everything else.

He waited for Kiyana to explain. And when she did, he hung on every word. "Now that we're mated, I can finally share something I've wanted to tell you for days. It has to do with the DDA."

Alistair's apprehension faded as he searched her eyes. "Oh, aye? Do they want you to keep working for them?"

She nodded. "Yes. But it's for a special project, one I hope you can help with from time to time when you're not busy teaching."

Both man and dragon's curiosity piqued higher. "What is it?"

"Remember how I discovered some information about the Dettifoss Gathering?" He bobbed his head. "Well, Rosalind Abbott wants to try to make that a reality again within a few years. Me, Max, and a few others will be working on it in secret, trying to find a way to make it happen."

The goal was a bloody big one, but if anyone could try to make it come true, it was his mate. "If—no, *when* you make it happen, it will help dragon-shifters all over the planet."

And his mate would end up in the history books.

His dragon murmured, *As she should.*

She shrugged. "That's the goal. However, I'm not sure if a few years will be enough time to accomplish everything, especially once the baby is born."

He hitched an arm around her waist. "I'll help with our bairn, as will my whole family. Don't worry, love. You'll have all the support you need."

She smiled at him. "I'm almost afraid to tell you how amazing you are again. I don't need a dragonman with a big head so soon after our mating."

He snorted. "Don't worry, I still need to walk with a cane most of the time, which keeps my head in check."

She looped her arms around his neck. "I don't care if you always walk with one. I love you just the way you are, Alistair Boyd."

"Just as I love you, Kiyana Barnes. And as a reminder, I'm going to do this."

He closed the distance between them and took her lips in a slow, devouring kiss.

Alistair had regained his family, once again had love in his life, and even had a child coming. On top of that, his mate was helping him to make his vow and dream a reality.

None of it would've been possible without the female on his lap, and he took his time letting her know just how much he loved and appreciated her for it.

EPILOGUE

Years Later

$\mathcal{K}$iyana stood in front of the ruins of stone, laid out in a rectangular shape. The building was near Loch Naver, and one of the first places Alistair had shown her back at the beginning of their courtship.

Well, sort of courtship.

Still, the cottage ruins held a special place in her heart and never more so than today.

Alistair stood at her side holding a small plaque. They'd come to honor what they had accomplished together, and to have a physical reminder of how they'd fulfilled Alistair's vow to Rachel.

At that moment, the nearly full-term baby inside her womb kicked. She smiled and placed a hand over the spot. It'd taken them so many years, but their second child was on the way and eager to join their sister.

Alistair placed his hand over hers. "Are you all right? Is it the bairn? I told you we should've waited."

She shook her head. "Why? I'm perfectly capable of walking a few minutes. The baby kicked is all. I think he or she wants to honor this moment as well." She met her mate's gaze. "Now I feel guilty for leaving Serena with your mother."

Serena was their daughter, the longed-for granddaughter Meg had always wanted. Of course, she had the most energy out of all the grandchildren so far, which was saying something.

Alistair snorted. "Don't be. Serena would probably run for the loch or try to climb these walls. And while I love her adventurous spirit, this moment is for us right now, love."

She glanced down to the plaque. "I feel like we should say something, but I have no idea what."

"I think getting so many dragon clans together without any sort of war breaking out is achievement enough." Alistair removed his hand and took a few steps forward, so he could place the plaque right next to one of the crumbling stone walls.

He returned to her side and hugged her against him. A wind blew, and she cuddled into his warmth. "Even though I was there, I still can't believe we made the gathering happen."

"Aye, but you were one of the main forces behind it, so of course I knew it would happen."

She hugged him tightly. "There's no need to flatter me. I'm a sure thing by this point, Alistair."

He chuckled. "It can never hurt to butter you up a wee bit. Especially since I think both my dragon and I are going to treasure every inch of your body again whilst we still can. I'm extremely happy about our second bairn, but once they get here, it'll be chaotic for a wee while. I need to drink up as much of you as I can whilst I still have the chance."

She lifted her head up, staring in Alistair's mismatched eyes, and grinned. "If I wasn't the size of a whale, I'd suggest those trees over there."

His eyes flashed to slits and back. "You know how my dragon likes claiming you in the woods."

"I bet if we find a log or rock for me to sit on, we can find a way to make it work."

He frowned. "But I don't want you to catch a chill."

She leaned more against her dragonman. "With you next to me, I'll never be cold."

With a growl, he took her lips in a demanding kiss. Each lick, nibble, and swipe a reminder of how much he still loved her, and probably always would.

And soon after, they found a suitable rock to help her balance, and he proved it even further until he had to swallow her screams.

Author's Note

This book is the most-delayed of any of my dragon books. I wish I could make my brain cooperate with a firmly set schedule, but it doesn't always happen. I hope the wait has been worth it. :)

Alistair and Kiyana's story is special in many ways, but most noticeable is the fact that it's the very beginning of the end of the series. (Before you panic, rest assured there are probably 4-5 years left of my current dragons!) While some people never want the books to end, extremely long series that never end usually end up monotonous, or worse, an author learns to hate it. I do, however, want to write about the kids all grown up at some point. The fact I can even imagine how some of them will be as fully fledged adults is another sign I am steering toward a conclusion. However, to reach it means peppering my Stonefire and Lochguard releases with more Stonefire Dragons Universe (SDU) books. If you missed the first of these, *Winning Skyhunter*, then let me explain—they are standalone books set in my dragon universe but in other clans around the world. Since the end will require the cooperation of more clans, I think it's best to give an idea of how they are doing presently and how they connect, ultimately, back to the British dragon clans.

Sometimes you get cameos from favorite characters, too. (Finn and Bram play an important role in the first SDU book.) As such, I need to address certain clans before progressing with the two main series. This is why *Persuading the Dragon* will be out in 2020 and not 2019. I need (and needed) to write about both Skyhunter and Snowridge (the other two British clans), not to mention Lochguard #7, before that book. I'm sure some people will be disappointed, but I can't help it. Ivy Passmore, the human in a coma on Stonefire, can't wake up until the other stories are done. There's a reason I put her in a coma. ;)

The other reason my dragon releases were delayed is because I took a seven-month break from writing paranormal and sci-fi romances and this pushed ALL my releases back. Crafting complex worlds and managing large casts of character is exhausting. I took the break to write some romantic comedies (Love in Scotland series) and to write some short, insta-love sexy stories under a new pen name (Lizzie England). All of those cleansed my palate and allowed my brain some downtime before facing the enormity of my other series. If I hadn't of taken that break, I'm honestly not sure if I would have written any dragon books this year. Or, they would've been crappy ones. *Craved by the Dragon* was such a chore to write I learned to hate it by the end. Yes, I grew to hate it. Thankfully, the break made it all new again to me and I love them once more. The reason I'm sharing all this is to give you a glimpse into a writer's life and how it doesn't always go to plan. I know there's a climate of instant gratification, but if someone wants quality, it takes some time.

Whew, thanks for reading all of that! As usual, I have some people to thank for getting this out in the world:

To Becky Johnson and her team at Hot Tree Editing. They always keep a sharp eye and don't hesitate to ask if ripping panties are really that easy.

To Clarissa Yeo of Yocla Designs. She is amazing at cover design and this one is no exception.

To all my beta readers—Sabrina D., Donna H., Sandy H., Iliana G., and Stephanie M. you do an amazing job at finding those lingering typos and minor inconsistencies.

And as always, thanks to you, the reader, for sticking with me. Writing is the best job in the world and it's your support that makes it so I can keep doing it.

Until next time, happy reading! I'll share some teasers for other books after this section, in case you need more books to add to the pile. ;)

Winning Skyhunter
(Stonefire Dragons Universe #1)

For more than a decade, Clan Skyhunter suffered under a cruel, power-hungry leader who did anything to advance his agenda. He was finally caught in an illegal scandal and sent to prison, and now the dragon-shifter clan in the south of England is ready for a new leader. And so the trials begin...

Asher King had been locked away under the former clan leader for speaking out against his cruelty. Now free, he wants to win the leadership and guide his clan to a better future. However, being the nephew of the old leader isn't easy, and if that wasn't enough to overcome, he's still recovering from the torture he endured while imprisoned. Still, he's determined to win and keep his clan from being disbanded by the humans, even if it means competing against his ex-girlfriend and denying how much he still wants her.

Newly returned from her stay in America, Honoria Wakeham puts herself up as a candidate to be clan leader. Not everyone approves of a female candidate, but that doesn't faze her. The old clan leader killed her parents, and in order to fully heal, she wants to bring the clan together and move their practices into the twenty-first century. What she didn't count on was running into Asher King, the male she loved over a decade ago, before she was sent away to stay with her American relatives for safety.

It doesn't take long for Asher and Honoria to give in to their attraction, but from it springs an idea that may be the best of all. Can they win the leadership trials and keep their clan together? Or, will one of the other candidates win and try to keep Skyhunter in the past?

————

Winning Skyhunter is available in paperback.

Do you enjoy laugh-out-loud romantic comedies? Then try the first book in Jessie Donovan's Love in Scotland series:

Crazy Scottish Love
(Love in Scotland #1)

Tired of the online dating scene and her nagging mother, Donella Spencer braves her eccentric extended family and heads for a month-long visit to Scotland to stay with them. As long as she keeps to herself and avoids her family as much as possible, it should be easy to relax, right?

What she doesn't count on is running into Robbie Campbell, the guy who tried so hard to ditch her nearly twenty years ago that it took a search and rescue team to save her. Not only that, she doesn't expect to fall for Robbie's daughter's big, brown eyes and agree to hold a themed costume party for Donella's 31st birthday. One that involves her relatives dressing in nineteenth century safari garb and dusty, old animal outfits.

And none of that even begins to address her grandmother's attempts to matchmake and marry off Donella within the month.

It's going to be one long, trying summer in Scotland. However, sometimes the strangest situations can show what someone needs in life. Because if Donella falls in love with a man who can put up with her family, her happy ending may finally be in sight.

Provided her relatives don't drive her crazy first.

Excerpt:

Chapter One

Unlike every other passenger from her plane, Donella Spencer didn't rush to leave the restricted area of Glasgow Airport in Scotland. She much preferred walking as slowly as possible, quite literally dragging her feet.

Sure, she'd love nothing more than a shower at her grandmother's house after a thirteen-hour flight from the US. But given the choice between a shower or dealing with her Scottish relatives, Donella would take being stinky around strangers any day.

For the moment, she merely enjoyed the calm and quiet of the nearly empty corridors. She would've closed her eyes if not for her murderous suitcase, which had wheels that stuck at random, as if making her fall flat on her face was its life purpose.

However, after only one close call with the blasted case, she eventually came to the exit. And unless she wanted to irritate security and possibly be deported, she needed to leave.

Although deportation might be the better choice in the long run.

Get a grip, Donnie. She'd come to Scotland to escape the endless line of jerks and asshats who made up the online dating pool. Well, at least for her. She only attracted the guys who liked to remind her of how her biological clock was ticking, preferred reliving their high school glory days over the present, or sat in silence as she ended up having a two-hour conversation with herself.

Running away to Scotland for a month and putting up with her extended family was definitely preferable to her mother asking twice a day, if she were dating anyone.

Taking a deep breath, Donella pasted a smile on her face and exited the restricted area. She scanned the surroundings and spotted her family in exactly three seconds.

Contrary to what most Americans might think, Scottish men didn't wear kilts often, if at all. And yet, every male member of her extended Scottish family wore a kilt. Not just a kilt, but the full she-bang of a dark coat, weird lace-up shoes that went up to midcalf, and the little sporran pouches covering their privates.

No doubt the men enjoyed them bouncing against their beloved penises.

Ew. She was not going to think of her relatives' penises.

Her Uncle Angus even had a set of bagpipes under his arm. Not to mention Aunt Flora had a tin of who knew what in her hand, ready to tell Donella she was too thin before proceeding to stuff something inside her mouth.

And then there was her grandmother, who probably had several schemes in place to try to marry her off to a nice Scottish guy by the end of the month.

Resisting a sigh, she debated sneaking away to grab a taxi, but her grandmother spotted her and yelled, "Donnie! You're here!"

A half-dozen sets of eyes all turned toward her and cheered, holding up a ginormous sign that said, "Welcome to Scotland, Donnie." Uncle Angus then fired up his bagpipes.

Deportation was suddenly back on the table.

She wasn't the only one to notice the racket. One of the airport security staff made a beeline for Uncle Angus. A normal person would stop playing and apologize.

But Uncle Angus increased the volume and started jogging away.

She had to give her uncle credit for never missing a note as he disappeared from her sight.

Her family didn't pay any attention to her runaway uncle. Her gran waved her hands above her gray-haired head. "Donnie, hurry yourself along. I want to hug my granddaughter."

Deciding that the sooner she could get her family out of the airport the smaller the chance they would be banned for life, she finished walking out the door and into the arms of an aunt, grandparents, and even two cousins.

The instant they released her and she could breathe again, Donella drawled, "I'm not sure this is a big enough welcome party."

As always, her grandmother chose to ignore her sarcasm. "Everyone else will come to Tobermory for your birthday next month. We even closed the restaurant for the day to celebrate your arrival. The Campbells will owe us a favor for the business."

Oh, great. Her gran would now have another thing to hold over her head. "There was no need to do that, Gran. The high tourist season's in full swing."

Her grandmother clicked her tongue. "Of course we needed to. It's been years since I've seen my oldest granddaughter, and we need to give you a proper welcome."

Not favorite or funniest. Or, even smartest. No,

Donella was always just the oldest.

The mention of a celebration made her wary. The Spencer shindigs were infamous, or so her father had said many times over in the past.

Aunt Flora spoke up. "It's just too bad your brother couldn't make it. Such a handsome lad. He'd be the star of the island."

Andrew had laughed for a full three minutes when she'd suggested he come with her. The bastard. "Andy has to work, Auntie. You know that."

Aunt Flora waved a hand in dismissal. "Americans work far too much. Besides, the air on Mull will add years to your life. Not to mention it's where you and your brother both belong and where you should've been born."

It'd been thirty-two years since her dad had moved permanently to the US with her mother, and her dad's family still held it against him. Memories were indeed long in Scotland.

Gran patted her arm. "I have plans of how to get your brother here. But for the moment, let's head home, aye? There are too many people in Glasgow for my liking."

Considering the Isle of Mull where her family lived had fewer than 3,000 people on it, a shopping mall would seem crowded to her gran.

As she followed her family out of the airport and to the parking garage, it took everything she had not to take out her cell phone and text her best friend back in the States. Her family had been nice enough to pick her up from the airport despite the combined four-hour car and ferry ride. She could smile and nod for a few hours.

The avoiding and ignoring would happen later.

Her granddad had been silent so far, but he elbowed

his way to Donella's side and grunted. "Humor your gran and I'll see what I can do about the rounds tomorrow."

She frowned. "Rounds? What rounds?"

"She plans to take you to every shop, restaurant, B&B, and hotel on the island before your birthday party."

She blinked. "The entire island? That will likely take days, if not weeks."

Her granddad gave a one-armed hug. "I hate to break it to you, but she has your entire month planned almost to the hour, Donnie."

She held back a sigh. There went any hope of relaxing and staying under the radar. Her grandfather could work magic with her gran, but he wasn't a god. Gavina Spencer would have her way more often than not.

Uncle Angus appeared from around a corner. He'd given up playing the bagpipes, but not jogging. Slightly out of breath, he shouted, "I'll ride with the wee ones."

The wee ones were his twin children, who happened to be twenty-one years old and were far from wee. Both towered over Donella.

Shouting came from the corner Uncle Angus had just rounded, which spurred her uncle to run out of sight. Two security staff stopped and looked around. One of them shook his head. "I think we lost him."

The other said, "As long as he's out of the building and not playing those bloody bagpipes, I call it a success."

The two headed back to the main building, throwing one last look over their shoulders as if to memorize her family for future reference.

When it came time for Donella to return to the

US, she made a note to keep her family away from the airport and instead use public transportation. Her dad would never forgive her if they were all arrested for giving Donella the send-off they thought she deserved.

She loved her family, but that love was a double-edged sword at times.

Donella, her grandparents, and Aunt Flora piled into a tiny car that her family swore was a "family car" in Scotland but would be used by teenagers to hotbox it back home.

Within seconds, her gran began to recount what had to be every family's gossip in Tobermory and the surrounding area. Even though she lost track of who was who within minutes, her gran's familiar Scottish brogue, in combination with her granddad and aunt in the car, comforted her. These people loved her as she was. There was no reason to put on a show.

Well, most of the time. Her gran wouldn't approve of some of the language she used inside her head.

On top of that, for the next month, there should be no first dates or accidental drop-ins coordinated by her mother. And despite her grandmother's ambitions, Donella was determined to work on her graphic design projects, read a few books, and explore the wilderness of Mull. Maybe she'd even get to see some of the sights in the nearby areas. After all, castles and centuries-old buildings weren't exactly a common sight back home, in a suburb just outside of Seattle.

However, her top priority remained avoiding dates and single men in general.

Even if there were single, non-creepy men on the island, her family would act as the perfect buffer. After all, few wanted to get involved with the Spencer brand of crazy.

Which meant for the first time in ages, Donella would have time to figure out what to do with the rest of her life. She was tired of the online dating game, and since she mostly worked from home, there was little chance there, either.

Marriage was most likely not in her future. A small part of her was sad at that realization, but she was also relieved to end the worst torture of the modern era—the first date from an online dating site. She had a decent job and would maybe get a cat or two. Maybe she could even work up the nerve to travel somewhere where they didn't speak English.

The only thing she truly worried about was breaking the news to her mother. Because if there was one thing her mother had wanted since Donella was a child, it was a big wedding and lots of grandbabies.

No. She wouldn't think of her mother's disappointment and ensuing guilt trips.

Taking one of Aunt Flora's scones from the tin, Donella took a bite and nearly moaned at the slightly crumbly texture. She added learning to make scones to her list of things to do. And if tasting every batch resulted in her having to buy bigger jeans before she went home, so be it. She was here to find herself, not to worry about calories.

——————

Crazy Scottish Love is available in paperback.

ABOUT THE AUTHOR

Jessie Donovan has sold over half a million books, has given away hundreds of thousands more to readers for free, and has even hit the *NY Times* and *USA Today* bestseller lists. She is best known for her dragon-shifter series, but also writes about magic users, aliens, and even has a crazy romantic comedy series set in Scotland. When not reading a book, attempting to tame her yard, or traipsing around some foreign country on a shoestring, she can often be found interacting with her readers on Facebook. She lives near Seattle, where, yes, it rains a lot but it also makes everything green.

Visit her website at: www.JessieDonovan.com